WINTER KILL

Special Agent Adam Darling (yeah, he's heard all the jokes before) was on the fast track to promotion and success until his mishandling of a high profile operation left one person dead and Adam "On the Beach." Now he's got a new partner, a new case, and a new chance to resurrect his career, hunting a cruel and cunning serial killer in a remote mountain resort in Oregon.

Deputy Sheriff Robert Haskell may seem laid-back, but he's a tough and efficient cop, and he's none too thrilled to see feebs on his turf—even when one of the agents is smart, handsome, and probably gay. But a butchered body in a Native American museum is out of his small town department's league. For that matter, icy, uptight Adam Darling is out of Rob's league, but that doesn't mean Rob won't take his best shot.

WINTER KILL

Josh Lanyon

VELLICHOR BOOKS

An imprint of JustJoshin Publishing, Inc.

WINTER KILL

November 2019

Copyright (c) 2015 by Josh Lanyon
Cover by L.C. Chase
Edited by Keren Reed
Boo0k design by Kevin Burton Smith
All rights reserved

ISBN: 978-1-945802-60-7
Published in the United States of America

JustJoshin Publishing, Inc.
3053 Rancho Vista Blvd.
Suite 116
Palmdale, CA 93551
www.joshlanyon.com

This is a work of fiction. Any resemblance to persons living or dead is entirely coincidental.

PROLOGUE

It was cold.

A bitter cold that stung his cheeks and made his eyes water. Even the ripe, low-hanging moon looked frosted over. He hugged himself, stamped his feet on the hard ground, and tried not to long for home and his warm bed.

Because that wasn't his home anymore. He and Buck were going to start a new life together. Away from here. Away from the big mouths and small minds, the people who couldn't mind their own business because they wanted you to be as miserable as they were.

Buck was his home now.

Yeah, he liked that idea.

An owl hooted from overhead and he jumped—and then laughed at himself.

But it was lonely out here. No doubt about it. Lonely and quiet and very dark. In the moonlight the snow on the surrounding mountains looked silver, and the tips of the blue-black pine needles seemed to glow.

Anybody who thought there was only one shade of black should try standing out in the middle of nowhere surrounded by shifting shadows and wavering light.

He wished Buck would hurry up.

Then he worried Buck might have changed his mind. It felt unlucky to let that thought form, but it had taken Buck a while to come around to his way of thinking. This wasn't an easy thing for either of them.

It would be worth it in the end.

The owl gave up asking for identification and flew away into the night.

The icy moon dipped lower behind the mountains.

He licked his lips nervously. The night tasted of snow. Hopefully he wouldn't die of hypothermia before goddamned Buck showed up. He pounded his boots some more on the rock-hard ground and stomped back and forth across the clearing.

Come on, Buck. Don't do this to me.

At last he heard the approaching rumble of a truck engine. His heart pounded faster and he felt a little sick with excitement and fear. It was for real. They were going to do it.

He smiled into the white glare of the approaching headlights.

CHAPTER ONE

"**I**t was a mistake bringing in the feds," Zeke said.

Rob thought it was a mistake too, but it hadn't been his call, and it was too late now, so what was the point of bitching? He said, "Feebs."

"What?"

"The FBI. They call them feebs now."

"I don't care if they call them fucking frankfurters."

Rob grunted.

From the observation deck at Rogue Valley International-Medford Airport they watched in silence as Alaska Airlines Flight 477 touched down, skimmed the rain-blackened runway, and taxied slowly toward the terminal.

Rob straightened. "Come on."

"There's no hurry." Zeke continued to gaze out the wet, streaked window.

The overhead speaker announced the flight's arrival just in case anyone in the small airport wasn't paying attention, and offered information on collecting baggage to the passengers still sitting on the plane.

A few long minutes passed before the mobile stairway was lined up with the plane doors. The cabin door opened. At last the passengers began to disembark.

Rob's stomach growled and he glanced at his watch. It was already twelve thirty and in this weather it would take about an hour to drive from Medford to the resort of Nearby. He sighed inwardly. It had been a long morning and it was going to be a long afternoon. Of that, he had zero doubt.

Zeke said suddenly, "Fucking Barbie and Ken!"

A woman carrying a briefcase exited the plane. The rainy breeze tousled her long, pale hair. She threw a comment over her shoulder to a man in an olive raincoat. The man replied and the woman laughed.

Rob smiled grimly because that time Zeke nailed it. Tall and blond and elegant in their His and Hers trench coats, these two looked more like they were auditioning for a hot new TV series than real law enforcement. But law enforcement they were. Real live FBI Special Agents come all the way from sunny Los Angeles to offer their wisdom and expertise.

Yep, it was pretty damned annoying.

"Come on," he said again, and this time he meant it. Zeke heaved a heavy sigh but followed him downstairs to the Arrival Gate where Barbie and Ken were impatiently scanning the waiting crowd for their welcome committee.

The bystanders parted before Rob and Zeke. There was nothing like a sheriff's badge to clear a path.

"Special Agents Gould and Darling?" Rob asked. Not that he had any doubt.

The man—Rob's height, green eyes, short, wavy fair hair—said crisply, "I'm Darling. This is Agent Gould."

"Deputies," Gould said. She had a very pretty smile. No question who played Good Cop on that team.

"Special Agent What'dyousay?" Zeke asked.

Darling directed a look that should have left Zeke encased in ice, and Rob preserved his poker face with effort.

"I'm Haskell. This is Deputy Lang," Rob said. "How was your trip?"

"Long," Darling said. "Shall we hit the road?"

"I could see getting that mixed up," Zeke interrupted with his usual godawful timing.

Darling looked almost human as his green gaze met Rob's. Gould's pale brows drew together. "I'm sorry?"

Zeke opened his big mouth again. "I could see how someone might think *you* were the d—"

Rob spoke over him. "We're parked in the lot across from the terminal." He gave Zeke a helpful, hard nudge in the direction of the exit. Zeke winced and glared at him. "You have any luggage?" Rob asked the feds.

Gould held up her briefcase. Darling didn't seem to hear the question, heading straight for the doors leading out to the rainy gray October day.

They piled into the Rural Patrol SUV, the FBI agents in the backseat and Zeke riding shotgun. Rob started the engine.

"How long a drive is it to the resort?" Darling asked.

"Not quite an hour. Maybe longer in the rain."

"With you driving, definitely longer," Zeke said.

Rob ignored him, pulling out of the parking lot and turning east.

"You really think our DB might be one of the Roadside Ripper's vics?" Zeke asked, looking back at their passengers.

"That's what we're here to find out," Gould said.

"What's the body count now?" Zeke asked.

"We believe we have twenty-one confirmed kills." Gould's voice was pleasant. She might have been discussing the weather.

"I almost applied to the FBI," Zeke said. "I didn't want to have to wear a fucking tie all the time."

Rob managed to swallow his snort. He glanced in the rearview mirror as he merged onto OR-62 West and briefly met Darling's eyes. Darling's mouth quirked in a sardonic not-quite-smile.

"Excuse my French," Zeke added for Gould's benefit.

"*Pas du tout*," Gould returned.

Zeke gave her his biggest, widest grin. She smiled back, but he was wasting his time there. Gould was so far out of his league she might have been from another planet.

Again Rob's gaze rose to the rearview and again he met Darling's ironic regard. Darling did not blink, did not look away.

Wasn't green supposed to be the most rare eye color? Rob could believe it in Darling's case. He'd never seen eyes quite that shade. Maybe Darling wore contacts.

Either way…that was one very direct, very intense regard. In other circumstances, it might mean a couple of things. Even in these circumstances that look might mean a couple of things. Unlikely, but still…

Zeke asked, "How many of those twenty-one vics were in Oregon?"

"Seven," Gould replied.

"But that doesn't mean they were killed here."

"True."

"They might just have been unloaded here. He's using the I-5 as his dumping ground, right?"

Darling was now directing his laser stare at the back of Zeke's head. Rob would not have been surprised to see Zeke's hair burst into flame, but then that was always a danger given how much hairspray Zeke used. Way more hairspray than straight guys generally went in for, in Rob's opinion.

"That's the current theory," Gould said.

"How many members on your taskforce?" Zeke asked. "The whole West Coast is involved, right?"

"It's one of the largest ever formed," Gould answered. "Even we're not sure of the exact number of team members."

Obviously not true, but more polite than what her partner was clearly tempted to tell Zeke.

"You guys okay?" Rob asked. "You hungry?"

"Yeah, I'm hungry," Zeke said.

"We had a two-hour layover in Seattle," Darling said. "We've eaten. And we're on a tight schedule."

Gould glanced at her partner. What she said was, "Gosh, it's green here. We could use some of this rain in California."

"We've never had a homicide in Nearby," Zeke said with an edge to his tone. "I know it's same old same old to you, but to us it's a big deal."

"We don't know we've got a homicide now," Rob said, with a warning look.

It was wasted, of course.

"Right," Zeke said. "Maybe it was suicide. Maybe John Doe buried himself beneath that rock pile."

Sunday afternoon, campers had discovered human remains buried in a shallow grave covered with rocks on a decommissioned logging road off Route 140. Not exactly the Roadside Ripper's stomping grounds, but for some reason Frankie— Sheriff Francesca McLellan—had decided to call in the feds just to be sure. Which just went to prove what a high profile case the Roadside Ripper was. High profile enough that even in their corner of the woods, they'd heard about it.

But the chances that this unlucky John Doe was one of the Ripper's? That seemed pretty far-fetched to Rob.

All the same, twenty-four hours later, FBI Barbie and Ken had shown up on their doorstep.

"How long have you been with the Sheriff's Department, Deputy Lang?" Gould inquired.

"Six years."

"How do you like it?"

There was nothing Zeke liked more than talking about himself, and he was off and running. Off at the mouth. Agent Gould kept him primed with the occasional comment, but it was clear to Rob she was just making conversation—or maybe avoiding discussing their case.

Their case being the operative attitude.

Well, let 'em have it. One of the advantages of working out in the boonies was he didn't have to deal with the territorial bullshit that came with larger LE agencies. No thanks. Best case scenario, in Rob's opinion, was that John Doe was one of the Roadside Ripper's vics, and the feebs could take over the whole damned investigation. But, though he hadn't followed the case, the bit he had picked up indicated the unlikelihood of that. John Doe had been found just too far off the beaten track.

Zeke was still offering the highlights of his career in the Sheriff's Office. Gould was still making polite sounds. Darling stared out the SUV window at the wet and glistening tall trees lining the road leading deep into the national forest. Rob pressed the gas and the SUV leaped forward.

"**W**e don't have a morgue in Nearby." Pulling up in front of Mountain Mortuary fifty minutes later, Rob interrupted Zeke's lengthy yarn about how he'd single-handedly nabbed the "butt-naked" RV bandit of Blue Rock Cove. Zeke gave him a reproachful look, but Rob ignored him. "Doc Cooper, the Klamath Falls ME, has a vacation home up here, and he's doing the autopsy."

"Quaint," Gould said. It was unclear whether she was referring to the autopsy arrangements or the black wrought iron fencing which made the small yard in front of the brick and white clapboard building look like a miniature graveyard.

Rob turned off the engine and undid his seatbelt. They climbed out of the SUV and went through the ornate gate, which shut behind them with an unmusical clank. The rain had stopped for the time being. The air was cold and smelled of pine trees. Sodden autumn colored leaves were plastered to the walkway; the white wooden steps were slick and wet.

As they reached the glass double door entry, Frankie pushed open the door and leaned out. "Did you take the long way? I was starting to think you got lost."

Before Rob could answer—not that he'd have bothered—Zeke said, "You shouldn't have let Grandma drive."

Frankie ignored him. She nodded in greeting at Darling and Gould. "Agents. Thanks for coming on such short notice."

She offered a tanned, freckled hand to Darling, who shook with her saying, "We appreciate the heads-up, Sheriff. I'm Agent Darling and this is Agent Gould."

Frankie held the door wide for Gould, who got a shrewd look—beige pumps to coiffed hair—as she passed. "We realize this is off your beaten track, but it never hurts to be sure."

Frankie had probably never worn a pair of heels in her life. Or at least Rob couldn't picture her in heels, let alone a dress. She was a short, stout woman in her mid-fifties with a ruddy, weathered face and frizzy, rust-colored hair. It wasn't her looks that had gotten Frankie elected to four consecutive four-year terms as Sheriff. But despite her non-glamorous appearance and brusque demeanor, she was liked and respected by the citizens she had served for so long.

"Doc Cooper is the Klamath Falls ME. He's doing the honors today."

"So we heard," Darling said as Frankie led the way through an obstacle course of empty caskets and urns stuffed with silk flowers. The showroom—if "showroom" was the right word—smelled of formaldehyde and air freshener, and Rob was glad in hindsight that they hadn't stopped to eat.

A gust of rain-washed air from the open door ruffled the silk petals and sent a couple of soulful portraits of praying children knocking against the walnut paneled walls. There was a weird ambiance to the place, an uncomfortable mix of commercial and mournful. An ordinary, modern morgue probably would have been less disturbing.

Even Frankie lowered her voice when she addressed Rob and Zeke. "I don't need both of you here. Zeke, I want you to get back over to the office."

Zeke instantly protested, "Why me? Why is Haskell always the one who gets all the perks?"

"Perks? You want to stay and watch Doc carve up John Doe, be my guest," Rob said.

"You two knuckle-heads shut up," Frankie growled. "There's no carving up to be done. And I'm not asking for volunteers. I said—"

"This is a great learning experience," Zeke kept on. "You're always saying we need more training opportunities."

Frankie began to splutter. She got control and said, "Keep your voice down! Mr. Eden has folks in the Arrangement Room right this minute."

Zeke looked so horrified that Rob probably would have laughed—except he caught sight of the two FBI agents' expressions. Clearly they thought they'd stepped into an episode of *Police Squad!* And no wonder. Instead, he muttered, "The bereaved, you dumbass."

"Yes, the bereaved," Frankie said impatiently. "Real live customers. What do you think I mean?"

Agent Darling, edging toward a white door with a placard that read *Employees Only*, said, "Sheriff, we're just going to—"

They didn't wait to hear Frankie's answer, which was just as well. The door swung shut behind Darling and Gould as Frankie said to Zeke, "For cryin' out loud, Zeke, if it means that much to you, you can stay." She nodded at his shoulder mic. "But keep your radio on. *Low*."

Zeke threw Rob a look of triumph, and Rob shook his head because there was no competition, whatever Zeke imagined. He would happily surrender his spot at the autopsy table to anyone who asked. He didn't know why Frankie thought he needed to be there in the first place.

"But I don't want to hear any complaints, if we get a call."

"What kind of call are we going to get?" Zeke muttered. "Jack Elkins got stuck in the mud again? Ruby Lowe can't find her dog?"

"You heard me." Frankie bustled toward the door behind which the agents had vanished.

The doorway swung onto a short set of steps leading downstairs. They found the agents in the Preparation Room speaking with Doc Cooper.

Doc was tall and rangy with gold wire spectacles and a white, handlebar mustache. He was older than Frankie; had been ME long before Frankie had first taken office. He wore cowboy boots, and drove a vintage red mustang. And he had a surprisingly pleasant bedside manner, given that the bedsides he generally attended were slabs in the morgue.

The body—more accurately, the skeleton—had already been removed from the large stainless steel refrigerator in the back of the sterile white room, and arranged on the metal morgue table. The yellowed skull—gaping jaw and dark, empty eye sockets—grinned sightlessly up into the remorseless white light of the overhead lamps.

The left front tooth was chipped.

The air was artificially chill, and the room smelled of chemicals and something that raised the hair on the back of Rob's neck.

It was not his first autopsy. Hell, this examination of old bones didn't even qualify as an autopsy, but he felt a strange sort of regret. Not pity—because death and decay was what happened to everyone in the end—but something. Something he'd heard on late night TV came to him, a quote from one of those English murder mysteries where a cranky, roly-poly detective went around solving all those gruesome slayings in cute little cottages.

Any man's death diminishes me.

Something like that. Anyway, no one else looked particularly moved—unless Agent Darling really had lost color and it wasn't just a trick of the light. Between the chill air and the smell of chemicals, anyone might feel kind of off.

Zeke sucked in a breath. "Well, shit," he said softly.

The FBI agents were still speaking quietly to Doc Cooper, but Darling glanced up at Zeke's comment. His eyes met Rob's.

This time when Rob felt that flash of awareness, he knew he wasn't imagining it. He had to repress an inappropriate smile. Not like this was a social occasion.

"Well, let's get started," Doc said. He nodded to his white-clad assistant standing by the door, and the assistant flipped the switch. An instant and heavy gloom descended on the room. Only the spread of bones on the table remained illuminated in that fierce circle of light.

"As you can see, despite the fact we have a nearly intact skeleton, we don't have a lot to work with," Doc said. "No personal effects or identification of any kind, and the clothing, what's left of it, is cheap, generic stuff. Boots, jeans, T-shirt, jacket."

"How old?" Frankie asked.

"We're looking at a male probably in his late teens or early twenties. You can see the collarbones aren't completely fused. The skeleton is sixty-nine inches long so he would have been about five feet nine inches tall. Not a big fella. I'm not an anthropologist, but I believe our victim to be Caucasian. I can't be completely sure."

"How old is the forensic evidence?" Darling asked.

Doc sucked in his cheeks, thought it over, and finally announced, "About twenty years, I'd guess. A couple of decades at least. I believe the bones are contemporary, but like I said, this isn't my area of expertise."

Darling's brows drew together. "You're sure the recovered specimen is that old?"

Doc gave him an exasperated look. "I'm reasonably sure. What I can't tell you yet is how he died. Aside from a chipped front tooth, there are no broken bones. No fractures. Nothing smashed, nothing crushed. No signs of skeletal trauma. Obviously we have no way of knowing what damage might have been done to his vital organs or soft tissue, but there is no immediately apparent cause of death."

Gould said to Darling, "Right age and the right sex. But either way—"

Darling nodded.

"Twenty years," Frankie said thoughtfully.

"I don't remember any twenty-year-old missing person cases," Rob said.

Frankie said to Doc, "Back in '98…what was the name of that college kid who backpacked into the woods and disappeared?"

"Jordan something."

"That's right. Jordan Gaura."

"You're forgetting," Doc said with grim satisfaction.

"What am I forgetting?"

"The whole reason everyone got worked up so fast. That kid'd had a hip replacement. I remember that very clearly because I thought at the time if his remains did ever show up, there wouldn't be any doubt about who it was. Our John Doe is virtually intact. Ninety-five percent of the skeleton was recovered on site, so we can see that there were no broken bones either prior to or after death. Hell, he's even got all his teeth."

Frankie swore. "Then I can't think of anybody else."

"That's good news," Doc said. "He's someone else's problem."

Doc and Frankie looked at Darling and Gould.

"But not ours," Darling said. "The age of the victim is about right, but his location is all wrong." He looked at Gould.

Gould concurred. "We haven't identified the type of knife used by the Ripper yet, but we're pretty sure it's some kind of hunting knife with a serrated blade. Possibly homemade. That type of weapon leaves its mark. The ribcage, the sternum, there wouldn't be any missing those grooves and depressions and striations."

"I guess not," Frankie said reluctantly.

Rob said, "He could have been carrying his ID in something else. A knapsack. A backpack."

All eyes turned his way.

Rob answered his own thought. "Except there's no knapsack. No backpack."

Frankie said, "No."

"No bike." They had a lot of cyclists come through their patch, especially during the summer months.

"The bike could be out there somewhere," Frankie said. "Someone could have pitched that bike off the mountainside. Or someone could have found it lying alongside the road. A bike is the kind of thing that might get carted off. Especially one of those expensive mountain bikes."

Darling said, "You're probably looking at a runaway."

"If we are, it isn't anyone from around here."

Zeke's radio suddenly crackled into life. The blast of static was followed by Aggie's tinny voice requesting his location. Doc jumped and glared at him. Zeke looked guilty and stepped out of the room, but he was back a moment later, gesturing to Rob. "Gotta roll. We've got a 12-16 on I-70 eastbound."

Hell. A traffic accident. And nobody else available to deal with it, if they were getting the call rather than the state police.

That was liable to keep them busy the rest of the afternoon and into the night. He threw a regretful look at Agent Darling who was frowning down at the skeleton, completely oblivious to Rob's presence anyway. So much for that imaginary awareness or connection or whatever Rob had nearly convinced himself of.

With an inward sigh, he followed Zeke from the Preparation Room and up the stairs to the main floor of the Mortuary.

"You think he's banging her?" Zeke asked in an undervoice they could probably hear in the Preparation Room refrigerator.

It was tempting to play dumb, but Rob answered honestly, "No."

"You sound pretty sure."

He probably *had* sounded a little too confident on that score. Rob shrugged. When Zeke glanced back at him, he shrugged again. "They probably have a non-fraternization policy at the FBI."

"No, they don't," Zeke said surprisingly. At Rob's look, he said, "I wasn't bullshitting. I really did think about trying out for the FBI. I just didn't feel like working with a bunch of tight-asses like Special Agent Fuckface."

"You've got a real way with words, Lang."

"I should have remembered there'd be babes like Barbie too."

Dream on, Rob thought. The shortage of eligible bachelors in Nearby had given Zeke an overinflated idea of his masculine charms.

"Anyway, what a waste of time," Zeke said, pushing open the double glass doors that led outside. The rain-laced air smelled sweet and alive after the chemical-scented chill of downstairs.

And Rob, thinking of Agent Darling staring grimly down at the skeleton on the morgue table, was inclined to agree.

CHAPTER TWO

"That was a waste of time," Jonnie said, following Adam into his cabin.

The rain had started again. It drummed soothingly on the roof, but the room was cold and damp. Was there a thermostat in the place, or were they supposed to rely on fireplaces and potbellied stoves for warmth?

"It usually is." Adam pulled his tie off and draped it over the back of a chair facing the small desk beneath the painting of the snowcapped Cascades. He unbuttoned his collar.

Jonnie sat on the foot of his bed and slipped her heels off. "You never know though. It could have panned out. Grant's Pass was definitely one of ours." She flexed her stockinged feet, pointed her toes, flexed again. She had long, narrow feet. *Like Audrey Hepburn*, she'd informed him. He smiled faintly at the memory.

"Grant's Pass is right on the I-5. Our guy likes to stick to the I-5 Corridor."

She groaned. "What a fiasco. From start to finish. I can't *believe* they just hauled those remains out of the ground and carted them over to Mortuary Madness or whatever that place was called. It's obvious it never even occurred to them to call in a forensic anthropologist. They *annihilated* the crime scene."

"I know." She was on a roll, and the best thing was to let her get it off her chest. Anyway, he agreed one hundred percent.

"One." Jonnie held up her index finger. "*One* chance to process the crime scene without contaminants. *One* single, solitary chance to retrieve all of the physical evidence. To photograph the grave site, map whatever evidence there was in relation to the remains and the terrain, collect all the necessary data—and they *blew* it."

"I know."

"Did they think it was Search and Rescue? Did they think there was some rush retrieving the remains? Don't they have any training? They're real sheriffs, right? This isn't some local militia thing? They've got the uniforms. I thought I was going to have a stroke when Doc Adams told me how they 'processed' that crime scene."

Adam grinned reluctantly at the "Doc Adams" crack.

"Minus any soft tissue we can't know for sure whether John Doe was mutilated in the same way as the Ripper's other victims."

The Ripper carved symbols into the chests of his victims. Flesh and blood proving a messy artistic medium, no one was sure what the symbols represented. The current widely held theory was that the ragged lines represented an incomplete cross and flower.

"No, we can't," Adam said. "Which is exactly what I was afraid of. But if the skeletal remains are as old as the ME seems to think, it's not likely that this is the work of our unsub. This doesn't affect our case. They just made their own job harder."

"You're just saying that to make me feel better," she said gloomily.

"No. If that was the work of our guy, what was the Ripper doing for those twenty years between this logging road John

Doe and Jackie Ramos winding up with his heart carved out in Redding?"

"Good question." She studied his face. "But you've got doubts. I could see it when we were in that creepy underground morgue."

"I've got doubts, but not about that. That kind of gap doesn't make sense."

Not that serial killers didn't go on hiatus. The BTK Killer was proof of that. Illness, incarceration, change of venue…and sometimes they just aged out of the game. Or died. But a twenty-year pause between kills was highly unlikely. And there were too many other anomalies.

So the Roadside Ripper's score remained twenty-one. FBI zero. Adam sighed.

"I didn't know whether to laugh or cry when they started talking about DNA." But Jonnie was starting to wind down. She sounded more weary than worked up.

"It's a rural patrol. At best a substation. I'm amazed they even bothered to call us."

She didn't answer. For a second or two they listened to the rain on the roof.

"Is that an actual painting?" Jonnie rose from the bed and moved over to the desk to inspect the wood-framed painting. She gave a disbelieving laugh. "Those are brushstrokes. When was the last time you stayed anywhere with actual art on the walls?"

"I think *art* might be an exaggeration."

"Point. But I mean, an actual original painting."

Adam shook his head. He studied the interior of the rental cabin. Knotty pine, woven rugs and blue plaid curtains, a potbellied stove and vintage red Formica countertops. "When do you think they built this place?"

"The fifties maybe?"

"I think you're right. I hope they've changed the mattresses since then."

"I hope they've changed the sheets." Jonnie walked back to the bed and slipped her heels on. "I can't believe there's no motel here. It's going to take forever to heat up these cabins."

"I can walk over with you and light the fire in your fireplace."

"Please. You're talking to a former Girl Scout."

Not for the first time, he was grateful that she wasn't one of those women who tried to find innuendo in the most innocent comments. He grinned. "I had no idea. Well, in that case, do you want to grab some dinner?"

She pulled a rolled-up magazine from the deep pocket of her trench coat, and held up a copy of *Bride's*.

Adam scowled at the airbrushed bride chortling on the cover. "Yeah, I still don't follow why getting married means you can't eat dinner anymore."

"Making sure I can fit into that Vera Wang size-four wedding gown is why I don't eat dinner anymore. I can't *wait* till I can have dinner again."

"Chris said he booked Outback Steakhouse for your honeymoon."

Jonnie laughed. "I'm all in favor of that. So long as it's on the way to Maui. Speaking of airports, when's our flight out?"

"Six thirty a.m., and it's a direct flight back to L.A. We do not want to miss it." Few things irritated him more than the time suck of having to fly to Washington State to sit two hours in an airport when their ultimate destination was Oregon—and they'd had a lot of it these last months, tasked with the unpleasant job of determining which of the dead bodies periodically discovered along the I-5 Corridor belonged to the Ripper.

But that's the kind of plum assignment you landed when you screwed up as spectacularly as Adam had four months earlier.

"Tell it to Dumb and Dumber. Although, frankly, I think they can't wait to get us out of here."

Adam said, "Oh, I don't know. I think you made quite an impression there."

Jonnie laughed. "I think anything in a skirt makes an impression there. See you at oh-dark-thirty." She headed for the door. "Don't do anything I wouldn't."

"Like eat dinner?" His smile faded as the door closed behind her. He really did hate eating alone. It gave him too much time to think about things he didn't like to remember. Which was kind of ironic when he remembered how once upon a time he had monopolized breakfast, lunch, and dinner with discussion of his cases.

Granted, back then he hadn't been on morgue patrol.

He checked out the cabin and was forced to accept the fact that the only source of heat was a potbelly stove that used pellets for fuel. By the time he got that thing going, it would be time for dinner, and rather than leave it burning and take a chance on burning down the entire resort, maybe the simplest thing was to take a hot shower and save waiting to deal with the stove until he got back that evening.

A hot shower helped, although two minutes in, the water started to cool. A lot. Adam toweled off, dressed, and combed his hair into place.

He grimaced at the effect. Good enough for government work? He would have thought that was funny once. But after all, it wasn't like he was headed for a night on the town.

In fact, he couldn't think of the last time he'd had a night on the town.

He pulled shut the cabin curtains, dragged back the bedding to let it air. In the lamplight, the cabin looked almost cozy: Pendleton blankets, myrtlewood oil lamps, and the old-fashioned paintings created the impression of stepping back in time. The furnishings reminded him of something. Maybe the one and only time his father had taken him camping?

Anyway, it was just one night, and then back to central heating and plentiful hot water. Civilization.

He gave the cabin a final appraisal, picked up his coat, and headed out to dinner.

The rain had stopped again. It was a dark and dripping world of towering pines and deep shadows. A few yards away he could see light in Jonnie's cabin. They seemed to be the resort's only guests. That was probably normal for October. Besides pretty scenery, this area didn't have a lot to offer visitors between water sports and winter sports.

The pine needles cushioned his footsteps as he made his way toward the restaurant by the lake. Through the trees he could see shining windows and smell the appetizing scent of roasting meat.

It was very quiet out here. So quiet he could hear the lap of lake water and the rustle of grass. Every drip seemed magnified.

He was not nervous. Not by inclination and certainly not given his training. He knew how to take care of himself, had every confidence in his ability to take care of himself. But something about this place made him uneasy.

Or maybe he was picking up Sheriff McLellan's unease. Because she was...troubled. Not alarmed exactly. Whatever was bothering her wasn't something she had identified; she couldn't—or maybe wasn't ready—to put it into words. But Adam didn't think what she was feeling was dismay about a twenty-year-old murder. She wasn't happy about it—and she hadn't been expecting it—but that wasn't what was worrying her.

No, she had been expecting something a lot worse.

And, maybe he was wrong, but he didn't think she had been particularly relieved by the outcome of that autopsy.

The breath of the lake misted up and drifted toward the shoreline. This would be one spooky place at Halloween.

He walked on. It was farther to the restaurant than he'd thought. Distances were deceiving at night.

He couldn't shake his feeling of disquiet. But maybe he was mistaking what he was feeling for something more sinister. Maybe what was really bothering him was the realization of how much he was going to miss Jonnie. She was still planning to resign after her wedding. The big day was four months away, but that no longer seemed like a safe distance. He did not want to lose their partnership. Not just because Jonnie was such a good agent, although that was certainly part of it. And not because she was a friend, although it was true he wasn't always the easiest person to get along with. He hadn't joined the Bureau to win popularity contests. But Jonnie was the first partner he'd had that he'd really clicked with. They had only been together four months, but they made a good team. They didn't have to speak to know what the other was thinking, and there was none of the antagonism or rivalry he'd experienced with other partners. He liked her, he respected her, he trusted her.

But he didn't get a vote. Jonnie said one FBI agent per family was enough, so she was resigning in February.

A white and rambling two-story building fronted by a ramshackle porch came into view. The boathouse sat on the edge of the water next to a long, low deck that gleamed like bones in the porch lights. The lack of moonlight made it difficult to discern more than a shingle roof and a lot of what guidebooks usually described as "rustic charm."

The Lakehouse Restaurant and Bar was open. That was all Adam cared about. Lights shone behind windows, and silvery smoke drifted into the black night sky.

He walked up a short flight of steps. The sign on the window of the front door read *We will be closed October 15th through March 15th. Happy Holidays. See you soon!*

Judging from the sounds inside, the locals were bidding the place a noisy and affectionate goodbye. He hesitated. He had been thinking quiet meal and a couple of drinks. According to Sheriff McLellan, his only other options were a hole in the wall pizza shop and a bar about the size of a tackle box, optimistically named Marina Grill—though if they grilled anything besides cheese and bread, he'd be surprised.

Adam opened the door and walked into warmth and loud voices.

A petite girl with a wild head of pale green hair greeted him and asked how many for dinner.

"Just one," Adam said.

The girl with the mermaid-colored hair gave him a look of pity, consulted a clipboard, and beckoned him to follow. He trailed her past the long and crowded bar—a lot of flannel shirts, down vests, hunting caps. There were a few women, but the grim, curious gazes meeting his own were mostly male.

A burly, big guy with a black beard and piercing blue eyes sized him up—and turned his back.

He got that a lot.

In a village the size of Nearby there would be no mystery as to who he was and why he was there. In fact, any one of these men boozing and laughing with their neighbors might be the unsub responsible for the logging road John Doe. The silver-haired man wearing a fringe jacket and flirting with the waitress? He ought to be arrested simply on the grounds of wearing fringe at fifty.

That was the problem with this job. You couldn't walk into a bar without wondering who was skipping out on their child support payments, who was knocking their wife around, who was dumping bodies on back roads. Was it easier or harder to live with the people you were policing?

Adam spotted Deputy Haskell and almost tripped over the first step of a small transition stairway leading into the dining room.

"Watch the step!" the green-haired hostess called belatedly over her shoulder.

Haskell was drinking what looked like Scotch and apparently taking a friendly ribbing from his companions. "Not guilty! Not guilty," he protested, laughing and shaking his head. His gaze happened to slide toward Adam, and while he didn't exactly do a double take, for an instant—an instant that seemed to last a very long time—their eyes locked.

Adam was aware his heart was suddenly beating very fast, and his face felt warm.

No use pretending that it hadn't crossed his mind that *maybe…* He hadn't really expected it. Things rarely worked out like that for him these days. And in a town as small as this one— too small to be called a town, in fact—he'd figured there might be a couple of obstacles. Like maybe a wife and kids.

And he could be wrong. In fact, he was probably wrong. He wasn't great at picking up those kinds of signals. Much better at reading psychos than normal guys, according to Tucker.

The last guy he wanted to think about now was Tucker.

"How's this?" the hostess asked, stopping before a small corner table positioned beneath a couple of Norman Rockwell fishing prints.

"Great." Not great though because he couldn't see Haskell, now blocked behind a wall of plaid and denim. It was the only empty table, so Adam sat down, picked up the battered menu, and stared blankly at the ketchup-stained pages.

"Can I get you something to drink?" inquired the hostess.

"Gin and tonic."

"Well gin okay?"

Still on automatic pilot he said, "Sure," and then, as the hostess disappeared, could have kicked himself. He hated cheap gin. Hated anything cheap, really.

Adam studied the menu some more. The chicken scratches came into focus, and he began to read his options. A lot of beef. Somewhere between the smoked tri-tip and the meatloaf was surely something he'd like to eat. Autopsies always took his appetite away. Even after all these years. Not that there was much to autopsy on a set of twenty-year-old remains. That really didn't make it a whole hell of a lot better.

The chair across from him scraped pine on pine as it was dragged out. Haskell—lean, compact, and broad-shouldered— sat down. "Hi."

Adam's heart jumped. "Hi," he said.

"Okay if I join you?"

It was a bit late to ask, but Adam wasn't objecting. "Sure."

Haskell offered his hand. "Rob." He was out of uniform, wearing jeans and a red tartan shirt. His hair was dark and thick and, despite the conservative cut, fell boyishly across his fore- head. Adam got another whiff of that very nice aftershave: a mix of sequoia and citrus. Understated and masculine. Like Haskell himself.

"Adam." They shook, and he liked the firm, easy pressure of Rob's grip. He really got tired of guys who thought crushing your fingers proved they weren't intimidated by a G-man.

"I recommend the tri-tip." Rob nodded at the menu.

"I think I'm going for the Chicken Alfredo."

"Everything's pretty good here." Rob finished his drink. His brown eyes met Adam's and he smiled. He was a handsome guy and he knew it. That was fine. Adam liked self-confidence and he liked self-assurance, being confident and assured himself. At least in most things.

Rob began, "How long have you been with the Bur—" The hostess, who was apparently pulling double-duty as waitress, showed up with Adam's G&T.

"Hey, Robbie," she said, dimpling.

"Hey, Azure."

Rob and Azure chatted for a few moments before Azure remembered to take Adam's order. "Good choice," she approved of the Chicken Alfredo. She fluttered her false eyelashes at Rob and departed.

Adam sipped his drink.

"So you're part of this Roadside Ripper taskforce?" Rob asked.

Azure must have thrown him off his stride, because that was a pretty lame opening. They both knew he already had the answer to that one. Maybe Adam's speculations about Rob still being in the closet were right. Easy to believe in a backwoods place like Nearby. Anyway, this wasn't a conversation Adam wanted to have. For a lot of reasons, not the least of which was…

dinnertime. He answered with his own question. "How long have you been with the Sheriff's Department?"

"Sheriff's Office? Twelve years."

Adam nodded. Rob looked to be in his mid-thirties. About his own age. A man at the peak of his abilities. Which were probably wasted here. "Did you grow up locally?"

"No. I'm from Portland originally. I moved here for the job. And the scenery."

Adam smiled.

"Amateur photographer," Rob explained.

"Ah."

"And what do you do when you're not chasing serial killers?"

"I jog."

Rob laughed and Adam laughed too, though he wasn't kidding. He didn't have hobbies. He jogged and went to the gym. That was as close as he got to a hobby. When he'd been a kid he'd collected vintage model airplanes. For a while he'd been into sailing.

And, again, thinking about the past was not productive.

The conversation wilted. Rob held up his empty glass, and across the noisy room one of the waitresses spotted him and nodded. Rob pointed to Adam. The waitress nodded again. Rob turned back to Adam and smiled briefly.

Adam racked his brains for a neutral topic of conversation. He was really bad at this part. The other part, the part that came after—assuming you got through this part—he was good at. Not so good that it counted as a hobby, but he did definitely enjoy it.

Finally he came up with, "So you've got yourself a cold case."

"Yeah. Well…" Rob shrugged.

That surprised Adam. "No?"

"Twenty years later and no ID?" Rob's smile was wry.

"The Sheriff's Office is not going to investigate?"

There was no hiding the note of disapproval in Adam's voice because Rob's smile thinned. "Investigate what? A twenty-year-old hit-and-run? Anyway, it's up to Frankie. Sheriff McLellan, that is."

What. The. Hell. However, Adam didn't want his disgust with this lackadaisical approach to law enforcement to get in the way of getting laid. "Right."

"Look," Rob said. "We'll do what we can, but we're not the FBI. We're not even Portland PD. We're a small, rural sheriff's office, and we spend most of our time dealing with kids setting fires and vandalizing property—or assholes who think shooting at ground squirrels in their front yard is all part of their right to bear arms. The fact that we even called you in ought to demonstrate how far out of our depth we are with this kind of thing."

"'This kind of thing' being a twenty-year-old hit-and-run?"

Rob's dark gaze was unsmiling. "Okay," he conceded. "Maybe it wasn't a hit-and-run. I've never known a hit-and-run driver to stop to bury his—or her—victim. But it wasn't your guy either. Right?"

"No. Right," Adam said. He had never known a hit-and-run victim to be struck hard enough to kill yet somehow not break any bones.

"People do crazy things in a panic."

"That's true."

The grave depth and use of terrain to conceal the body did indicate panic and haste. The remote location, however, indicated premeditation.

"I'm still not sure why Frankie instantly assumed this was one of your whatdoyoucall'em? Unsubs."

Adam grimaced inwardly. Rob wasn't as overtly hostile as Deputy Lang, but nobody in LE liked the FBI circling their crime scenes. It didn't matter that the FBI usually had to be invited in by someone in charge; they didn't just barge into a homicide investigation for the hell of it. He said neutrally, "We're getting a lot of that these days."

"It's a fact the freeways, the interstates, are popular dumping grounds for bodies."

"Yes. Correct."

"So why Frankie jumped to the conclusion that one lone DB in the middle of nowhere had to be part of your investigation… that I don't get."

Adam shook his head. Rob was mostly arguing with himself anyway.

They had come up here knowing it was a longshot. The Ripper selected his victims carefully, mostly preying on the young men who worked at or frequented gay clubs and bars in the cities and large towns connected by the Interstate 5. He chose a vulnerable segment of the population. Victims who were unlikely to be missed. Victims who, even if they were missed, local law enforcement was unlikely to investigate the circumstances of their disappearance.

And the Ripper had been at it a long time. With no end in sight.

Azure appeared with their drinks and Adam's dinner. The speed at which that entrée had been delivered was not encouraging. Adam dug in anyway. Azure, now flirting with the guys at the next table, removed their empties and departed.

Rob said in a different tone of voice, "Not that I mind you being here." He smiled with deliberate charm at Adam and Adam smiled back, relieved that they were getting back on track. If there had still been a case here, they would not be doing this dance. He didn't believe in getting involved with coworkers and team members. Not after Tucker. Not after the way that relationship had ended. Never again.

But this was not their case, and he would never see Deputy Rob Haskell after tonight.

He smiled back and said, "Good. Because this is right where I want to be."

Rob's smile widened.

Three drinks and one mediocre plate of Chicken Alfredo later, Adam and Rob walked back through the soaked grass and tall trees to Adam's cabin.

The lights were out at Jonnie's, which Adam was glad to see. Not that Jonnie would have much, if anything, to say about this. That was another reason he hated losing her as his partner. He liked keeping his private life private. *I think the word is covert*, she'd said when the topic had come up in regards to who he'd be bringing to the wedding.

Adam fumbled with the key and Rob laughed.

"You bothered to lock it?"

"Paranoia is good for the soul."

"Probably not."

"Probably not," Adam agreed. He pushed the door open and groped around for a light switch.

Rob brushed past him, and a moment later one of the table lamps flared into life. "There we go." He smiled and the triangle of light threw a sinister shadow across his face.

Not his first rodeo, clearly. Not even his first rodeo in this cabin. Which was fine. It didn't matter to Adam. He was curious though.

"So you *are* out then?"

Rob, in the process of unbuckling his belt, laughed. He yanked down his jeans and shorts. "I am tonight."

Yes, he was.

Adam laughed too, shrugging out of his tailored suit jacket and removing his shoulder holster. He couldn't help noticing that Rob was not wearing his own weapon.

"You're not carrying?"

Rob tossed his own shirt onto Adam's computer case. "I'm off duty."

Once again Adam bit back a comment that might potentially put a crimp in current events. Maybe his very lack of expression was a tell to another LEO because Rob grinned and said, "It's okay. You'll protect me, right?"

He realized that he kind of liked Rob's goofy sense of humor. "Yeah. I'll protect you."

Rob, now totally and, frankly, magnificently naked, walked over to him and wrapped Adam in his arms. He whispered, "But who's going to protect you?"

Adam wound his arms around Rob's broad shoulders, and bumped suggestively, cock to cock.

Rob's shoulders were broad, his arms muscular. His thighs were muscular too, pressing against Adam's. He had a strong, athletic body—tight and toned beneath skin like hot silk. Adam let his hands wander, enjoying touching, exploring…

Rob groaned. "Jesus, there's something about a man who isn't in uniform."

That made Adam laugh. Rob was a funny guy. He was not used to sex being a light and playful thing. Pleasurable yes, definitely. Also biological necessity and stress relief. Rob's jokes caught him off guard—as did Rob's attempt to kiss him.

He liked the scent of Scotch on warm breath. Rob's full lips were both firm and soft, but it was too personal. Too reminiscent of someone else. He dodged Rob's mouth, nuzzling him beneath his ear, beneath his jaw, bouncing against him again, pointedly now. More thrust than bounce. Whatever they were doing, he wanted to get on with it.

"What do you want?" Rob's voice was deep and rough. "Just say. Whatever it is…"

That was generous. Unusually generous. "Have you got a condom?"

"Uh…yeah. Hold on…"

"Not going anywh—" Adam broke off, breath squeezing out in a wheeze as Rob ducked, hauling him into a clumsy shoulder carry, and dumping him onto the bed. Something beneath him gave a loud crack, and the mattress sank in the middle like it was deflating.

Rob's expression was priceless and Adam started to laugh.

"Pretend you didn't notice that." Rob was chuckling too, hunting through his jeans. He met Adam's eyes, mimed frantic haste and ripping his jeans in two, and Adam laughed again.

He didn't fail to notice though that when Rob landed on the bed next to him, he was perfectly sure of his welcome, amused, and a little smug. Not a clown, but not afraid to play the clown if it got him what he wanted.

"You've got really green eyes," Rob commented. "I can tell the color even in this light."

"You've got a really big cock," Adam returned, reaching for him. "I can tell the size even i—"

It was good. Just what he'd needed. *Exactly* what he'd needed.

Adam wore the condom and Rob let himself be taken, hairy legs propped on Adam's shoulders as he gazed dark-eyed and intense into Adam's face. Not submission. Just being a good ambassador. *Welcome to Nearby. Come for the serial killer and stay for the lousy Chicken Alfredo.*

If Adam *were* staying another day, Rob would wear the condom the next time and Adam would be the one getting pleasurably nailed to the musty mattress.

But if Adam was staying another day, they wouldn't be doing this anyway.

He glanced down and Rob's cock was huge, engorged, and ruddy, thrusting up needy and eager over the taut plane of Rob's abs. His skin was unexpectedly, disarmingly snowy white. Like he didn't get to spend much time in the sun. Which, this being Oregon, he probably didn't.

"Yeah, come on," Rob whispered urgently. "Bring it home."

Something like that. Adam wasn't listening. No one ever said anything intelligent during sex. Including himself. It was all about physical sensation, his own mostly, though he hoped it was good for Rob too. From a distance it sounded like it was.

Adam threw his head back and rolled his hips. Rob was pushing back, matching his rhythm easily, and the slick heat of him was just…

"Good. So goddamned *good*," Adam muttered. He was down to short strokes now, hips rocking, pumping furiously, a labor of delight. The base of his spine tingled, his balls tightened, *hold on…just a few seconds longer…*

The world shrank to this. A sweaty, lathered midnight ride, hell for leather, racing through the dark toward—

Oh God.

Hot, wet burst of *exquisite* release. He saw stars. He *felt* stars.

He yelled, and somewhere in the night Rob yelled back.

And the urgency, the need that had been driving him slowed, slowed, stumbled to a walk and then a limp, and then stopped, trembling and woozy.

Rob arched, yelled again…only it turned into a yodel. *A yodel?*

"Yodel-Aye-EEE-Oooo!"

Yeah, a yodel. Followed by laughter. This guy had been in the mountains too long.

"Jesus fucking God that was great," Rob proclaimed finally. Even in the gloom his eyes were shining and his teeth were white. Maybe he got laid even less than Adam.

Wet, sticky, spent, Adam crashed down beside him. "You were great," he said, and squeezed Rob's shoulder. Or he hoped it was Rob's shoulder. Maybe it was his knee. His eyelids felt weighted. The room smelled of sex and old linens and Rob. That was one hell of a nice aftershave. He closed his eyes.

When he lifted his lashes, he was under the fusty blankets, and the cabin felt warm.

He was surprised that he'd allowed himself to fall asleep at all, let alone deeply enough not to notice Rob stoking the fire in the stove. He was more surprised when he felt a delicate touch on his wrist. He turned his head.

Rob rested on his side, head bent, tracing a fingertip along the silver links of Adam's bracelet. His eyelashes threw dark crescents on his cheekbones.

"Pretty." He raised his head and met Adam's gaze.

Adam quirked a smile.

"Very...refined."

That was probably not a compliment. Adam didn't answer. Rob studied him. He said slowly, "Are you saying the federal government doesn't have a problem with this?"

"With this?" It took Adam a second to remember their earlier conversation. "If you mean does the Bureau discriminate against gay personnel, no."

Rob raised his brows. Unconvinced? Unimpressed?

"J. Edgar Hoover has left the building. Quite a while ago, as a matter of fact."

"Yeah? Well, there's official policy, and then there's reality."

That was true. No argument there. There probably wasn't a profession in the world where the rank and file didn't struggle to balance ideals with practice.

He was vaguely disappointed when Rob rose from the rumpled bed in a quick, lithe movement. He moved around the room, picking up his clothes and dressing.

Adam opened his mouth to say... What? *You can stay?* Probably not a good idea even if Rob showed any indication of wanting to linger. Which he did not. And Adam didn't particularly want that either. It was just that sometimes...after sex...he felt lonely.

And tonight in particular. These woods, the darkness beyond these four walls, the unnatural quiet that made him dread the moment when he would be on his own with nothing but thoughts and memories for company.

"So you're not out then?" He watched Rob shrug into his red tartan shirt.

Rob looked up, startled. "Huh? Well, I'm sure as hell not *in*, as you may have noticed."

"Okay." It didn't matter to him, after all. Curiosity was part of his job description.

Rob pulled on his jeans with efficient speed, fastened his belt. "I don't like people knowing my business. That's all. I like to keep my private life private."

"Sure. Same here."

Rob winked. "If I see something I like, I don't mind going for it."

Adam smiled. He could understand that, and it had been a very agreeable encounter. "I'm glad about that."

"The pleasure was all mine," Rob said. Then he grinned. "Well, I hope not, but a lot of it was mine." Before Adam could respond to this unexpected gallantry, Rob had the door open and was stepping into the pitch-black beyond. He called cheerfully, "Nighty-night. Don't let the bed bugs bite."

The door swung gently shut.

CHAPTER THREE

Promptly at five o'clock the next morning Rob rapped on Adam's cabin door. Adam, looking uptight and well-groomed—so well-groomed that Rob, had he not personally seen him naked as a blue jay, would have guessed he'd never undressed the night before—threw open the door and scowled his disapproval.

"Cutting it close, Deputy."

Rob smiled cheerfully. "Good morning to you too, Darling."

Darling's face grew grimmer still. He'd probably had a life-time of lame jokes like that one. Still. However, as Rob glanced past Adam he realized Agent Gould was sitting in his cabin, drinking instant coffee and eyeing them in surprise.

"Uh, sorry," Rob said. "It's not going to take more than forty-five minutes to get to the airport. And at this hour on a Tuesday morning you're not going to be dealing with any long lines."

"Good morning, Deputy," Gould called. She put her coffee cup down and picked up her computer case.

"Yes, it is, ma'am. Any morning it isn't raining is a good day."

Adam grabbed his trench coat, gave Rob an austere look, and followed his colleague out the door.

Well, hell. No offense intended. He guessed that even if he'd been early, Adam would have been much the same. A very tightly wound guy, Special Agent Darling. And nights like the evening before were probably a rarity. They were a rarity for Rob too. That was the off season lack of opportunity, not lack of inclination. With Adam…well, he probably didn't like anything that messed up his five hundred dollar haircut.

Rob sighed as he fell into formation.

The drive, as promised, took no more than forty-five minutes. Rob was left to his own thoughts, punctuated by the crackle of the radio, while the agents conferred quietly in the backseat. He was disappointed that all lines of communication had been cut off between himself and Adam—not that there was anything he wanted to say. *If you're ever in the area?* Not very likely. If they wanted to treat him like a chauffeur, so be it.

When they reached the airport parking lot, Agent Gould said thank you and goodbye, offering that very pretty smile, and then briskly crossing the street to the terminal, without waiting for her partner. Smart and tactful. He liked that in a woman.

"You have a nice flight home," Rob said to Adam.

Having reached the airport in plenty of time, Adam had relaxed. He looked tired, there were shadows beneath his green eyes, but he smiled at Rob. He had an attractive, quirky smile—despite noticeably sharp incisors—and Rob was sorry again that the night before had been a one-time thing. There was a guy in Klamath he saw now and again. No one special. And Adam did seem…special. Or at least different from anyone else Rob knew.

"Yes, thanks," Adam said. "Thanks for your help. And last night." There was a hint of color in his face, which Rob found sort of endearing.

"Thank *you*," he said, which unfortunately came out sounding more lewd than he'd intended.

Adam only laughed. "Good luck," he said, and turned away.

Rob considered those final words as Adam strode across the road and vanished through the glass doors. Maybe Adam was wishing him good luck with his cold case, or maybe he was wishing him good luck being the only gay man within thirty-six miles.

Either way, he could probably use all the luck he could get.

*　*　*　*　*

"Say what you want," Frankie called from her office when he finally got back to the station around three o'clock that afternoon. "There are advantages to living in a small town."

"Nearby is too small to qualify as a town," Rob retorted. That was just being grouchy, and there was no reason for it. No reason for feeling out of sorts, but he did. Had felt that way ever since dropping off Darling and Gould at the airport. His last call—helping Jack Elkins dig his pickup out of the mud yet again—hadn't improved his mood any. Not that he was bored. Not that he regretted choosing the peace and quiet of rural policing to the excitement and glamour of chasing down junkies and hookers in Portland. There was no denying he was feeling restless.

Maybe he'd visit his pal in Klamath Falls this weekend.

Frankie's good mood was undiminished. "*Sometimes* living in a small town works in your favor. We sure wouldn't get these kinds of results in the big city."

She was waving a manila folder, and Rob walked over to lean on the frame of her office door. He folded his arms. "Meaning what?"

Her smile was wide and uncharacteristically jovial. "Dental records. We matched 'em to our logging road John Doe."

"Already? You're kidding."

"Nope."

"Nice," Rob approved. "So then he was local?"

"Yep. He sure was. Dove Koletar." She was staring at him like that ought to mean something.

Rob glanced over his shoulder. The station was empty though. Zeke had called in sick that morning, which was why Rob had drawn taxi duty. And Aggie was on family leave, attending her father's funeral in Las Vegas. He turned back to Frankie. "Who?"

"Dove Koletar. His parents used to own the cabins down by the lake. Marion sold to Sid Lodi after Roger passed."

Rob shook his head. Long before his time.

"Dove was…you know," Frankie said.

Rob guessed, "Not right in the head?"

"Gay."

Now Rob understood what that meaningful look meant. *One of yours.* "Same thing in some people's minds," he said easily.

Frankie laughed her deep, smoker's laugh. "Back then for sure. Which is why nobody was surprised when he left town."

"You mean when he disappeared?"

"No. No, there was no mystery about it. Dove left a letter. I remember that very well. He left a letter for his parents saying he was leaving this hick town forever. I remember that particularly because the 'hick town' comment pissed off all us hicks."

"He was a runaway then?"

"Nope. He would have been in his early twenties. I was about twenty-two, and we were in school together, so he was of legal age. Dove was unhappy, and he didn't fit in. Nobody was surprised when he left. The surprise was that he waited as long as he did."

"He didn't get very far."

"No, he didn't." Frankie looked grim.

"Any further evidence as to how Koletar died?"

Frankie shook her head. "His remains are being transported to Klamath Falls where Doc can conduct a real examination. He's going to bring in a forensic anthropologist too."

Rob grunted. Better late than never. He said, "So we've got a cold case."

"It appears so." Frankie tossed the folder to her desk, and Rob reached over to pick it up. "What happened with the break-in at the museum?"

"Attempted break-in." Rob opened the file. It was nothing but the preliminary autopsy report and a copy of dental records. His gaze sharpened as he studied the dates on the dental records. "Wait a minute. These are from *thirty* years ago."

"Yep."

"Doc had it wrong then? This guy disappeared thirty years ago?"

"Nothing wrong with your math skills. Now how about the museum break-in?"

"Somebody who didn't know what he was doing tried to pick the back door lock. When that didn't work, they tried to kick the door in. That's when Mrs. Joseph woke up and scared them off."

"She should have called us last night when it happened. I'm not sure what she thought we could do seven hours later."

"She said she knew he wouldn't come back, and she didn't want to wake anybody up when we wouldn't be able to see anything till daylight anyway."

"There's such a thing as being too considerate," Frankie said.

"Yeah." Rob was glad Mrs. Joseph hadn't called them out in the middle of the night. For a lot of reasons. And the truth was, they wouldn't have been able to do much till daylight. The kid or kids who'd tried to break in would have been long gone by the time he or Zeke made it over to the museum.

Anyway, the museum was technically on federal land, so any problems were as much the jurisdiction of the park rangers as theirs. Not that there was a surplus of park rangers these days. Not with all those good old government cutbacks.

Frankie frowned, thinking.

Rob said, "They need an alarm on that place."

"An alarm system would cost more than anything in that museum is worth," Frankie said, and that was probably true. "You dusted for prints?"

"I tried. Aside from the fact that it was pouring rain for most of last night, a lot of people have touched that lock. I couldn't get anything usable. I made a cast of the boot prints outside the broken window. Size nine-and-a-half hiking boots, nothing distinct or unusual there."

Frankie was still frowning.

"What?" Rob asked.

She said slowly, "You know, Robbie, one day you're going to be Sheriff of Nearby."

"What? *Me?* No way." He felt a genuine stab of alarm at the idea.

"Who then? Zeke? Aggie?" Frankie shook her head.

"It's not a hereditary title, you know. The city council could hire someone from outside." He tossed Koletar's file back on the littered desk.

"They could and they probably will if you don't step up."

"Step up?" Rob protested. "How am I not stepping up?"

Frankie's frown deepened. "Everything is not a joke."

"I don't think everything is a joke." He began to get irritated. "I don't think there's anything funny about an attempted break-in. I don't know if the plan was burglary or vandalism, but I'm not laughing. I tried to get fingerprints. I made a cast of the boot prints."

Frankie waved a dismissing hand. "I'm not talking about that."

"Well, what then?"

She shook her head, as though it wasn't worth answering. "Marion Koletar is living in Klamath Falls now. She needs to be notified."

He said curtly, "All right." There was nothing he hated more than a notification run. Having to break that kind of news to a loved one? There was a bright side though. He could probably arrange to meet up with his friend while he was there. Maybe have dinner together. Or better yet, skip dinner altogether.

"I want you to take lead on this investigation."

"Roger that." Like there was any question? What the hell had got into her?

"And don't sulk."

Now that really was uncalled for. Rob opened his mouth, caught the glint in her beady little eyes, and said instead, "Well hell, Frankie. You've already said you knew the victim. I guess maybe I should start by interviewing you."

Frankie threw her head back and laughed that deep, alarming laugh. "Maybe you should. There's not a lot I can tell you. Dove wasn't a friend. He didn't have many friends. Kind of a loner, like I said. No one was surprised when he took off."

"What about enemies? You said everybody knew he was gay. Thirty years ago that might not have gone over well with some people."

Frankie looked thoughtful. "I don't remember him being bullied in school. Not more than anyone else. Mostly people just left him alone. He was odd. Apart from being gay, I mean."

Yeah, well that was a convenient way of looking at it. Rob said, "So no friends and no enemies? He was just a ghost?"

She shrugged. "You might say that."

"You said you went to school together. Was there a school in Nearby back then?"

"Ha! A little red one-room schoolhouse? Is that what you're thinking? No. Back then the kids up here rode the bus to Klamath Falls same as they do now. We went to Haney Elementary, and then Haney Middle School, and then Haney High School."

That was a relief. There might be some kind of a lead there. Or at least a hint as to the character of the victim. Who was Dove Koletar? He needed something more than dental records and vague memories. "Okay. I'll contact the mother and make arrangements to interview her."

"Good deal," Frankie said.

* * * * *

"You're not telling me anything I don't already know," Marion Koletar said. "I knew Dove was dead. I've known for years my boy was dead."

She was a small, washed-out looking woman with faded hair and faded eyes. Dry eyes. She wasn't shedding any tears. Her voice was tired, muted; Rob found himself leaning forward to hear better every time she spoke.

It hadn't taken him long to track her down, but getting her to answer the damn door? *That* took some doing. He'd tried knocking twice, and then he'd tried leaving a phone message. Finally he'd parked in front of the apartment building where she lived and waited for her to show.

And she looked so different from what he'd imagined that he'd nearly missed her when she had finally strolled up, pushing her shopping cart. He'd been expecting someone older and more affluent. After all, Frankie and Dove had been classmates, and she'd sold the thirty-four lakeside cabins for a small fortune. She didn't look much more than Frankie's age, and she didn't appear to be particularly affluent judging by the contents of her grocery bags. A dozen boxes of Lean Cuisine spaghetti and a two-gallon jug of fruit punch.

"How's that, ma'am?" he asked. "What made you think Dove was dead?"

She gave a vague shrug. "He never called. He never wrote."

When he'd identified himself, she had seemed to weigh whether to let him into her place or not. Finally she'd opened the door, and he'd stepped into hoarder heaven. Newspapers were stacked everywhere. They lined the walls and formed precarious towers all the way to the ceiling. Numerous shorter stacks created a paper maze across the length of the living room.

This was taking keeping up with current events to a whole new level.

"You were close to your son?"

"No. But I still think once he grew up he'd have contacted me. If he'd lived."

She wore a flowered house dress, the kind of thing that nobody wore anymore. Nobody her age, at least, because, again, she wasn't *that* old. He glanced at the clock—only the top half showed above the towers of newspapers—he had to meet his friend in twenty minutes.

"Do you have any idea of who might have wanted to hurt Dove?"

"No."

"Do you remember the exact date he left home?"

"November."

November was an exact date?

She irritated him. Everything about her irritated him. Her vague manner, and the stacks and stacks of newspapers, and the fact that she'd taken it for granted her kid was dead—that she'd never made any attempt to *do* something. Anything. It all irritated him. And he was irritated that he was irritated. If he couldn't summon up a little compassion, where at least was his professional detachment?

He just wanted to get out of there.

"Do you still have the letter Dove left for you and your husband?"

Marion looked around the magazine-lined room as though she hoped to spot the letter lying on a stack of newspapers. "He did leave a letter," she agreed. "I'm sure it's here somewhere."

"Do you have any photos of your son?"

Another of those dubious looks. "Somewhere…"

Rob sighed. Marion Koletar wasn't deliberately obstructive, but she might as well be.

He was doing a half-assed job and he knew it. Special Agent Darling would have that supercilious look on his face were he observing this interview. But Special Agent Darling was not here, and Rob was going to miss meeting his friend if he didn't wind this up pretty quick. His friend would not take kindly to being stood up for "police business" again. It wasn't like Rob was making any headway with Marion. Maybe if he pushed her and kept pushing her.

Tell me about your son. What was Dove like? Those were the questions he should be asking. And had it not been a thirty-year-old cold case, he would be asking. However, this was a victim whose own mother hadn't bothered to keep a photo of him. Someone who had fallen off the grid and no one had ever questioned it, let alone made an attempt to find him. He was sorry. Genuinely sorry about Dove Koletar. Life would not have been easy for that young man. And neither would death.

There was only so much you could do, and this was an uphill battle all the way.

"Could you put together a list of your son's friends?"

"Oh. I..." She trailed off helplessly.

Rob gritted his teeth and forged on. "Actually, could you put together a list of anyone you can remember who might have been close to your son?"

"Close to him?" She looked alarmed.

"Right. Friends. Or whatever. Or not friends. Anyone he didn't like. Maybe he had a run-in with someone? I know it was a long time ago, but anyone you can think of. Friend or foe. If you could put that list together for me and try to dig up a couple of photos—and maybe find the letter he left you—"

"Why?" she interrupted. She looked bewildered.

"*Why?* Because we're investigating his death."

"But...it's too late."

"I'm not sure what you mean. It's a cold case, yes."

"He's *dead*," Marion said. "It's too late to do any good. What's the point of digging all that up?"

He honestly didn't know what to say to that. *Because your dead son deserves justice.* How about that one? *Because it's my job*. Not noble, though the truth. *Because it's not good for any of us when someone gets away with murder.* That was also the truth.

He rose. "If you could just put those things together for us, ma'am?"

She continued to blink up at him in noncomprehension. He knew she would not put that list together, would not find the photos, would not look for the letter. In a few days she probably wouldn't even remember his visit.

"Sorry for your loss," Rob said.

Just as Rob figured, Marion Koletar did not provide him with any of the information or materials he requested. He tried a couple of follow-up calls, but Marion did not answer the phone or return his messages.

He didn't give up. Not immediately. He got the forensics back on Koletar. Aside from a couple of almost microscopic nicks on the rib cage that might or might not have been inflicted by a knife, there was no indication of how he had died.

There was even a tiny chance it had been a natural death, and some Good Samaritan who couldn't afford any public scrutiny had found the body and buried it.

Yeah, right.

He got copies of all Koletar's school records. There was nothing useful there. The victim had been an average student—which was a feat in itself given he typically missed about twenty days a semester. No wonder his teachers had nothing to say about him. They probably wouldn't have been able to pick him out of a lineup.

He asked around, talked to people about Dove. No one but Frankie seemed to really remember him. And she didn't seem to remember much except that he hadn't fit in and hadn't been happy.

"What about his father?" Rob asked. Unfortunately, when something happened to a kid, the parents were the first and obvious suspects.

"I doubt it," Frankie said. "Maybe they slapped him around now and again. He wasn't abused. Not for that day and age. More like neglected, I'd say."

"What about friends? He must have had friends."

"I don't know that he did," Frankie said.

Rob was drawing blanks in every direction. He could have kept pushing. But then the holidays came, and the first snow of the season, and then the tourists were back. Everybody was busy. Even Frankie lost interest in the subject of Dove Koletar.

Nobody actually ever said the words "case closed," but when Rob tucked the skinny manila folder in the lowest drawer of the filing cabinet, no one questioned it. Or pulled it out again.

November, December, January.

And then Cynthia Joseph was murdered.

CHAPTER FOUR

"**I** don't get it," Russell said. "Why us?"

Tall, dark, and handsome, Russell could have served as a poster boy for the modern FBI. He was smart too. And personable. Though he didn't waste much of that personability on Adam.

"Murder on federal property," Adam replied. Most of his attention was on the road ahead. It was starting to snow. Not hard, though it was sticking, and he wasn't used to driving in these conditions. A born and bred California boy, he preferred sailing to skiing. He knew enough to know he didn't have winter tires, and all the training in the world didn't help when the other people on the road were idiots.

Not that there were a lot of other people on the road. Right there was probably an indication.

They'd arrived in Medford that afternoon, rented a car, and were now on their way to Nearby. The curator of a small museum at the edge of the national forest had been found dumped in a Native American exhibit with her throat cut. Sheriff McLellan had invited the FBI—and Adam personally—into the investigation.

It was hard to know what was bothering Russell more: that the Bureau had been dragged in, or that Adam had been requested. He asked again, "Why you? Why ask for you specifically?"

"I don't know. I guess we'll find out." He was glad though. Grateful. It stung that his SAC had no hesitation in releasing him from the Ripper taskforce, but frankly it was a relief to get off morgue patrol. It wasn't that he didn't think they were doing useful work helping to compile the database of the Ripper's victims for eventual possible federal prosecution. It was work a probationary agent could handle. Just about tolerable when he'd been partnered with Jonnie. He and J.J. Russell had been at odds from the moment they shook hands. Russell resented morgue patrol even more than Adam did, and Russell nearly *was* probationary. First office agent. Bu-ease for an agent who didn't know enough to realize how little he knew.

Maybe what really bugged him about Russell was he reminded Adam too much of himself. Or at least the self he'd used to be.

"If they're a substation then they're too small to handle a homicide investigation, and they need to hand it off to the state police. Or to a larger sheriff department in the county," Russell said.

Which was perfectly true.

"There's nothing about this that justifies bringing in the Bureau."

"Murder on federal property," repeated Adam.

"We're from Los Angeles. This is Portland's case, if it's anybody's."

"They asked for us. They requested our help. Portland signed off on it."

"Because Portland doesn't think it's worth their time or manpower."

Russell was probably right about that too. Adam said neutrally, "Maybe we should wait to draw any conclusions."

Russell's silence was stony.

So that was the drive from the airport. It took about an hour. Then another two minutes after they reached Nearby to locate the sheriff's office tucked between the library and the optimistically named Tourist Center.

Over the past months Adam had been inside so many of these small town police departments and sheriff stations, he could have described the interior without ever opening the door. It was always the same setup: from the female deputy frustrated with being the one stuck manning the phones, to the bulletin board papered with the crimes and tragedies of distant metropolises. *Be on the lookout for…*other people's problems. Because nothing bad ever happened in these small towns.

Until it did.

This time the deputy was tall and boyishly thin, with dark hair tied back in a tight ponytail that would be a liability in a street fight. Since she would probably spend most of her career doing paperwork and answering phones, her hair style was likely not a concern. Her eyes widened at the sight of Adam and Russell.

"Frankie!" she called without glancing at the identification Russell proffered.

From an office on the other side of the long wood-paneled building, Sheriff McLellan called back, "Yep?"

"They're here."

Russell put his identification back. Sheriff McLellan bustled out of her office to meet them. She was shorter, stouter, and redder than Adam remembered. "Thanks for coming on such short notice, Agent Darling."

It was always short notice. Nobody planned for a murder or a kidnapping or a bank robbery. Adam shook hands and said, "Of course, Sheriff. This is Agent Russell."

McLellan nodded a curt hello to Russell. She looked haggard. Like she hadn't slept in forty-eight hours. Which was probably accurate. There were bags beneath her eyes and lines carved around her mouth. She pointed to the front desk deputy. "That's Aggie. Deputy Hawkins. You know the rest of the team. Zeke is out interviewing residents of the homes nearest the museum. Unfortunately, we've got a number of vacation properties out that way with nobody home this time of year. Rob and I have been going over the crime scene photos."

Adam didn't like the way his pulse gave a kick at the mention of Deputy Haskell's name. That was the last thing he needed. He'd enjoyed their previous encounter, but it had been a one off. It had to be.

"Help yourselves to some coffee." McLellan led them into her office. "So far the media hasn't caught wind. We're hoping it stays that way."

"That won't last," Russell said. "Some blogger will get hold of it. Somebody's going to go on Twitter."

Rob was sitting to the side of McLellan's desk. There was a coffee cup and a half-eaten sandwich on a paper plate near his elbow. He was poring over a gruesome selection of crime scene photos. Glancing up, he met Adam's eyes, gave a tiny nod, and returned to scrutinizing the photos.

That was a relief. Nothing to worry about there. Rob clearly shared his desire to keep things on a strictly professional basis.

So why he felt ever so slightly piqued, Adam wasn't sure.

Funny thing: he hadn't recalled Rob being so handsome. He was. From that strong, square jaw to those expressive, dark eyes, he was by anyone's standards a very nice looking guy.

"Rob, you know Agent Darling. And this is Agent Russell."

"Agent Russell." Rob glanced again at Adam. His mouth quivered ever so slightly as he added, "Darling."

"Who processed the crime scene?" Adam asked. "State police?"

"That's right," McLellan said.

Russell said, "Sheriff, why is a substation attempting to conduct a murder investigation? Why has this not been handed over to the Medford or—"

"Because Medford is Jackson County," Rob said, and all good humor was gone from his face and voice. "You're in Klamath County. And we're not a substation. Nearby is an incorporated village. We've got our own civic charter, and we've been recognized by the state legislature. Frankie is the duly elected sheriff of this community."

Russell turned red, met Adam's eyes, and looked away.

Adam said, "Whatever advice or assistance you need, Sheriff. Say the word. This is your investigation."

"Good," Rob said. "Because one way to guarantee media coverage is inviting in the FBI."

"Robbie," McLellan cautioned.

Rob shrugged.

"You called us, remember?" Adam said.

"*I* didn't call you," Rob said. "If it had been up to me—"

"No, *I* called Agent Darling," McLellan cut in. "Duly elected or not, we're out of our depth. And the last thing we want is to have to turn this over to State or KPD."

"Then let's stop pissing on trees and start working the case," Adam said.

Rob said shortly, "Suits me." He pushed the photos across the desk. His hands were strong, capable. Nails clipped short, cuticles a little ragged. Adam experienced a sudden, vivid memory of those hands stroking his back, caressing his ass.

He swallowed and said to McLellan, "Is the body in the mortuary?"

"No. Not this time. The remains have been transported to Klamath Falls."

Adam turned to Russell who said, "I'll interview the ME." Adam nodded.

Russell wanted to return to civilization ASAP, and Adam didn't really blame him. Russell believed they were on a wild goose chase, and Adam thought he was probably right. The difference was he was grateful for the break. Russell, on the other hand, resented spending time on anything that would not potentially bring him to the attention of his superiors and possible promotion. Adam got it. Once upon a time he'd felt the same way.

As Russell left the office, Adam picked up the crime scene photos.

You got used to them, of course. You couldn't do the job if you didn't manage to develop a high threshold for other people's pain. Not so high that you stopped caring, but high enough that you could look at the slaughter of a woman like Cynthia Joseph and not lose your lunch.

It did make it hard to sleep sometimes.

Cynthia Joseph had been about forty. A dark-haired woman with strong rather than pretty features. Granted, it would be impossible for anyone to look pretty with her throat cut.

He opened his mouth and Rob said tersely, "He hit her over the head with a metate. Hopefully he knocked her cold."

Hopefully, yes. Adam said, "A metate?"

"Handheld grinding stone."

"Did you recover a weapon?"

"No," Rob said. "We think he used one of the knives in the museum. A display case was smashed open, and it looks like one of the knives is missing."

"Do you know time of death yet?"

"Not yet. Just that she died sometime during the night. She was found a little after nine o'clock yesterday morning." McLellan said, "Pete Abrams was delivering propane to the Josephs. He saw the museum door standing open and went inside. He found Cynthia." The lines on her face grew more pronounced. "Our killer dropped her body on one of those displays—"

She looked at Rob who answered, "Diorama."

"That's right. It was a funeral display. Well, the Modocs cremated their dead so it was supposed to show the body being prepared for the ceremony."

Rob said, "He dumped her body on the funeral pyre."

Adam said thoughtfully, "Hm. He didn't light the pyre."

"Jesus," Rob muttered.

Adam asked, "Was there a mannequin in the display? What happened to it?"

"No. No mannequin." McLellan was watching him as though awaiting some grand pronouncement. He didn't have a pronouncement for her. Initial observation maybe. Nothing they wouldn't have noticed themselves: that it had been a crime of opportunity, and that they were dealing with someone likely both deranged and disorganized.

McLellan said, "Cynthia and her daughter lived next door to the museum. Back in October someone tried to break into the museum, and Cynthia scared them away. We think that may have happened again."

"Only they didn't scare this time," Rob said.

Adam asked, "What's so valuable in that museum?"

"Nothing." McLellan met his gaze and repeated, "Nothing. No precious metals, no gemstones. There are a couple of stuffed animals displays—dioramas—a few maps, a lot of information about nature and the woods. And there's a collection of Modoc antiquities that belonged to Cynthia's family. Bowls and baskets. Costumes and beads and feathers. She donated the lot to the Park Service when she married Henry."

"Henry?"

"Henry Joseph. Henry and Cynthia were both park rangers. Henry died five years ago. Cynthia stayed on as a tour guide and the museum curator."

"You said there's a daughter?" Adam questioned.

"Tiffany. Aged seventeen. She's staying with friends in Klamath Falls this weekend."

"You said you believe a knife was taken from a display case. Was anything else taken from the museum?"

Rob said, "That's what we're trying to determine. It looked like maybe a couple of items have been removed. Cynthia may have pulled them for her own reasons. We're hoping Tiffany can shed some light on that."

Adam said slowly, "You haven't spoken to her yet?"

"We're working on it. She didn't go to school yesterday, and we don't know the last name of the friend she was staying with. Aggie's tracking her down now."

Not good. In fact, suspicious. Although the previous attempt at a break-in did offer an alternative scenario. A preferable scenario.

Adam shuffled through the photos, considering the possibilities. He said finally, "I'd like to walk the crime scene if that's all right?"

"Sure. That's the idea. Rob will do the honors," McLellan said wearily.

Rob rose at once, removed his jacket from a hook on the wall, and pulled it on. "Let's do it," he said.

In silence, they left the sheriff's office, walked around the corner of the building, and climbed into a white SUV with the official green and gold Sheriff's Office insignia. The snow had turned to a slushy rain. The interior of the vehicle was cold. Adam could smell Rob's aftershave—that blend of green citrus and sequoia—and he was disconcerted at how familiar it seemed.

Given that he hadn't had anything but solo sex since the night with Rob, it was probably a Pavlovian response.

"So. How've you been?" Rob's gaze was on the rearview mirror as he reversed, the wide tires leaving deep tracks in the snowy mud and gravel. "How's your Roadside Ripper doing?"

As a matter of fact, the Ripper had been taking it easy lately. Nearly five months since his last kill. Not his longest cooling off period. That had been six months. Long enough to make you hope he'd finally picked up the wrong guy. Not that you were supposed to hope for that. The aim was always to catch the offender.

"Good. Busy," Adam said. "Sorry we're meeting again under these circumstances."

Rob's laugh was short. "Are there any other circumstances we would have met under?"

Well, no.

"Did you know the victim?"

"Yep." It was a flat smack of a word. "Everybody knows everybody in Nearby. Cynthia wasn't just 'the victim' to people around here."

"I realize that."

"No, you don't." Rob threw him a hard, white smile. "This is personal for us. For you, it's just another case. Not that we don't appreciate the expertise you bring. I don't doubt you'd rather be working on your high profile taskforce."

"You'd be surprised."

Rob's gaze slid sideways. The windshield wipers beat out a few moments of silence before he said—sounding more friendly, "You got a new partner?"

"God help me." Adam hadn't meant to say that aloud, but when Rob laughed, he laughed too. Still. Not professional. Adam asked, "Did you ever find out the identity of your logging road John Doe?"

Rob half lifted a hand from the steering wheel in absent greeting as they passed a couple of elderly men in cowboy hats. "Yes, we sure did." His grin was mocking. "Surprised?"

He was, yes. It wouldn't be diplomatic to say so. "He was local?"

"Yes. Dove Koletar. According to local legend, the only other gay man to ever live in Nearby. His parents used to own the campground cabins by the lake. He left for the big city thirty years ago. Left a goodbye forever note and everything."

"A hate crime?" Adam asked. If that was the case, there was a good chance Koletar had been killed by someone local. Maybe even someone still living in Nearby. Thirty years was a long time, but it wasn't a lifetime.

"That, we'll probably never know. Koletar was the invisible man. Nobody remembers anything about him. Even his own mother forgot about him."

"Everybody copes in their own way."

Rob made a noncommittal sound.

They had left the brief stretch of small businesses that made up the village proper and were picking up speed as they headed toward the national forest. Despite the sleety rain, the snow was sticking, glazing the ground and powdering the trees. Behind walls of fir and pines, Adam glimpsed the roofs and windows of large, expensive homes.

"What's the year round population up here?"

"A little over fifteen hundred. It's shrinking steadily. During the summer season we see over a hundred thousand visitors annually."

"What?"

Rob laughed at his expression. "Not all the same week luckily."

"One hundred *thousand* visitors?"

"This is a very popular recreation spot in Southern Oregon."

"This is? What the hell do they do here?"

Rob was clearly amused at his ignorance. "Hiking, biking, and horseback riding. Among other things. People come here to swim, fish, canoe, water ski. You name it. If it can be done in water, they do it. And a lot of winters we get them ice fishing. Not this year. This is warm winter."

"It is?" Adam doubtfully eyed the windshield wipers briskly beating back the fall of fat, icy raindrops.

"Yep. Very warm."

They were only about five minutes out of the village when the SUV slowed and Rob turned off the main highway. The road was still paved, though the asphalt was wearing thin. The SUV hit a couple of teeth-rattling potholes in quick succession.

Rob said, "There's the museum up ahead."

The museum was an A-framed log cabin which sat in a clearing surrounded by deep forest. Two wickiups sat to one side of the main structure. The main building was constructed of wood that shone almost golden in the dreary light. Window frames, door, and steps were all painted in bright primary colors and adorned with Native American symbols.

"It's small," Adam commented.

"Yeah. Pretty much a one-woman enterprise. Cynthia was the curator and sole employee. Most of her time was donated. A few years ago—when the economy was better and we had more visitors—she had part-time help, but for the last few years it's just been her."

"And it's way out in the middle of nowhere."

Rob made a sound that was somewhere between a laugh and a snort. "That's right, city boy."

Adam glanced at him. "Correct me if I'm wrong. Isn't Portland the largest city in Oregon?"

"Why yes, it is. I'm flattered you remember that I'm from Portland."

"I remember." He held Rob's gaze for an instant.

A yellow crime scene banner and rope stretched across the road. Parked by the side of the road, a state trooper was pouring himself coffee from a thermos when they pulled alongside.

The trooper and Rob spoke briefly, and then he unhooked the rope, and Rob drove through and parked in the small parking area reserved for visitors.

They got out and crossed the empty lot, boots crunching the thin crust of snow.

"Was it snowing Thursday night?" Adam asked.

"Raining. We didn't get any usable tracks from the lot or the road."

"Maybe he didn't drive up." Though it would be a long way from anywhere to walk.

The wooden steps creaked forlornly as they walked up to the porch. Rob pointed out one of the tall windows along the side of the structure. The window was covered by a tarp.

"That's where he got in. Nothing fancy. He just smashed the window. Cynthia must have heard the glass breaking. The Josephs live over there." Rob indicated a small single-story white house on the far side of the clearing. "Out here sound carries at night."

Adam studied the house. It was not immediately visible from the road. "You said in October there was an attempt at a break-in?"

Rob nodded, opening the door and holding it for Adam. "Though it doesn't prove this was the same guy."

"You'll want to put together a list of everyone who ever worked in the museum," Adam said.

"Why didn't *we* think of that?" Because of the high ceiling Rob's sarcasm seemed magnified, echoing emptily as they walked past the reception desk with its tidy display of maps and NPS brochures. Adam's nostrils twitched at the scent of raw wood, old leather, and crime scene chemicals.

"This way," Rob said, and they turned left, passing a tall display case containing a full-size mannequin wearing ceremonial dress and a fierce and elaborate black and orange bear mask. The mannequin held aloft a painted staff which he seemed to point at the viewer. Glass case or not, the masked figure was pretty intimidating. The eyes behind the mask glittered with life-like alertness.

"Imagine seeing that out of the corner of your eye all day long," Rob commented.

"Maybe she considered him a coworker." Adam stared up at the cathedral ceiling with its steeply sloping open beams. "I'm not seeing surveillance cameras."

Rob said, "That's because there aren't any."

For God's sake. In this day and age?

Rob stopped in front of a dugout canoe propped on pedestals a few feet above the glossy floor. Behind the canoe was the broken window, now secured with tarp and heavy duty tape.

Adam stepped forward to examine the shattered, scattered glass on the floor behind the canoe, careful not to disturb any of the plastic crime scene markers.

"He'd have to know he was in full view of Joseph's front window. If this was the same intruder, he'd certainly realize there was a chance she might see him breaking in."

"Maybe he thought he was invisible. Or maybe he didn't give a shit if he was seen or not."

Adam nodded absently. Maybe there had been a plan. Maybe that plan had been to get Joseph over here on her own. "Why wouldn't she call for help? Why did she storm over here on her own?"

He was thinking aloud, but Rob answered. "She wasn't afraid."

He turned and Rob was right behind him. Not really enough room for two grown men in this small confined space. They looked uncomfortably into each other's eyes. Rob backed up and Adam squeezed past the canoe. He was conscious of the warmth of Rob's body. He remembered how it had felt to lie in Rob's arms.

It took him a second to remember what they had been talking about. He said, "She should have been. This was a bold and aggressive intruder. Why wasn't she afraid?"

"She thought she could handle the situation."

"Did she? Because that's the question. Is the X factor here Joseph's character or the character of her killer?"

Rob raised his eyebrows. "Maybe both. Maybe she thought she knew who the intruder was."

Adam's gaze zeroed on Rob's. He nodded. "Maybe she did. Yes. Where did he leave the body?"

"The other side of the museum." Rob turned away, and Adam followed him past a display of baskets and woven bowls and bottles, and then a wall of maps and black and white photos of early Twentieth Century Oregon.

The rain was coming down hard now. He could hear it drumming against the sloped roof. The light through the windows cast an eerie blue tinge over the rooms and their contents. It felt much later in the day than it actually was. An artificial twilight.

Rob paused, pointing out a few dots of red brown on the knotty paneling. "We think she came around this corner, and he hit her using one of the stones from that display."

The display dealt with diet and food preparation. The Modocs had been hunter-gatherers subsisting on everything from grizzly bears and pelicans to rye grass and yellow pond lilies. There were fishing spears, bows and iron-tipped arrows, boiling stones and grinding stones.

"He picked up a stone instead of an arrow or a spear," Adam said. "It's possible he didn't initially intend to kill her."

"Or, on the spur of the moment, a rock seemed less complicated."

Adam murmured acknowledgement. Rob was right. The unsub's election of weapon could have been based on something as simple as the grinding stone being closest to hand.

Rob said, "He knocked her out. Stunned her at the least. You can see by the smeared blood that he dragged her over here." He skirted the gruesome stains on the wood floor and led the way past a couple of glass cases to the far end of the building.

This final exhibit was a beautifully conceived diorama. The raised flooring was covered with dirt and grass. The painted backdrop depicted trees, lake, and wickiups in the far distance. In the center of the diorama was a funeral pyre of real wood piled several feet high. Very lifelike.

The most unrealistic element were the plastic crime scene markers surrounding the pyre. Now there was irony for you.

Rob said, "I've been reading up on this. The Modoc washed their dead, wrapped them in tule mats, and carried them head-first out of their homes. The body was taken to the cremation grounds and laid on a funeral pyre with the head pointing to the west. That's supposed to be where the entrance to their under-world was."

West. The direction of the setting sun. That made sense.

"Was Joseph's body arranged so that her head was pointing west?"

"Yeah. He undressed her, but wasn't able to wrap her in the tule mat, so he just draped it over her. She was lying with her head to the west."

Had it been a real attempt to adhere to ritual, or just a sick joke? Impossible to know. The staging of the body suggested someone familiar with Modoc death ceremony and/or the museum. Given that this was a very small museum in a very small town, it was possible that everyone in Nearby had visited the museum at some time or the other.

Watching him, Rob said, "So is this the part where you close your eyes and a grainy flashback of how the crime was committed comes to you?"

Adam smiled faintly. "Complete with Theremin soundtrack and slashing sound effects? No."

"You're sure? Because that would be convenient."

"Wouldn't it?"

"Seen enough?"

"I think so."

"I want to show you something else."

They started back toward the front of the museum. Adam paused at one of the smashed cases. There were three masks similar to the one worn by the mannequin near the entrance doors. Old and elaborate concoctions of carved cedar and brilliant plant dyes. They were large and would be very heavy and awkward to wear. Visibility would be nil. You couldn't wear them hunting or fighting. Their purpose would have to be ceremonial only.

On the far right was a bear mask, similar to, though larger than, the one worn by the mannequin in the front lobby. The second was of a dog or a wolf, and the third seemed to depict a bald man with a pierced lip and goggling eyes.

"What was he after here?"

"We think he took a mask," Rob said. "That's what it looks like. If so, he took the card with it. If he took one, I don't know why he wouldn't take all four. They're probably the most valuable things in the museum. Collectors pay big bucks for these ceremonial masks."

Beside the case was a placard with browned paper. Adam leaned forward to read it. "'Spell of the Laughing Raven'?"

Rob shrugged. "A story. A Modoc legend."

Adam read.

> *At "dance place" when the Klamath Lake people danced, many people were there.*
>
> *Kemush, Old Man of the Ancients, went there. Then Old Raven laughed at them, laughed when they danced, and all people dancing there became rocks.*
>
> *Gray Wolf entered Kitti above, from the north. There he stopped and lay down, although not yet having reached his home. In full dress, at that spot, moccasins with beads on toe, stopped and rested.*
>
> *Then Old Grizzly approached Old Gray Wolf while lying asleep. And Old Grizzly stole from Gray Wolf his moccasins, beads also, and put them on to go to the fishing place.*
>
> *Upon this, Old Gray Wolf, waking up, threw Old Grizzly down hill. He rolled him down over the rocks for having robbed him of moccasins and beads also. Thus killed he Old Grizzly.*
>
> *Upon this, the Klamath Lake people began fighting the Northerners because Old Grizzly had been killed by Old Gray Wolf.*
>
> *Then Old Raven laughed at them when fighting and they became rocks.*

He looked over at Rob who was watching him with an odd expression. "What does it mean?"

"You're asking me?"

"You said you've been reading up on this stuff."

"I just started," Rob said. "We've been a little busy around here, you may have noticed."

Adam turned to examine the case contents again. "I'll tell you what he took," he said. "He took the raven's mask."

CHAPTER FIVE

Of course. It was so damned obvious when you weren't trying to find a logical reason for murder and robbery. Adam's almost impatient certainty was annoying. So Rob said stolidly, "Yep. That's one theory."

As though reading his thoughts—right down to that flicker of childish *You don't know everything!*—Adam smiled. It was a tiny smile, true, just a glimpse of those white and too pointy incisors. He said gravely, "Oh? What's your other theory?"

"Simple theft. Like I said, these are valuable collector's items."

"Like you also said, why take one mask and not the others?" And now Adam was not bothering to hide his smile. He was full out grinning, full of confidence and superiority.

"No idea," Rob said curtly. "Why take the card describing the mask, but not take that placard, if it's related to the mask?"

"True."

Only partially mollified, Rob turned away. "I want to show you where we think he found the actual murder weapon. Although maybe you'll decide it was actually a tomahawk he took."

Adam said nothing. In fact, his silence was so complete that Rob wished he had kept his mouth shut. The problem was the G-man thing was a little intimidating, and Rob was not used to feeling out of his league. He was also not used to running into a guy who could apparently take or leave him without a second thought. Because *he* had given Adam a second thought. And maybe a third and fourth too.

He stopped in front of another damaged case. This one contained iron knives of different sizes and shapes. Some had simple handles of bone or wood. Others were carved with more elaborate designs.

Adam said nothing, waiting for Rob to do the honors, apparently.

Rob said, "He didn't break into every display case, so we believe that the cases he did break into held items he wanted."

"That makes sense," Adam said politely.

"Every one of these knives matches up to one of those descriptor cards. So either he didn't take anything, or he took the card along with the knife."

Adam nodded.

"For whatever reason, he doesn't want us to know what he took, although he clearly wasn't worried about hiding the fact that he took something."

"It doesn't seem like he was in any kind of a hurry either," Adam said.

"Well, he wouldn't be. There's nobody for miles around. And Cynthia's daughter was spending the weekend with friends."

"How would he know that though?"

"Tiffany is a cheerleader for the basketball team, and Haney High is in the playoffs. The kids up here usually stay with friends in Klamath when there's a Friday away game."

Adam seemed surprised. "That would be common knowledge?"

"Yep."

Adam smiled tentatively. "Small towns."

Rob smiled back. "That's the truth."

Adam returned to studying the broken case. "Joseph must have kept a catalog of the museum's contents and their provenance. We should be able to look at her files and see what's missing."

"Frankie's working that angle. The last photos of the exhibits are outdated. Joseph sold a few artifacts a couple of years ago to come up with funding to keep the museum open. And items have been moved around. A lot of Cynthia's notes are handwritten, and Frankie's one of the only people who can decipher her handwriting."

Adam started to say something, then seemed to think better of it. "It would be useful to check out Joseph's home. I suppose we don't have access yet?"

"Sure we do. We can walk over right now."

It took about three minutes to walk the snowy and uneven expanse from the museum to the small white house at the edge of the forest. Adam appeared to be deep in thought, so Rob left him to it. The afternoon air was bitterly cold, and it turned Adam's face pink and the tip of his nose red. Rob forgot his irritation. Maybe Adam was a know-it-all, but at least he wasn't as big an ass as his partner.

Though the land between the museum and the house where the Josephs lived had been left wild, a neat square of lawn surrounded the house. Clumps of snow covered the flower beds. The flag pole in the center of the front lawn was bare.

"Cynthia's NPS truck is still in the garage," Rob said, unlocking the front door. "This door was left unlocked. There's no indication her killer came inside. No mud or rain water on the floor, nothing out of place as far as we can tell."

The house was dark and quiet, the only sound the rain on the roof and the clock ticking patiently away in the living room. The first room off the entry hall was the kitchen, dated but tidy.

The dishwasher was sealed, green light indicating dishes were clean. A small wood burned sign above the refrigerator read: *A man travels the world over in search of what he needs, and returns home to find it.*

"Happiness is found in your own backyard," Adam said.

Rob gave him a puzzled look. Adam nodded at the sign.

"Maybe it's true," Rob said. "It depends on the backyard. Her bedroom is down the hall."

The master bedroom faced the museum. One set of window blinds were tangled as though they had been opened in a hurry. The bed was unmade. A pair of slippers rested on the woven rug beside the bed. The shirt of a Park Ranger uniform was tossed on the floor.

Rob said, "It looks like she ran over there in her nightshirt, jeans, and her uniform jacket and boots. Her pistol is still in her holster, hanging over the chair at her dressing table." He remembered Adam questioning him that first night about not carrying his weapon. He didn't think he'd ever leave it at home again.

Adam said, "Again, indication that she didn't fear the intruder."

"She was a gutsy lady," Rob said. "And if it was the same guy who tried to break in the first time, she'd scared him off by yelling. She may have thought that was all it would take."

Adam asked, "Did she actually say the offender was male?"

"She wasn't certain. She thought he was male. She didn't see him close up. He ran the minute she started shouting."

Adam nodded. "Were her clothes found?"

"In the Dumpster behind the building."

"Interesting."

"Or just weird."

Adam shrugged. "Or just weird, yes. The girl's room is on the other side of the house?"

"That's right." Rob led the way. "Anyway, you can see for yourself there's no sign of any disturbance."

As they walked through the small dining room, Adam stopped beside the oval table to sort through the small pile of mail. There was a summons for jury duty, a couple of credit card bills, and a number of newsletters from organizations like Modoc Nation—"The sole legitimate government of the Modoc People of Southern Oregon and Northern California."

"She was politically active," Adam's tone was thoughtful.

"Not particularly."

Adam glanced up. "You don't think so? It looks to me like she was a regular subscriber."

"Look," Rob said. "Don't go there. She's the victim here, and her political beliefs are—were—her own business. She wasn't an activist. She wasn't a militant. She wasn't a terrorist."

Adam's eyes narrowed. "Did I say she was?"

"You've got that *ah ha!* look on your face. Everybody knows the FBI's mission changed after 9-11. You're all about homeland security now."

"Actually, Homeland Security is all about homeland security now," Adam sounded uncharacteristically short. "I'm trying to understand who Cynthia Joseph was. You say she wasn't a terrorist, and I believe you. Her interests indicate—and I don't find it surprising or disturbing, by the way—that she had an inclination toward activism."

"She wasn't killed because she thought the Klamath Tribes got a raw deal in some of the disputes over water and our other natural resources. Believe it or not, a lot of people feel the same way."

"You could be right. Then again, a couple of Native American artifacts were stolen out of a museum, so it's not impossible that Joseph's cultural heritage and political beliefs are a factor in her death."

Rob couldn't really argue with that. He didn't buy it, but he couldn't disprove that theory. "Fair enough," he said. "Personally I think we're wasting time."

Adam's brows rose. He laid aside the Modoc Nation bulletin. "It's your investigation, Deputy."

"So far, yeah. I think we'll get further focusing closer to home."

"Was she seeing anyone?" Adam asked. "Was she in a relationship?"

"No."

"You seem pretty definite."

"It's a village," Rob said. "Cynthia and Frankie both belonged to the Women's Club. They both tried to set each other up—and they both got nowhere with their matchmaking."

"They were friends a long time?"

"They both grew up in this town."

Adam said, "A place where everybody knows your name? Tiffany's room must be down this hall." He moved past Rob.

The second bedroom had been done in candy box shades of pink, lavender, and mint green. There were a lot of pillows and stuffed animals. No posters of rock stars or TV actors. A backpack with school books leaned against a surprisingly tidy desk. Clothes spilled out of a gym bag on the neatly made bed.

"That's Tiffany." Rob indicated one of two photos tucked in the corner of a square mirror over the painted chest of drawers.

Portrait of a young girl. Tiffany was small and cute, like a kitten. Big dark eyes and straight dark hair. And at seventeen, very, very young.

Adam barely glanced at the photo, his attention on the other snapshot. It was old. That went without saying. These days kids used their phones to preserve the moment. This looked like it had been developed from one of those disposable cameras.

"Do you recognize either of the boys in this photograph?"

Rob frowned at the image. "The kid on the left is Terry Watterson. He drowned at Blue Rock Cove a few years ago. The kid on the right is Bill Constantine."

"What kind of relationship did Tiffany have with Terry?"

"Nonexistent, I'd say. This picture is at least five years old. Tiffany would have been twelve. Terry and Bill would have been nineteen or twenty."

"What kind of relationship does Tiffany have with Bill?"

Rob said dryly, "I don't think there's a relationship there."

"Why not?"

"To start with, Bill's too old for her. For another, he's geeky and shy, and Tiffany is outgoing and popular. She's an honor student. She's a cheerleader."

"She wouldn't be the first popular girl who fell for an older man. Or a geek."

"No." Rob was positive. "No way."

"She kept the photo for some reason."

"Well, maybe she had a crush on Terry. I don't know. As far as I'm aware she isn't dating anyone. I don't keep track of the social lives of teenaged girls."

Adam looked unconvinced, though hopefully not about the part about not keeping track of teenaged girls. "This will be the en suite?" He headed for a small bathroom—also painted pink—off the bedroom. Pink and black tiles, white fixtures. The bathroom smelled of girly shampoo and soaps—and Adam's expensive aftershave. A combination of fragrances that did not exist in nature.

There was a faint draft in the bathroom. It barely stirred the pink polka dot shower curtain.

Rob edged past Adam, distractedly noting that his initial impression had been wrong. Though tall, Adam was not really a big guy. Not a Ken doll at all, though he was strong and nicely built. Whipcord muscle and tensile strength. Rob could vouch for that. He gave off an aura of authority and power. That aura was at least fifty percent attitude—bolstered by ten percent blue and gold credentials. The rest of it…hard to say, but it was effective.

Rob checked the latch on the window by the toilet. The window wasn't quite closed. And the latch…

Not locked.

Shit. He glanced at Adam who had stooped to feel a pink and white striped towel on the floor beneath the sink.

Adam looked at Rob. "This towel is still damp."

"You leave them on the floor, they stay damp." Rob was a guy who had a lot of experience in that branch of the sciences.

"She would have showered for school on Thursday morning. This is Saturday afternoon. Even with the heat turned down, that's more than forty-eight hours later."

Rob was only half listening, still thinking about the unlocked, not-tightly-closed window.

A horrible thought came to him. *Book bag.* "Wait a minute," he said, and squeezed past Adam heading back to the bedroom. There must have been something in his voice because Adam followed, silently watching as Rob went to the desk.

Rob picked up Tiffany's book bag.

They stared at each other.

"She came back," Adam said.

This was the kind of thing that had made Rob decide to chuck Portland for the wide open spaces. But evil—and this was fucking evil, no question about it—was no respecter of city limits or county lines.

Rob said in a voice that didn't sound like his own, "She could have seen everything. And the killer could have seen her."

There was a white line around Adam's mouth. Rob had never seen anyone lose color quite like that. When Adam spoke he sounded unemotional, almost cold. "There's another possibility. Tiffany may be involved in her mother's murder."

Rob opened his mouth, but Adam was right. It wasn't impossible. A kid in California had beheaded his mother only a few weeks earlier for nagging him about cleaning his room. The adolescent brain was a scary thing.

He said—not arguing, just offering another possibility, "She could have witnessed the slaying and fled."

Adam nodded. "Yes. Though it's hard to understand why she hasn't come forward, if that's the case."

"Maybe she can't."

"Meaning?"

Rob shrugged. "She's injured?"

Adam opened his mouth to point out the obvious: there was nothing to indicate a second struggle. Rob headed him off. "Either way, we need to get back to the station."

"Is her cell phone here? Laptop?"

They conducted a quick search. The laptop sat on Tiffany's desk. There was no sign of her cell phone.

"If she's carrying her cell, it gives us a starting point. If we can get a court order—and I'm sure we can in the case of a missing minor—the phone company can try pinging her. So long as her battery is charged—"

"That's a great idea," Rob interrupted. "But you may have noticed reception is sketchy out here. I don't think we can put a lot of hope on that cell phone."

Adam conceded this point reluctantly.

They left Tiffany's bedroom and walked through the quiet rooms toward the front of the house. Adam didn't say a word, and that was actually a relief. Not that Rob believed the world was all sunshine and lollypops. This wasn't routine for him, and it wasn't an academic equation. He knew these people. This was his community, his home. These were his friends and neighbors. At the very least they were his charge, his responsibility.

And he had failed to keep them safe.

The front door lock scraped, and the door inched open. A crack of wintry daylight framed the entrance. Rob reached for his weapon, unhappily aware that he should have unsnapped the flap, should have been ready to draw—he was distantly aware that Adam was doing the same, had already pulled his weapon.

"FBI," shouted Adam with a ferocity that raised the hair on Rob's neck. "Identify yourself."

Jesus Christ, has he—? Yes, he had. Rob knew with absolute certainty that at some time in the past Adam had had to shoot to kill.

At the same time Rob yelled, "Sheriff's deputy. Don't move!" as the tall figure froze inside the entrance hall.

"Fuck!" Zeke's shocked and angry voice floated through the gloom. "What the fuck are you doing, Haskell?"

Good question. Until that instant, Rob hadn't recognized how uneasy he was, how on edge. Not just him. Adam too. In fact, Adam more so. Spooked. They had both been spooked, even though there was every likelihood that whoever was on the other side of the door was fellow law enforcement.

"What the fuck are *you* doing?" Rob retorted, lowering his weapon. He noticed Adam was a lot slower about standing down, and he was glad. Zeke deserved a good scare for this one.

"Looking for Tiffany," Zeke said. The snow-scented breeze swirled through the hall. "Aggie finally got hold of the friend Tiffany was supposed to be spending the weekend with. Tiffany claimed she was coming down with some kind of stomach bug. Her mom drove down and picked her up Thursday night."

"Why would no one at the school know that? How could there not be a record of that?" Rob asked.

"How the hell should I know? Because teenagers don't always follow rules? And sometimes parents don't either?"

Adam holstered his weapon. "You said that, according to Tiffany's friend, Tiffany *claimed* she was feeling sick. Did the friend not believe her?"

Zeke said sourly, "She said this flu bug came on Tiffany suddenly. No, I don't think she believed Tiffany was really sick."

"I see." Adam didn't look at Rob.

"Let's get back to base," Rob said.

"There's no sign of her here?" Zeke stared from Rob to Adam.

"There are signs she *was* here," Rob said. "There's no indication of what happened to her, or where she may have gone."

"Maybe she's our perp," Zeke said.

Rob stared at him. Adam had suggested the same thing, but somehow hearing it from Zeke made Rob angry. "That's the first thought that occurs to you? How do you figure a small girl like Tiffany overpowered a tall woman like Cynthia and then lifted her onto that burial display? And why would she do such a thing?"

"Kids are crazy. Look at that kid in California. Anyway, she's a cheerleader, and everybody knows cheerleaders are all homicidal maniacs." Zeke grinned, looking maniacal himself.

Adam said, "If she's not involved, she's a potential victim. In any case, we need to find her." His flat, unemotional voice recalled Rob to the job at hand.

"Agreed. Let's get back to the office and bring Frankie up to speed."

"What did you find?" Zeke asked.

"Exactly what I said. Proof Tiffany was here."

Zeke hesitated, and then preceded Adam and Rob outside.

* * * * *

Rob was preoccupied with his own thoughts, so he was only vaguely aware that Adam was even quieter than usual on the drive back to town. They reached the station only a few minutes before Agent Russell phoned in his report.

"Tell him he better not try driving back up here tonight," Frankie told Adam, breaking off the debate on whether or not to activate an Amber Alert. "We get black ice on these mountain roads this time of year."

"I'll tell him." Adam left the room to phone Russell back. They could hear snatches of a short and businesslike conversation as Russell reported the ME's preliminary findings. Adam returned to Frankie's office to relay the news that Cynthia Joseph had probably died just before midnight Thursday evening.

"That early?" Frankie sounded shocked.

Adam nodded. "The blow to her head wouldn't have killed her, but she was likely unconscious for everything that followed."

Rob recognized that Adam was trying to be tactful, conscious of what he would consider small town sensibilities. He asked, "What did follow?"

Adam flicked him a look. "Her throat was cut with a not very sharp and not very clean knife. It took a couple of tries."

"Well, at least she won't get tetanus," Zeke muttered.

They all ignored that. Adam said, "She was not sexually assaulted."

"Thank God for that." Frankie muttered thanks as Aggie refilled her coffee cup.

Rob said, "Just before midnight. Which means Tiffany could very well have still been up and moving around the house."

"She should have been in bed if she was so sick," Zeke said.

"The State crime scene team needs to get back here and process Joseph's residence," Adam set his coffee cup aside, untouched. "Among other things, we need to find out who their cell phone carrier is so we can try to track Tiffany's phone."

Frankie groaned. "Let me summarize. We've got a murdering nutcase on the loose and a missing girl. Does that sound about right?"

"And they may be one and the same," Zeke said cheerfully.

Frankie glared at him.

Unworried, Zeke sipped his coffee. He made a face. "Aggie, you know I take sugar!"

"Get it yourself!" Aggie called back from the front desk.

Frankie said, "At least it's not tourist season. Thank God for small miracles." And to Adam, "In my opinion there are too many question marks here to justify activating an Amber Alert. If I'm wrong, I've got to live with it."

Adam replied, "I don't believe this is an abduction. If it is, I don't believe the girl has been taken out of the area. So either way—"

Rob finished, "We've got to organize a search for Tiffany while there's still daylight."

Nobody had to say aloud what they all knew. If Tiffany *had* been abducted, the chances of her safe return were dwindling with every hour. The fact that this was a rural and isolated setting only upped the odds against an innocent victim. Frankie turned to look out the window with its gray and unencouraging vista, and then bellowed, "Aggie, get me the State Police. And then get me Sheriff Clark in Klamath Falls!"

"On it," Aggie called back.

"Sure as hell, it's going to snow tonight." That was Zeke.

Rob glanced at Adam. He was surprised at how bleak he looked. Adam sounded unemotional as he said, "If the girl is involved, there's a strong possibility that she had help. Which means there's a good chance she'll have food and shelter tonight."

Rob said, "And if she isn't involved, there's a good chance she's going to freeze to death."

Frankie said, "You don't have kids do you, Agent Darling?"

"No," Adam said.

"I didn't think so. There's no way in hell that girl had anything to do with her mother's death. I'd stake my badge on it."

Adam seemed strangely at a loss for words, and Rob surprised himself by saying, "In the interests of accuracy, you don't have kids either, Frankie. So nobody better stake their badge on anything till we find Tiffany and hear what she has to say."

Adam threw him a strange look, and Rob wished he was better at reading emotion in another guy's eyes because he had no idea what that dark, almost uncertain glance meant. It gave him a funny feeling in his solar plexus.

Adam had already turned his attention to Frankie. "Why are you so sure the Joseph girl isn't involved?"

"A cop's instinct. I just am."

"No," Adam said slowly. "It's more than that. Why did you feel that you needed the FBI's support for a simple homicide?"

"It's a homicide on federal land, for one thing."

"That's not the reason though," Adam said. Patient and persistent. He was probably very good at his job. The thought hadn't occurred to Rob before. Maybe because it hadn't mattered to him before.

Though he still couldn't decipher Adam's expression, he knew Frankie well enough to know when she was lying. Well, prevaricating, she'd have said.

"Why us?" Adam pressed.

Frankie seemed to struggle internally before bursting out, "Because I don't think she's the first."

"Not this again," Zeke groaned. It was all Rob could do not to echo the sentiment. When it came to this, he and Zeke were in total agreement.

"The first what?" Adam asked.

Zeke was shaking his head. Frankie looked at Rob.

Adam said, "Somebody ought to bring me up to speed."

Once again Frankie nodded to Rob, only more forcefully.

Rob sighed. "Back in December, a college student staying with friends at one of the forest ski chalets claimed that a man tried to abduct her."

"Abduct or assault?"

"Abduct."

"You don't sound convinced," Adam said.

"It was a house party. These were kids on winter break. They were all drinking. A lot. I think it's possible one of the guys took a joke too far."

"A joke?" There it was, that look of disapproval.

"Or maybe it was a genuine attempt at sexual assault. It's impossible to know for sure. The girl was frightened but unharmed. And largely incoherent."

Adam said, "You checked the alibi of everyone in the house for the time of the alleged abduction?"

"Gee, I never thought of that," Rob drawled. "Too bad you weren't here."

Adam's face tightened.

"Haskell," Frankie said in warning. If she was using his last name, she was genuinely irked. So was he. Maybe they weren't the FBI, but they did understand basic police work.

"Yes," Rob said. "We checked the alibi of everyone in the house. And since everyone in the house was blitzed, it doesn't mean a whole hell of a lot."

"And in January?" Frankie prompted.

Rob sighed and said, "And on New Year's Eve a couple of girls walking back to their lake cabin claimed that a man jumped out of the trees and tried to grab them. Or one of them. Again, alcohol was involved."

"If you get over one hundred thousand people here during vacation season, sexual assault can't be a rarity."

"Well, as a matter of fact, it *is* a rarity," Frankie said. "Between us, the park rangers, and the state police, we do a good job of keeping our community safe and secure."

They did. Still, in the interests of fairness, Rob felt compelled to say, "Yeah, we do deal with the occasional assault, sexual and otherwise. We've even had to handle an attempted murder. These two incidents were maybe different."

Zeke groaned.

"How so?" Adam asked.

Frankie was watching him with that *go on!* look. Rob said reluctantly, "In both cases the girls described their assailant as wearing war paint."

In the silence that followed he could hear the fax machine spitting out paper in the next room, and Aggie's muted voice still speaking on the phone.

Adam said at last, "Is it possible these women mistook mud or an attempt at disguise for something else?"

"Camo face paint," Rob agreed. "I thought that was one possibility." And he had a most likely suspect in mind too. He hadn't been able to prove anything against Sandy Gibbs—and in any case, he'd never been convinced that the girls were reliable witnesses.

"In both cases those girls described Indian war paint," Frankie said. "Those were their exact words. *Indian war paint.*"

Adam raised his brows. Maybe at the political incorrectness of the word "Indian."

Zeke said, "Three drunk-off-their-asses chicks, two who, we know for a fact, had been to the museum—"

"Two possible attempted abductions during the past two months," Adam said thoughtfully. "And now the Joseph girl is missing."

"Hold up," Rob protested. "We were both agreed that there were no signs of struggle at the Joseph house." He thought of the unlocked window. "Maybe she saw something and fled. There's no indication that Tiffany was abducted. She may not have even been on the premises when her mother was attacked. For all we know, she skipped out on one friend for a ski weekend with another. Kids do that stuff. But even if that's not what happened, even if Tiffany's disappearance is related to Cynthia's death, it's still a stretch to claim that this is part of a larger pattern of half-assed attempts at abduction."

"True," Adam said to his surprise. "The house needs to be processed. Until any—"

"Sheriff Clark on line one!" hollered Aggie.

Frankie gestured to them to be quiet and picked up the phone. "John? You heard? Well, I need some help."

Rob looked at Adam. Adam offered an odd, self-conscious half smile.

"Was that all Agent Russell had to say?" Rob asked, for lack of any better topic.

"It was all he had to say pertinent to the investigation."

There were unspoken volumes behind those precise, clipped syllables, and Rob repressed a snort.

In the background, Frankie was crisp and to the point. When she disconnected nine minutes later, she said, "Here comes the cavalry. And there goes any chance of keeping the media out of this."

"There was never any chance of keeping them out," Adam said. "Anyway, we can use the media to our advantage."

Zeke said, "Yeah? Then you can be our press secretary."

"State Police!" screeched Aggie. "Line two."

Frankie reached for the phone, pausing to say, "Rob, you and Zeke need to round up every available body to help with this search. We don't have time to wait for reinforcements. Anyway, what we really need are locals, people who know the area. We don't have many hours of daylight left."

"Roger," Rob said.

"We'll do what we can tonight and, if we don't find her, we'll start all over in the morning. But let's find her." Frankie reached again for the phone.

* * * * *

They did not find her.

They did not find any trace of Tiffany Joseph.

It wasn't for lack of trying. Everybody who could walk was out searching for the girl even before the state police and Klamath Falls reinforcements arrived.

Bert Berkle brought his dogs and began to work the woods around the museum and the Joseph house. There was a lot of snuffling and baying and running in circles, however, the dogs did not pick up a hot track. They did not pick up any track at all.

"Too much rain," Bert told Rob. "Too much rain, too much snow, and too much time."

"Hey, you tried," Rob said.

Bert looked more dour than ever.

If there was anything good about a situation like this, it was the way a closely knit community came together in times of crisis.

Rob noticed the Constantine men speaking to Zeke, and he remembered Adam's theory that Bill and Tiffany had some kind of relationship.

He studied Bill. He wasn't a bad looking kid. Actually he wasn't a kid. He had to be about twenty-five or twenty-six now. He looked young for his age, still as tall and gawky as he'd been as an adolescent. He was like an awkward version of his older brother Dan. Now Dan was a handsome guy, and if Tiffany had stuck a photo of Dan on her mirror, nobody would have questioned it. Like his old man before him, Dan had been a heartbreaker—although these days he did his heartbreaking in Springfield. But Bill?

If they didn't find Tiffany soon, they would need to interview him. That was going to be an awkward conversation. Rob was still hoping they'd find her. How far could a teenaged girl get in this terrain and in this weather? Then again, she was physically fit, and her parents had both been park rangers, which gave her certain advantages.

Rob glanced over at Adam who was practically vibrating with nervous tension. He reminded Rob of Bert Berkle's sleek, eager hunting dogs in the seconds before Bert turned them loose.

He grimaced. It bothered him how aware he was of Adam. He noticed things about Adam he'd never noticed of another man before. The stubborn, sun-streaked wave in his stylishly cropped hair. That discreet loop of silver around his wrist. What was the story there? He'd thought it might be a medic alert bracelet. It wasn't; he'd checked that night they'd spent together. Adam's cheekbones, for God's sake! Since when did he notice another man's cheekbones?

Even when he wasn't looking at Adam, Rob knew where he was standing, who he was talking with, what he was watching.

Well, the last one wasn't hard because Adam was watching everyone and everything—watching with suspicion.

And as little as Rob liked it, he couldn't help looking at his neighbors and friends through Adam's eyes. Law enforcement made you cynical. That was the reality of the job. Good people did bad things. And bad people got away with doing bad things.

He had joined the sheriff's office because he was fit, active, and had a hunger for adventure. He had wanted to spend time in the outdoors, and he had wanted to do some good in the world. And that was pretty much the way things had worked out. Frankie was easy to work for most of the time. Off season, life was quiet. Never monotonous. And during their busy months… well, there were other compensations. He never lacked for company, that was for sure.

They searched until nine that night, and then reluctantly, Rob called a halt. The snow was coming down again, like ghostly leaves glimmering in the gloom. The temperature was falling. It was bad news for Tiffany if she was out there, if she was still alive. Rob hated to think of her frightened and freezing. Nobody wanted to give up, but it was dark, and it was getting dangerous.

"We'll meet back here at daybreak," Rob promised. He didn't like being the guy who had to pull the plug on the search effort. Most of the would-be rescuers were not professionals, not trained, and he was responsible for their safety too.

"What about the cabins by the lake?" Adam said on the drive back to town. "Did anyone search them?"

Rob shook his head. "If she walked back to town why would she hide out in the cabins? Why wouldn't she come to us for help?"

"I think we should check the cabins."

It was too dark to read Adam's face. He didn't appear to be kidding. "In that case we might as well break into all the vacation homes in the area too. Hell, we might as well do a door-to-door search of every house in Nearby."

"It may come to that," Adam said. "You don't mind me checking out the cabins, do you? I'll be staying at the campground anyway."

Rob was cold, hungry, and tired. He hung onto his patience though. "No, I don't mind. I'll check with you. I think we're wasting our time."

And yes, they were wasting their time.

But by God they checked out every single one of the thirty-four cabins that weren't being commandeered for use by Klamath Falls Search and Rescue. They looked behind dusty shower curtains. They checked closets that smelled of mothballs. There was no trace of Tiffany.

Rob resisted the desire to say *I told you so*. Adam had been tireless in his efforts to help with the search. He could have stayed back at base, warm and comfortable, advising and consulting, which was what Frankie had dragged him up here to do. But he'd been out there hiking up hillsides and digging through brush and bush, cold and wet and weary as the people who actually knew and cared about Tiffany.

"You want to grab something to eat?" Rob asked when they had closed the door on the very last empty cabin.

Adam said regretfully, "I've still got a couple of reports to file tonight."

Rob's day wasn't over either, and tomorrow would come early, but they had to eat, and they had to sleep at some point. Or at least lie down. He said, "I have to get back to the office. I could come by later."

As he threw it out there casually, his heart pounded with a mix of hope and adrenaline. He was startled at how much he wanted to spend the night with Adam.

Adam said slowly, "I'd like to, but I make it a rule not to get involved with work colleagues."

Rob gave a disbelieving laugh. "Since when?"

"Since I got involved with a work colleague, and it ended badly." Adam's smile was wry. He sounded polite and regretful.

It was unexpectedly painful—and it felt unfair. "What the hell was last time?" Rob asked.

Adam hesitated. He said still quiet, still courteous, "We weren't work colleagues. Your John Doe wasn't connected to my case. We're working together on this, and I don't think it's a good idea to mix personal with professional."

"It doesn't have to be personal," Rob said. He didn't want to be a dick, but his ego was definitely smarting. If anything, Adam's attempt to be tactful made it worse. "It could just be sex. Really good sex. Like last time."

"That's very tempting." Adam sounded less tactful now and more irritated. "No thanks."

"Okay." Rob already regretted his previous comment. He said pleasantly, "Maybe next time."

"Yeah, maybe." Adam turned away.

Your loss, Rob thought. Mostly it felt like his own loss.

CHAPTER SIX

He woke to the echo of a scream.

Adam's eyes flew open, and it took a second to remember where he was. He had been dreaming about Bridget; the familiar confused, frantic scramble to get to her in time. Somehow, knowing how it all ended didn't change the horror of the race to reach her. Only this time he was arguing with Rob Haskell about his decision to hide in Conway's car. What the hell Haskell was doing in his nightmares, Adam didn't know, and he had been starting to question it when the scream woke him.

For a confused instant he thought it was Bridget screaming. The darkness was complete and absolute. The bed was not his, and the room smelled of pine and fire pellets and musty linens. He remembered that he was in Oregon, and that Bridget had been dead for nearly a year.

Had he dreamed that bloodcurdling shriek?

It had been so loud. So close.

Adam pushed back the blankets and reached for his pistol on the bed stand. The cabin was cold despite the red glow behind the grate of the potbelly stove, and the wooden floor was chilly beneath his feet. He found his way to the door, unlocked it, opened it, and gasped at the rush of icy air. That blast of frigid night air took his breath away and woke him up completely.

No lights shone behind curtains in any cabin. Snow powdered the ground, shining eerily in the half light.

He listened tensely. Not so much as a pine needle dropped. The stillness was nerve-wracking.

Was that a natural silence? Was it *too* quiet?

Well, yes, from his perspective it was too quiet. How did people sleep when it was this still? Was he mistaking bad dreams and guilt for the real thing?

Goosebumps sprang out across his arms and shoulders, and he shivered. He hated the cold. He hated the silence.

Maybe he should get dressed anyway.

Nothing moved in the darkness. There was not a whisper of sound.

Adam swore under his breath, closed the door, and dressed quickly. A couple of minutes later he eased open the cabin door and slipped outside. There was no moon. The shimmering snow threw a surprising amount of illumination—except where the wall of tall trees cast deep and disorienting shade.

He had no target destination and no plan. As tired as he was, he knew he was done sleeping for the night, so he might as well put his mind at ease.

Not that anything that happened in the next forty minutes put his mind at ease.

The fact that the surrounding cabins remained dark was surely a promising indicator that the scream had been a product of his nightmares. Even so, he set off toward the Lakehouse restaurant, the thin crust of snow crunching stealthily underfoot.

He did not find the source of the scream, but he did find footprints once he left the shelter of the trees. Lots of footprints. In fact, they seemed to be coming and going in all directions.

"What the hell?"

He couldn't tell when the footprints had been made— maybe Rob or Zeke would have had better luck with that. The tracks were filling with soft white even as he tried to follow them in what appeared to be circles.

He walked past the boathouse, and then walked back to his cabin and went the other direction. There was no sign of anyone.

Finally, cold and more tired than when he'd gone to bed, Adam returned to his cabin.

The rustic interior was comfortingly warm compared to the snowy night. He threw more pellets into the stove and made coffee.

The footprints meant nothing on their own. And if there had really been a scream, why had no one else heard it?

The truth was this case was triggering bad memories. There were just enough similarities…

There were also key differences, and that's what he needed to remain focused on.

He studied the room décor. It was a different cabin from the one he'd stayed in back in October. He thought of the broken bed slat and smiled faintly. He wished now he'd let Rob stay.

Rob was right. It didn't have to mean anything more than shared companionship and sex. Both of which he was in desperate need of. His rejection of Rob made no sense given that he did find Rob very attractive. More attractive than he'd found anyone in a long time.

Or maybe that *was* the problem?

He glanced at the painting over the bed and remembered Jonnie's comment about "real art." This was another landscape, only the lake was front and center rather than the mountains. He rose and examined the brushstrokes.

In the corner of the landscape was a black slash of signature. DK. Dove Koletar? Rob had said Koletar was the son of the original owners of the campground, so it was a possibility that he'd been the artist. If that was the case, if the painter had been an untrained twenty-something, Adam was a bit more impressed by the craftsmanship.

He sat back down on the chair beside the stove and picked up his coffee cup.

Maybe Koletar simply had really bad luck. It was possible. Anyone could be a victim. That was the terrible truth. Sometimes it was just a matter of being in the wrong place at the wrong time.

In Koletar's case…

Adam had been conjecturing Hate Crime. That was thinking like a gay man versus an investigator. Because if it had been a hate crime, why wait until Koletar was leaving town?

There was a certain type of predator that liked to play with his victim, and it was just barely possible that Koletar had run afoul of one of those. Stalker or psychopath, this offender had seen his victim escaping and acted. That type of predator existed in film and books. The Chianti-swilling, classical music-listening, omnipotent serial killer was a fictional creation. Mostly, these predators eluded capture because of the inherently random nature of the victim selection process, and a combination of luck and the lack of both manpower and imagination on the part of law enforcement.

Like a horrific Monty Python skit; nobody ever expects a serial killer.

Which didn't change the fact that Koletar had been killed *after* he made the decision to leave.

Why?

Because someone *didn't* want him to go?

Looking at it from that perspective…well, it changed everything.

It cracked open the can of possible suspects, and now everyone from parents to peers had to be considered equally. If he was correct, instead of looking for Koletar's enemies, Rob should be looking for Koletar's *friends*.

Adam considered this and swallowed another mouthful of bitter coffee.

*　*　*　*　*

"If you've not been assigned a grid location, come see me." Frankie was shouting through a bullhorn from the stage of the gazebo in the small park at the center of town. "Remember, this is a team effort. Don't go wandering off on your own. And if you do find something, *anything*, contact your team leader immediately. Team leaders, mark it and call it in."

"This is going to be chaos." Russell did up his blue jacket in irritable snaps. He had returned to Nearby at first light along with reinforcements from Medford and Klamath Falls. "Too much ground to cover. Too many civilians. Too much time since the girl disappeared."

Adam nodded. Russell was probably right, but the situation couldn't be helped. The terrain was what it was—and there was a lot of it. And because there was so much ground to cover, they needed every volunteer they could get. The team leaders were park rangers, state troopers, and law enforcement from neighboring towns, but they couldn't be everywhere at one time, and no matter how often you instructed people to *touch nothing*, someone always did.

"He could have escaped before the perimeter was ever set up."

"I don't think he's going anywhere."

Russell either didn't hear him or wasn't interested in what Adam thought. "Has anyone mentioned bringing in Portland?"

"So far we've got a homicide and a missing girl," Adam said. "Not exactly a case for the FBI."

"Yet here we are," Russell said. "And like you said, it's murder on federal land." His blue gaze was challenging. That was Russell's default with Adam. In Russell's opinion—in a lot of people's opinion—Adam's career was on a downward trajectory, and Russell seemed to feel that being partnered with Adam was a reflection on *him*. So he did his best at every opportunity to challenge or distance himself.

Adam didn't care. He was relieved to be off morgue duty and happy to actually be investigating something, *anything* again. He was intrigued by the situation at Nearby. And there was—well, stick to the case.

He was hoping that Russell might come up with an urgent reason for returning to L.A. That was unlikely. If Russell was recalled, Adam would likely be recalled too.

He met Russell's critical look and said, "This is the sheriff department's turf. We're here in a support capacity. It's not our case."

Russell opened his mouth, no doubt ready to argue this point, but Rob, looking unreasonably well-rested and energetic, came up to speak to them.

"You two can work alongside me or Zeke," he said briskly. He glanced briefly at Adam and directed the rest of his comments to Russell. "Up to you. I'd stick with someone who knows the area. It's easy to get lost in these woods, and we've got a lot of ground to cover."

"I'll work with you," Adam said. Rob's brown gaze veered back to him. He nodded curtly.

Russell said, "In that case, I'll assist Deputy Lang."

"Good enough." Rob turned away.

Apparently he hadn't forgiven Adam for turning him down the night before—which was the very reason Adam didn't like to get involved with coworkers. When it went wrong, it went really wrong.

Anyway, they were here to do a job. Anything else was just too bad.

Except he liked Rob. And perhaps in the back of his mind he had been hoping that after this case wound up, once he had his plane ticket home, maybe… But it looked like no.

That was really better anyway.

Russell moved over to join Zeke's team, and Zeke looked about as thrilled as Adam figured he would, which was about as thrilled as Rob had looked. Maybe the two of them would bond over bitching about their senior officers.

Volunteers and law enforcement moved to the edge of the search radius, formed search lines, the final round of instructions were given, and the hunt for Tiffany resumed, bolstered by the reinforcements from neighboring counties. There was nothing like a pretty, teenaged girl gone missing to mobilize the troops, and the weather was on their side. It was a bright, sunny February day. The night's snowfall had been light and was already starting to melt in patches.

The difficulty of course was they did not know for sure whether they were looking for a victim or an offender. Did Tiffany *want* to be found? That remained a question.

The air was thin and sharp as they left the grassy lowland and began to climb through the trees and hillsides. It had been warm in the sunlight, but that changed fast. The snow was pristine and pillowy beneath the trees and in the crevices and creases of landscape. The temperature dropped sharply as they worked their slow way up the mountainside. The clear air was invigorating, and it felt good to stretch his muscles and really push himself.

About ninety minutes in, Rob joined Adam. "You doing okay?"

"Fine." He was. He was in good shape—he'd passed his biannual fitness exam with flying colors in January—and he was enjoying pushing himself. Even so, this was one hell of a workout. They were going to start losing volunteers in another mile or so.

He shoved his damp hair back, and Rob said, "Your nose is red. I hope you're wearing sunscreen."

Adam wrinkled his nose. "That's from the cold not the sun."

"Cold!" Rob scoffed at the idea that this was cold weather, although the way his breath hung in the air didn't exactly support his argument. Nor did the fact that he was wearing his heavy uniform jacket and gloves. Adam wasn't sure he even owned a pair of gloves. His entire winter wardrobe consisted of a couple of wool sweaters, one of which he was wearing now under his FBI jacket. Thank God he'd remembered to pack jeans and boots. This was not a trek he'd want to make clad in Business Casual.

Rob nodded toward Adam's left. "That's Billy—Bill—Constantine. And over to his left, near that stand of sugar pine, is his dad." Rob added neutrally, "You should be aware that Buck Constantine is a big man around these parts."

Buck Constantine looked vaguely familiar, though it took Adam a few seconds to remember where he'd seen him before. The lakeside restaurant. Constantine had been wearing the same ridiculous fringe coat the night Adam had dined there.

"How big a man?" he inquired.

"Most of the undeveloped land around here that isn't national forest belongs to Constantine."

"I see."

"Which means we need to be careful when we interview Bill about Tiffany."

"Are we interviewing him?" Adam hadn't missed that *we*.

Rob nodded. "It's looking that way. Anyway, we have to start somewhere. I did some checking last night. Bill used to tutor Tiffany."

"In what?"

"Science. She flunked biology her freshman year."

"Interesting."

"I figured you'd think so."

"There's obviously a connection. Nobody keeps a photo that doesn't mean anything." Adam glanced sideways. Rob was smiling. It was a grim smile. "I've been thinking though. It's an odd photo."

"What is?" Rob asked.

"The photo of Bill Constantine and the other kid. The one who drowned. Watterson. It's not the kind of photo you give someone."

"So?"

"So Bill probably didn't give that picture to Tiffany. She probably found it somewhere and appropriated it for her own use."

Rob was frowning. "Appropriated it? What are you getting at?"

"I'm not sure exactly."

They were silent as they reached a spill of rocks.

"You think Tiffany had a crush on Bill, and maybe Bill didn't know about it?" Rob was watching Bill. As though feeling the weight of Rob's gaze, Bill glanced over at them. Rob nodded at him in greeting.

Self-consciously, Bill nodded back.

"He may or may not have known about it," Adam said. "I don't think he gave her that photograph. You have a scenario where she wants a photo of him—assuming it wasn't the Watterson kid she was interested in—but doesn't have access through the normal channels."

"Access through the normal channels," Rob said wonderingly. "Is that FBI-speak? Whatever happened to simple English? You mean she couldn't ask him so she snagged it from somewhere else?"

"Correct."

"Possibly the target of her emotional interest was not equally engaged and experiencing reciprocity?" Rob suggested.

"Oh, shut up," Adam said.

Rob laughed. He patted Adam on the back and dropped behind to speak to a couple of volunteers who were starting to lag.

Bill was looking his way again. Adam nodded politely. He didn't blame Constantine for feeling uncomfortable. Even innocent people started acting paranoid when they came under the scrutiny of law enforcement.

"Do you think we'll find her?" Bill called.

"We'll do the best we can," Adam replied. Equivocation was a big part of the job description. *Don't make promises you can't keep.* That was one of the lessons they didn't teach you at the Academy. You learned it facing the bereaved families of the victims you failed to save.

"We'll find her," Buck Constantine said grimly.

His son didn't look reassured.

"Let's try and keep this line together," Rob directed. "We want to be sure that we've covered every inch of ground in our sector."

Everyone assented. They were losing volunteers from their eight-member team. The terrain was too rough, and people were starting to say aloud what Adam privately thought: that there was no way Tiffany had come this far. Not at night. Not in the pitch dark.

Regretfully, apologetically, some of the older and less fit searchers were turning back. Rob's radio crackled into life and he stopped to answer it.

He whistled sharply. Adam glanced back and Rob waved to him.

Adam turned to start back down the slope. The combination of snow on pine needles didn't provide much purchase for the soles of his hiking boots. His right foot slipped, the rocks under his left foot crumbled away, and the next thing he knew, he was crashing face first down a ravine.

Somewhere in the distance he could hear Rob yelling. It happened so fast Adam didn't have time for much more than a gasp—mostly of disbelief.

"Shit!" His landing knocked the wind out of his lungs and cut short his protest. Brush and snow softened the collision, but he saw stars. His ears and nose seemed stuffed with snow, and for a few dazed seconds he feared he was going to smother.

"Adam? Adam!" Rob's voice floated down to him. He sounded as short of breath as Adam.

Adam rolled onto his side, heaving in a mighty lungful of oxygen. Pain flashed along his ribs, and his gloved hand hurt where he had smacked it hard on a rock.

He wiped snow off his face. A few glittering flakes stuck to his eyelashes. "I'm okay," he croaked.

"Are you okay?" Rob yelled.

"Great!" Adam yelled with more force. *Fucking fantastic. Why do you ask?*

He looked up. The ravine was not nearly as deep as it had felt like when he'd fallen down it. Maybe twelve feet. At most. Rob was kneeling at the edge, gazing down at him, eyes wide in his alarmed face.

"Don't try to move. I'm coming down."

Someone ought to tell Rob how great he looked in that vaguely western style sheriff's deputy hat. Then again, he probably knew.

"No. I'm okay. Stay there," Adam called. In fact, he felt okay enough to be mostly incensed with the whole situation. What the hell was it that people loved so much about the great outdoors? It was just one fatal accident after another waiting to happen.

Other heads were popping up alongside Rob as the rest of their search team arrived. He began to receive unsolicited advice on how to climb out even as Rob cautioned everyone to stay clear of the edge.

Adam sat up, and the brush and snow he had mistaken for the floor of the ravine gave way. He dropped another foot, landing on his tailbone in a pile of rocks and rubble.

That hurt and he swore loudly.

"Adam?"

"Still here," Adam yelled.

And he wasn't the only one.

He sucked in a sharp breath. Not rocks and rubble. Or not only rocks and rubble. He had landed on the rotting remnants of an old backpack.

"Haskell, you better get down here," he called. He got to his knees and crawled forward.

The outcrop of boulders and tree roots and brush made a nice dry, sheltered recess, and in that recess was another pile of rags. Rags and scattered bones. A skeleton.

Heart thumping, he sat back on his heels. Hollow, empty eye sockets met his own.

Rocks and snow rained down, followed by Rob who half jumped, half slid down to join him.

"Where the hell—?"

"Right here," Adam said.

Rob shoved aside the brush and dropped down beside Adam. He put his hand on Adam's shoulder. "I told you not to try to move."

Rob was a toucher. A hands-on kind of guy. But Adam realized he didn't mind Rob touching him. In fact, that brief, warm clasp was kind of comforting. He said briskly, "What was the name of the hiker who disappeared back in 1998? The college kid with the hip replacement?"

"Something Jordan. No. Jordan Gaura."

Adam indicated an article that looked like a bent metal and plastic mushroom amidst the strewn stones and bones. "I think we just found him."

Rob followed Adam's line of sight to the remains beneath the boulder overhang.

"God damn it," he said. He sounded more weary than shocked. But then there were only so many possible outcomes for hikers missing for very long in these woods. He added after a minute, "The good news is, it's not Tiffany."

"Yeah," Adam said. "The bad news is you need a crime scene team up here. Including a forensic anthropologist."

Rob stared at him.

Adam said, "Come on, Rob. One body maybe. *Two bodies*? Your forest is turning into a bone orchard."

Rob frowned. "You can't think this has anything to do with Dove Koletar."

"That's exactly what I think."

"What's happening down there?" Silver hair and fringe jacket. Bill's father looked down at them, frowning. "Anybody hurt?"

"Hang on, Buck. We've got a situation here," Rob called. To Adam, he said, "Let's not jump to any conclusions. This could have been an accident."

"Rob."

"We have no idea how this kid died. He could have fallen and cracked his skull. At that time of year he wouldn't have had snow to cushion his tumble."

"Maybe. His skull looks okay from here," Adam said. "I'm no expert. And neither are you. Which is why you want to get one up here. ASAP." He held Rob's troubled gaze with his own.

After a moment, Rob nodded. "Agreed." He rose.

Adam felt for him. He really did. For all his lackadaisical attitude, Rob cared about the people he was entrusted with serving and protecting. And though this crime—if it was a crime—had not happened on Rob's watch, he would take this to heart. He said, "And you've got to protect this site."

Rob nodded wearily.

Adam got to his feet, wincing, and Rob said, "You sure you're okay?"

"Yes. I landed on my pride."

Rob smiled faintly. "I've gotta say, I've never seen anyone look so dignified in midair."

Adam snorted and hastily wiped his nose. Rob laughed.

That was the only humor in the situation, and neither of them was smiling as they scrambled back to the top of the ravine. It wasn't a difficult climb, but Adam was starting to think longingly of a long, hot bath and a comfortable mattress—neither of which was waiting for him at the campground cabin.

Rob walked a way down the hillside to radio for reinforcements.

"You were lucky," Bill said. "What did you find down there?" He leaned over the edge, and his father grabbed his jacket.

"What the hell are you doing? Did you not just see what happened here?"

Bill freed himself, throwing his father a resentful look. He looked at Adam. "Is it Tiffany?"

"No."

Everyone's relief seemed genuine. Of course some people were better actors than others. Adam had plenty of experience with that.

"You and Tiffany were friends?" Adam asked. He kept his expression and tone sympathetic. Even so Bill looked vaguely alarmed.

"I mean, I know her," he said. "I used to tutor her."

"Can you think of anyone she'd run to if she was in trouble?"

"I don't know her that well."

Bill's haste to distance himself from Tiffany was understandable in the circumstances. His defensive posture and inability to hold Adam's gaze might indicate deception, or might indicate extreme discomfort at being questioned by the FBI. And in any case, this wasn't the time or place to try and interview him.

"Are we still headed up toward the peak?" One of the other searchers asked.

"I don't know," Adam answered.

"The climb is a lot harder from here on out. I don't believe that girl could have made it this far."

"She could have," said the only woman on their search team. "If she had to."

"Why would she have to?" Buck Constantine said.

Nobody had an answer for that. In fact, no one said much of anything at all. Mostly they were watching Rob. He had his back toward them, so there wasn't much to see. A couple of searchers found resting places on fallen timber. Canteens were handed back and forth.

After a minute or two, Rob hiked back up to where they waited.

"We're going to start back down," he announced. "What I was about to tell you before Agent Darling decided to pursue his own line of inquiry is that one of the teams searching to the south found what appears to be Tiffany's cell phone."

This information sent a ripple through the circle of remaining searchers.

"I've been saying that from the first," the older Constantine said. "What are we doing up here when sure as hell he'd have dragged her down to the highway? Nobody would stick around waiting to get caught."

"If we knew exactly where to search, we wouldn't need all of you," Rob said crisply. "Let's get moving. We need everyone focused on that quadrant." He met Adam's questioning gaze and nodded affirmative.

Rob stayed behind to mark the ravine and log its coordinates, while Adam and the rest of their party started back down. They were all moving a lot more quickly now that they were sure—rightly or wrongly—that Tiffany had never been up there. The problem with a search like this was both predator and prey were trying to outthink possible pursuit, which very often meant doing the last thing anyone would expect. Stupid things. Dangerous things.

When Rob caught up to Adam, he said, "We should have a crime scene team up here within a couple of hours."

"Good."

"Constantine is right. The most likely scenario is she was dragged to the highway."

"She wasn't dragged to the highway. She wasn't dragged anywhere," Adam said. "Whoever cut Cynthia Joseph's throat would have been covered in blood. There's no blood in the Joseph house. We both agreed that nobody came inside after her. She may have fled and later been caught and abducted. Or she may have been an accomplice."

Rob threw him a grim look. "You really do think she was in on it."

"I don't know. I think her sudden decision to come home that night doesn't look good."

"That's completely circumstantial."

"Yes. But you and I both know circumstantial evidence is every bit as valid as direct evidence."

Rob grunted.

They continued in silence marred only by the thud of their boots and the wind in the pines. From up here the view of the valley was spectacular, and it gave Adam a better understanding of how scattered most of the houses and dwellings were. In this land of snow and pine trees "neighbor" was more concept than reality.

Rob said grudgingly, "You're not doing too bad for a city boy."

"Thanks." Adam grinned, and after a second Rob grinned too. Their smiles faded at the sudden crack of gunshots.

CHAPTER SEVEN

A couple of yards ahead, the rest of the search party stopped walking and began to look around.

"Less than a mile away," Norris Peterson called.

"That's a semi-automatic," Adam said as Rob spoke into his radio.

"Who's firing?" Rob demanded. He wasn't sure he would be able to hear the answer over the thunder of his heart. His mouth was so dry it was hard to unstick the words from the roof of his mouth. "This is Deputy Haskell. We're hearing shots—"

Zeke's voice cut in. "Rob, we're taking fire."

What the hell? Once upon a time Nearby had been a nice, quiet, peaceful place to live and work. Now it was turning into a war zone. "You're…? Are you sure it's not some asshole hunter?"

"Hell yes, I'm sure!" Zeke returned.

Rob swore. "From where? What direction are the shots coming from?" He hastily unfolded his map. "What's your position?"

"Widow's Peak. Somebody's up there with a fucking assault rifle taking potshots at us."

The shots sounded tinny and distant over the radio compared to the crack and rolling echo of their real life counterpoint.

"We've got to get these civilians off this mountain," Adam said.

Rob nodded distractedly, trying to coordinate with the other team leaders. Everybody was hitting the airwaves at the same time. He was dimly aware of Adam jogging down the hillside, ordering everyone down to the shelter of the trees, and it was a relief to know that at least he had solid and sensible support at hand. Right now he needed all the support he could get.

"Zeke, is anyone hit? Hurt?" he asked.

There was a burst of static. "Negative," Zeke said.

The relief left Rob weak.

"We need everybody off this mountain right now. Move it!" Adam called. How the hell did he manage to sound so calm—like he did this every day?

That official permission seemed to be what everyone was waiting for, because the remaining searchers began a hasty descent, slowed only by the terrain. Thank God for that. Thank God for Adam.

Rob was calculating how long it would take to cut across the ridge, when Adam loped back up, squatting down beside him.

"Are they pinned down?" Adam asked. "Can they withdraw?"

Rob shook his head. *I don't know.* "Zeke, get your party out of there," he ordered.

Zeke's voice came over the radio with sudden and exasperated clarity. "I would LIKE to do that, Haskell. We're pinned down. Copy?"

"God damn it," Adam muttered.

"Roger that," Rob answered both Adam and Zeke.

"Deputy Haskell? This is Deputy Sheriff Sergeant Laird with Medford—"

At the same time another voice burst in, "This is Klamath Falls Sheriff's Deputy O'Neill. We are moving to intercept."

He looked at Adam in alarm. Moving to intercept? Did these cowboys think they were playing Xbox? All he needed was Zeke's group of civilians getting caught in interterritorial crossfire.

Adam was frowning over this exchange. "This doesn't fit," he said.

"Uh… Yeah. Well, tell it to the asshole with the rifle."

"What do you want to do?" Adam asked.

Rob had to smother a surge of something alarmingly close to hysterical laughter. Adam was asking *him*? How the hell was he supposed to know what to do in a situation like this? Things like this did not happen in his world.

He pointed to the map. "This is Widow's Peak. This is Zeke's position. Roughly. And this is us."

Adam met his eyes. "You want to try to circle in on the shooter? Sweep in from behind?"

Rob drew in a deep breath. He nodded tightly. "I do. Yeah." He folded the map again. "It's not much of a plan, but it's all I've got. It sounds to me like Medford and Klamath Falls will provide all the distraction we need. What I know for sure is we—I—need to get over there before someone gets killed."

He was thinking rapidly. He knew the area well—he'd taken a lot of photographs up here through the years—the snow would slow them down. Ten minutes? Maybe fifteen? Even so, he and Adam were Zeke's best chance of reinforcements.

"Right." Adam nodded. "Let's do it."

He sounded like he thought it was a perfectly reasonable plan. "Pistols against an assault rifle," Rob felt obliged to point out.

To his surprise, Adam's mouth twisted in a chilly smile. He rose, saying, "All that matters is who holds the pistol."

* * * * *

They made good time, and in twelve minutes they crested the ridge behind Widow's Peak and began their descent. Physical exertion—the useful expenditure of all that adrenaline—and time to think had helped Rob regain his equilibrium. He wasn't happy, but anger and determination had replaced his fear that he was not equipped to handle this crisis. *Someone* had to handle it. And by God, it looked like it was going to have to be him.

He was just glad he had Adam as backup. This way, at least one of them maybe knew what he was doing.

The slope was slippery with pine needles, loose stones, and wet earth. The snow had melted where the sunlight speared through the tree branches. Most of the hillside was in deep shade, and there was still ice in sharp crevices of rock. Even so, they moved swiftly, keeping about fifty feet between them.

The wind rushing overhead through the sugar and ponderosa pines sounded like the ocean. The spaces between shots were longer now. Every time Rob hoped the standoff was over, another crack of gunfire split the wind-scoured emptiness.

After several hundred yards they stopped to catch their breath. Below them was a large log cabin in a grassy green valley dotted with tall pines. The metal roofs of a couple of outlying buildings flashed in the irresolute sunlight.

Rob motioned to Adam. When Adam joined him, he handed over his field glasses. Adam took the glasses.

Rob said quietly, "That's Sandy Gibbs's place. He's what you might call our local survivalist nut. The they'll-have-to-pry-my-gun-from-my-cold-dead-fingers type."

Adam studied the spread beneath them. "You think Gibbs is our shooter?"

"I think there's a damn good chance."

"Has he got weapons stockpiled in there?"

"Oh hell yeah. I don't doubt he's got a goddamned arsenal in there. My concern is that he may also have Tiffany."

Adam's pale brows drew together. "Tiffany?"

"Maybe. Maybe he went courting the old-fashioned way. I can't think of any other reason he'd do this."

"You think this Gibbs kidnapped a teenaged girl and murdered her mother?"

"He's racist. Out and out. And he sees himself as a modern day mountain man. I know it probably sounds like a stretch, but I could see how killing a Native American woman and taking her child would fit his movie script."

Adam was silent, thinking it over. "Maybe," he said. "It's possible." He didn't sound convinced. "Cynthia Joseph's body was staged. Artifacts from the museum were stolen. The kind of offender you're talking about wouldn't bother with either of those things."

"You'd know more about that than me. I can tell you that Gibbs has a history of harassing women, especially young women. Nothing major, nothing serious, he's just obnoxious and persistent."

Adam scowled, possibly at the notion of obnoxious and persistent harassment not being serious. "Maybe," he said again, but he still sounded skeptical. "Here's another theory. Gibbs noticed the woods were crawling with law enforcement and jumped to the conclusion we were here for him."

Rob's eyes narrowed, considering this theory. "Maybe."

"Paranoia is part of the profile."

"That could be true. You've also got to admit that this is a pretty big coincidence."

"I wouldn't call it a coincidence. I'd call it cause and effect." Adam handed back the field glasses. "If Gibbs *is* the shooter, he's got a sniper tower set up somewhere along that treeline."

Rob trained the glasses on the mature trees overlooking the slope leading from the valley plateau. As he watched, he caught a metallic glint in the branches of a tall stand. Sunlight on a gun barrel. "Good call. Ten o'clock high."

"One or more shooters?"

"Looks like just one. I can't be sure."

"It sounds like one. Any movement from below?"

"Negative. That doesn't mean they're not on their way."

"True. How do you want to handle it?"

Rob said slowly, "He's not going to stay up there forever. He'll be coming back to earth even if it's just to rearm. More likely, he'll dig in for a siege. I say we get down to that cabin and wait for him."

"Hm." Adam frowned.

"We could end this fast and without anyone getting hurt. He won't be expecting us. And we'll have a chance to look for Tiffany."

Adam's face jerked to his. "We don't have a warrant to search that cabin."

"We have probable cause. He's up there shooting at law enforcement. How much more probable cause do we need?"

"I'll tell you what we *don't* need. Another Ruby Ridge."

Rob had been eleven at the time of Ruby Ridge. He barely remembered the details. What he did remember was that government agents had overstepped, and presumably innocent people had died. Adam would have been about the same age, but apparently Ruby Ridge was a sore spot with the FBI.

"This is not the same situation. I mean it's not parallel."

That didn't seem to reassure Adam. "If we do end up trying to prosecute Gibbs for Joseph's death—after we barge in there without a warrant—you know as well as I do that anything we find will be inadmissible."

That was true. Adam was looking at the bigger picture. That was probably the FBI way. Rob said, "You know what? If we can save that kid's life, I don't care about the rest of it. I'll deal with the rest of it when I get there."

"Rob…" Adam rubbed his fist against his forehead.

"Listen to me," Rob said. "We could wait for a warrant, and in the meantime Gibbs is going to barricade himself in that cabin. Maybe with Tiffany trapped inside there with him. Or maybe he sits up there in his sniper tower, and we sit here waiting for everybody else to get into position, and then KPD trots a trained negotiator up here to try and chat with him for a few hours. Or maybe a few days."

Adam shook his head. He was weakening, though, and Rob kept talking. "From what I know of Gibbs, I think we're looking at a lengthy standoff, and eventually, either way, we're going to have to shoot him or tear gas that cabin and go in after him. Unless he kills himself first—and anybody else in there with him."

After a moment, Adam said, "Do you have a plan or are we just going to break a window and climb inside to wait?"

Rob raised the field glasses once more and studied the cabin. "My plan only stretches to us hightailing it down there and intercepting him on his way back to the cabin."

"On his way to the cabin or inside the cabin?"

Rob lowered the glasses. He looked at Adam. "We play it by ear." It wasn't as reckless as it probably sounded to Adam.

One or two guys who knew what they were doing could get into that cabin and take down Gibbs before he ever realized what hit him. Maybe it wasn't the way they'd do it in the FBI. It wasn't protocol, but Adam wasn't running this case. He'd said himself that he and Russell were there to offer support and backup as required. And what Rob required was…he met Adam's intense, dark gaze…probably unfair to ask.

"Does Gibbs live alone? Do we know for sure there aren't other occupants in that cabin?"

"Gibbs is a loner. If there is anybody else in there, it's Tiffany."

Adam shook his head though it was unclear whether he was denying the possibility that Tiffany was in the cabin or Rob's plan in general.

It was a tough one for him. Rob could see that. He already knew Adam well enough to know Adam preferred protocol. Fair enough. Protocol existed for a reason. But bad guys didn't play by the same rules, and with or without Adam, Rob was going in there and getting Gibbs.

He didn't say that though. He didn't try to pressure Adam. And not only because he suspected it wouldn't go over well.

Adam said reluctantly, "The kind of blitz attack that you're considering could be the best bet in a situation like this one. Gibbs won't be expecting it. Neither will anyone else. We'll be on our own, and if anything goes wrong, one or both of us is liable to end up dead."

In other words, it was a hell of a chance to take on a guy you barely knew. Rob continued to watch Adam, waiting for him to decide.

Adam sighed. "Okay."

Rob's eyes widened. "Yeah?"

Adam scowled. "Yeah. Affirmative."

Rob grinned and put a hand over his heart. "Agent Darling, I think I may be in love."

Adam made a derisive noise. "If Gibbs is half the survivalist nut you think he is, he's probably got that place booby-trapped. You do realize that, right?"

"Yep." Rob shoved his field glasses into his backpack. "Don't fall over any tripwires."

"If I do, you'll be the first to know," Adam said darkly, and Rob laughed.

They did the last twenty yards on their bellies, and those three minutes were the longest of Rob's life. Halfway across the wide clearing that formed the firebreak around the cabin, he started thinking about what would happen if Gibbs looked behind and spotted them. This slow motion crawl made them sitting ducks. Sweat broke out on his back and shoulders, and it was all he could do not to rush, even though he knew movement would be the most likely thing to catch Gibbs's eye. What really scared him though was the belated thought that he might get Adam killed.

That blue and gold FBI jacket did not look like any kind of vegetation in this neighborhood, and somehow the fact that Adam had voluntarily put himself and his goddamned jacket in mortal danger made it worse.

But then they were safely behind the cabin and back on their feet. There was an armload of wood on the low deck running the length of the building, as though Gibbs had been bringing in firewood when he'd noticed the search party working its way up the mountain.

"What kind of vehicle does Gibbs own?" Adam asked, hands braced on his knees as he caught his breath. The crawl across the firebreak had not been fast. It *had* been strenuous.

"A pickup and a snowmobile."

"He's probably got them garaged in one of those outlying buildings. We need to make sure he doesn't get to them."

Adam straightened, lifted his foot to step onto the deck, and Rob caught his arm. "Look." He pointed to a nearly invisible strand of wire running along the edge of the deck. One end was fastened to a nail. The other was threaded through a stack of rusted pie tins perched casually on the far end of the deck.

Adam swore softly.

Rob said, "The good news is we know how to get his attention if we want it." He stepped over the tripwire.

Adam followed, still looking chagrined. He drew his Glock and said curtly, "You take left. I'll cover the right."

Rob said, "Allow me." He delivered a swift, hard kick to the door. The door, which turned out to be unlocked, burst open in bits of broken frame, and sagged on its hinges.

Adam dove past him, going to the right and sweeping the room with text book efficiency. Rob went left, following suit. It was a long time since he'd done anything like this—well, he'd never done anything quite like this—and his heart was thumping, his brain buzzing with adrenaline.

Adam had already moved to the next room. "Clear," he said.

Up in his sniper's nest, Gibbs began firing again. The good news was, he was still shooting down the mountainside, so it was unlikely he'd spotted them. The bad news was, he still had plenty of ammunition.

"He's got a homemade grenade launcher in his bedroom," Adam called.

"I guess it's true about the size of a man's gun," Rob called back.

"No grenades."

"That's usually the way of it."

The kitchen he stood in was so ordinary, it was almost disappointing. A pot of beans sat burning on the stove. Clean dishes dried in a rack on the wooden counter. It could have been any holiday rental, barring the target practice sheet of Osama Bin Laden pinned to the refrigerator. Now there was a collector's item.

Gibbs stopped firing again.

"Haskell, you need to see this."

Rob left the kitchen and followed Adam's voice to what appeared to be a large pantry or stock room. Near the corner of the room was an open trapdoor.

Adam peered down into the room or rooms below. "It looks like he's building a bomb shelter."

Rob joined him. "Or a dungeon."

They looked at each other.

Rob squatted down. "Tiffany?" he called.

There was no response. A cold, earthy draft seemed to rise through the opening.

"I'll check it out."

He half expected Adam to object. Adam nodded curtly. "Watch yourself."

Rob climbed down the metal ladder and found himself in what appeared to be a very old cellar. He switched on his flashlight. The bright beam highlighted a kerosene lantern hanging on the wall, and floor to ceiling shelves stocked with still more water jugs and canned goods. There was nothing particularly sinister, unless a lifetime supply of SpaghettiOs held some dark significance.

"She's not here," he called.

Adam replied, but Rob missed it. Something had caught his eye. A shovel leaned against one of the shelves. Rob stepped forward to investigate and realized that he had mistaken the gray sheen of a trash bag for the stone wall in the gap formed between the sides of two shelves.

"Wait a minute," he said. "I think there might be a doorway here…" He yanked the trash bag aside and sure enough there was an opening in the wall, though *doorway* would be an exaggeration.

"What the hell…" He looked upward. "I think he's digging a tunnel." Through the dark opening he called again, "Tiffany?"

He heard a faint, indefinable noise that might have been a response—or the winter wind finding its way through the creaking timbers holding up the roof.

Rob held the flashlight high. His own shadow loomed against the uneven surface of rock and earth. "I'm going to follow this tunnel."

Adam didn't respond. Or maybe Rob missed his reply. His attention was on the black hole looming before him. He proceeded with caution. Good thing he wasn't claustrophobic… At least he hadn't thought he was claustrophobic. Maybe he would be by the time he crawled out from between damp walls of earth and stone that formed a passageway so narrow he had to turn sideways to get through parts of it.

Whose idea had this been again?

The light from the cabin faded. Now there was only the jittery beam of the flashlight to guide him. He kept moving.

A couple of pebbles dropped from the low ceiling and hit the ground in front of him.

Not the most stable of passageways. Whatever Gibbs was doing down here, it wasn't meeting building code, that was for sure.

"Tiffany?"

He stopped. Without warning, he had reached the end of the tunnel. He stared in disbelief at a solid wall of rock and roots and dirt.

She was not here.

For a few minutes he had been convinced they were going to find her. He had been wrong. She wasn't here—there was no indication she had ever been here. In fact, there was no reason to think she'd ever made it up the mountain.

So why the fuck was Sandy Gibbs sitting in his tower shooting at a search party?

He realized he couldn't hear if Gibbs was still shooting or not. In fact, he couldn't even hear Adam.

Rob turned around in the narrow tunnel and started back the way he'd come. He had traveled several hundred yards, but he could still see the light at the end of the tunnel pooling in the cellar, illuminating all those cans of chili and corn and baked beans.

"She's not here," he called. "The tunnel is only about 500 yards long. It's a dead end."

Again no reply from Adam.

Shit. Had Adam gone dark for a reason?

Rob had gotten so carried away by the idea that Tiffany might be a prisoner in this hole in the ground, that she might be hurt, injured, dying... He'd forgotten that Gibbs was still a real and present danger.

He pulled his phone out and silently texted, *Clear?*

No go. The blue bar halted halfway across the screen. *Message not delivered.*

Given that Rob was standing in a hole in the ground, surrounded by mountains where reception was unreliable at the best of times, that really didn't mean much.

He reached the cellar. No sign of Adam. He listened.

Silence. That was probably a good sign. One thing for sure: taking Adam out would not be a silent process.

Rob stepped onto the ladder. One hand on the railing, one foot on the first rung, he glanced up and froze as he gazed into the barrel of an M4.

The black hole of the sniper's carbine barrel was no emptier than the eyes watching him over the gun sight.

"It's a dead end for you, that's for sure," Sandy Gibbs said.

Rob unglued his tongue and said, "That would be one hell of a mistake."

"Why's tha—"

Adam silently materialized behind Gibbs, placing his Glock against Gibbs's temple. "Because I'll blow your fucking head off." His voice was flat and there was no question he meant every word.

Gibbs's shock was matched by Rob's relief. For one hellish instant he'd thought that Gibbs had somehow managed to take out Adam, despite the fact that he'd heard no shot.

"Lower your weapon," Adam said. Gibbs complied. "Hands on your head and lace your fingers together."

Gibbs let loose a stream of obscenities, the gist of which seemed to be the Constitution granted a man the right to protect his home and property by whatever means necessary—

"Don't worry. You'll have your day in court, jackass." Adam locked a hand in his collar and dragged him back from the cellar opening.

By the time Rob scrambled the rest of the way up the ladder, Gibbs was face down on his stock room floor, hands locked behind his head, still protesting his right to bear arms.

"Since when is the national forest your private property?" Rob roughly cuffed Gibbs. "You better hope to hell nobody got hurt out there." He resisted the temptation to bang Gibbs's head against the floor a few times. For a couple of seconds he had been about as scared as he could remember, and it wasn't a feeling he liked.

Sandy continued to curse everyone from Frankie to the president, his voice growing hoarser and hoarser.

"Anything?" Adam asked Rob, ignoring the ranting and frothing going on at their feet.

Rob shook his head. "No. There's no sign she was ever down there."

"Now we know," Adam said, which was certainly a lot more pleasant than *I told you so.*

Reinforcements arrived, and for a while Rob was kept very busy with the briefing and debriefing—though *brief* was a misnomer if there ever was one. By the time he finally managed to radio Frankie, there were all kinds of crazy rumors circulating: Deputy Haskell had found a cache of weapons beneath Gibbs's cabin, no, the FBI agent had captured a domestic terrorist, which was his real reason for coming to Nearby.

"Just tell me the girl is safe," Frankie demanded. "Tell me you found her."

"Negative. She's not here. There's no sign of her."

"Then what the hell are you doing up there?" Frankie shouted, and in all the time Rob had known her, that was the closest he'd come to hearing her sound frantic.

He tried to explain yet again what they had been doing.

"What about Gibbs? Did he get away?"

"Hell no, he didn't get away. I already told you he's in custody."

There was an intelligible burst of words, and then Frankie said clearly, "Back to base…we've got worse trouble."

Worse trouble?

Rob felt someone's gaze. He looked up. From the other side of the room, Adam was watching him. He said crisply into his radio, "Copy. What worse trouble?"

Frankie's voice was harsh. "We've got another dead girl."

Chapter Eight

So much for never being able to find a cop when you needed one.

The streets—street—of Nearby was crowded with official and government vehicles. Everywhere you looked there was a man or a woman in uniform. Far from reassuring the citizenry, the police presence seemed to escalate tension and anxiety.

Although two, possibly three, dead women in nearly as many days probably had something to do with people in Nearby feeling under siege.

"This needs to be kicked upstairs ASAP," Russell had told Adam when they reconnected back at the search staging area. In the distance they could see the museum and crime scene technicians moving back and forth between their vehicles and the Joseph house. The property was being searched front to back for hairs, fibers, anything that might give a clue what had happened to Tiffany.

"That's not our call," Adam replied. Frankly, it was the last thing he wanted. If the Bend Satellite Office was brought in, it would be only a matter of time before the Portland Resident Authority was involved, and then he and Russell would be on their way back to Los Angeles.

"We've got a suspected terrorist responsible for the deaths of three women—"

That was a leap even for Russell. "Hold on. First of all, Tiffany may still be alive. In fact, there's every reason to believe she's still alive."

"Every reason? Give me one."

"Let's start with the fact that there's no body. Secondly, *suspected terrorist?* What hat did you pull that rabbit out of?"

Russell's blue gaze flickered.

All the weeks of putting up with Russell's dismissive attitude were coming to a head. Adam had not allowed himself to react or respond to Russell's constant challenge of his authority. He strove to keep it professional and impersonal at all times, and he was generally pretty good at that, but he suddenly realized how much he disliked Russell.

And how much Russell disliked him.

It was personal, and now that they both knew it was personal, it was going to be hard to keep the cracks from showing.

Russell said, "The hat where Sandy Gibbs was screaming anti-government doctrine after spending a couple of hours trying to kill us? How about that rabbit out of that hat?"

At that point Rob had yelled from his SUV, "Adam, are you with me?"

"Adam?" repeated Russell.

There was no reason Rob—Deputy Haskell—shouldn't call him by his first name. Adam's face warmed all the same.

"Be right there," Adam had called. To Russell he said, "This is not the time or the place to start throwing the weight of the federal government around. We do not have jurisdiction here. This is not our case."

"It needs to be our case," Russell said.

Oh. Right. *Now* it made sense. Russell was starting to see the career-making potential of the situation in Nearby. Well, good luck with that. It was going to take one hell of a lot of PR maneuvering to turn an antisocial gun-toting hermit like Sandy Gibbs into a political movement.

The second murder was a different matter. Adam was worried about the second slaying. And when he jumped into the SUV, Rob's words did nothing to reassure him.

"Zeke doesn't know yet. Frankie's going to tell him herself. The dead girl is Azure Capano."

"Azure?" The name was faintly familiar.

"She's—was—the hostess at the Lakehouse restaurant. She and Zeke have been on and off for a few years."

"Were they on or off now?"

"Off." Rob threw him a grim look. "Zeke is going to take this hard."

Maybe. Or maybe Zeke would pretend to take it hard. He didn't say it aloud. He knew Rob would be shocked and probably angry at such a suggestion. Adam knew he possessed a jaded world view. That was the trouble with their line of work. You couldn't help being suspicious of everyone. Even the people closest to you. Adam had been a shy, quiet boy, but anytime he'd been late or failed to call when he was supposed to, his father had accused him of everything from sneaking out to meet girls— which was actually pretty funny—to embarking on a career of juvenile delinquency.

Zeke had struck Adam as kind of a prick; even so he liked Rob's concern for his fellow deputy.

In fact, he thought Rob was a very decent guy. He had been impressed by the way he'd handled himself on the mountain. This had not been just another day at the office. Rob had stayed surprisingly cool under fire. Adam had met plenty of big city cops who hadn't been nearly as calm once the bullets started flying.

True, Rob's decision to explore the tunnel beneath Gibbs's cabin indicated an impulsive streak. He was probably too soft-hearted. A man could have worse flaws.

"A couple of Medford deputies found her down by the lake," Rob was saying.

Adam's heart sank. "Where by the lake?"

"Near the restaurant. She was floating half under the dock."

"You don't have time of death yet, I suppose?" The SUV hit a pothole and Adam winced at the reminder of the day's collection of bruises. And it looked like the day was going to get a lot worse.

Rob threw him a disbelieving look. "You suppose right. Sometime during the night. That much they could tell. She was nude and," his face grew grimmer still, "her throat was cut."

* * * * *

Rob was right. Zeke did not take the news of Azure's death well.

By four o'clock Sunday afternoon, Sandy Gibbs was cooling off in a jail cell, the search for Tiffany had moved south, forensic anthropologists were excavating the remains Adam had discovered, and Frankie had given her first press conference.

Nearby was beginning to look like the crime capital of the northwest.

Shortly after the gentlemen of the press—or at least the Medford *Mail Tribune*, the Klamath Falls *Herald and News*, and the Nearby *Nickel*—were dismissed, Adam met with the Nearby Sheriff's Office for a war council.

Crime scene technicians were still combing the Joseph house. So far there was no indication that Tiffany had met with foul play.

"Well, there's no way that she went off on a ski weekend," Frankie said. "I think we can rule that theory out once and for all. Our best bet now is Bert Berkle's dogs and the teams searching the Back Bend area." She cleared her throat. "We only have the preliminary findings on Azure, but we do have to consider the similarities between her case and Cynthia's."

"Was there a connection between Azure and the Josephs?" Adam asked.

"Not that I'm aware of," Frankie said. "It's a small town. Everyone knows each other. So in that way, I guess there's a connection."

"Azure and Tiffany didn't get along," Zeke said. His eyes were still red. Otherwise he seemed composed. "Back when they were both on the cheerleading squad. Azure said Tiffany was a snotty, spoiled brat."

"Azure was how old?" Adam inquired.

"Nineteen," Zeke said.

Zeke was probably in his mid-to-late-twenties. Not that that meant much. Zeke seemed a bit young for his age and Azure, at least from what Adam could remember, had struck him as seasoned.

"Okay." Frankie shuffled the papers in front of her. "Well." She glanced at Zeke. "Zeke, maybe you ought to take the afternoon off."

"The hell!" Zeke returned hotly. "I'm not going anywhere."

"All right then. Have it your way." Frankie cleared her throat. "Both Azure and Cynthia Joseph had their throats cut. Cynthia was knocked out first. Azure went down fighting. The weapon used on Cynthia was dull and rusted. The weapon used on Azure was razor sharp, and that's about all we can tell."

Rob suggested, "Cynthia's death was a crime of opportunity. Someone went hunting for Azure."

Frankie nodded. "That's how it looks to me too." She glanced at Adam.

Adam agreed. "That doesn't rule out the same offender though."

"I guess that's true."

"Or," Rob said, "somebody could be trying to make it look like the same offender."

"Yes." Adam studied the crime scene photos now tacked and taped across the wall of Frankie's office. The artistically arranged crime scene wall was Aggie's contribution. There were several disturbing shots of the girl with the mermaid hair floating in the lake. Meanwhile, in the background, he could hear Aggie at the front desk doing her best to keep up with the flood of phone calls coming in.

"Was Azure sexually assaulted?" Adam asked.

"We don't have that information yet."

"She was nude. So." He really wished Zeke would go home. This was tough enough on them without Zeke sitting there struggling to control his face and breathing. There just wasn't that kind of room for sensitivity in a homicide investigation.

Rob said, "According to you there was an attempt to stage Cynthia's body. But there wasn't any attempt to stage Azure's crime scene. She was left floating in the water."

"If there was an attempt to stage the body," Adam said, "I may have interrupted it."

"You? How?"

"I heard what sounded like a scream around three thirty this morning. I went down to the lake, had a look around. I didn't see anything. It was still dark." He didn't want to make excuses. He was angry and sick thinking about it.

There was silence, and then Rob said, "For all you knew it could have been a screech owl."

Adam gave him a speaking look. Rob had kind instincts. Adam knew he had not heard a screech owl. He had heard a scream. He had convinced himself he'd dreamed it.

"What were you up to at three thirty in the morning?" Zeke demanded.

"I wasn't up. Whatever sound I heard woke me."

"And you didn't think you should call anyone? That you should have fully investigated?"

"I wasn't sure what I'd heard. I spent forty minutes looking around. There were no sounds, no movement. I thought I might have dreamed it."

Zeke sneered, "You have a lot of bad dreams?"

"I do. Yes."

That left even Zeke without a comeback.

"Agent Darling wasn't the only one bunking down by the lake," Rob said. "None of us would have handled it any different, Zeke. And it wouldn't have made any difference to Azure. If she'd still been fighting, Adam would have seen or heard something."

"She wouldn't still be fighting after that wound," Adam said.

Zeke's eyes filled with tears again—a good part of that was rage, in Adam's opinion. Which didn't make his feelings any less powerful or real.

Frankie said, "I guess we need to try to understand what links these victims together. Because there has to be something."

"I'll tell you what links them," Zeke said. "They're the victims of a serial killer."

Frankie scowled at him in warning. "What we need to do is find Tiffany."

Zeke stared at her. "You think Tiffany murdered her mom and then went after Azure?"

"I didn't say that!"

"I think you're right," Adam interjected. "I think finding Tiffany has to remain a priority. The second killing does change things significantly. We still need to understand what ties the murders of Cynthia Joseph and Azure Capano together. These are two women of different ages, backgrounds, professions, appearance."

"Victimology," Zeke said knowledgably.

"Well, okay. Yes."

Adam's acknowledgement seemed to anger Zeke all over again. "You're no profiler."

"No, I'm not. Anyway, that's television. There's no such position at the FBI. But I do know—"

Zeke spoke over him. "Why is he even here? Why are we listening to him? I Googled this asshole. You know what his last big case was? A kidnapping. And the victim died because he fucked up. Royally."

It blindsided him—though really it shouldn't have. Not these days when anyone with a combination of curiosity, persistence, and rudimentary surfing skills could find out just about anything about anyone.

The bigger surprise was Rob, who was suddenly on his feet, hands braced on the table as he leaned into Zeke's face. "We're listening to him because he's the only one here who has a clue of what to do in this situation. Why are you so afraid of hearing what he has to say?"

"Rob…"

If Rob heard him, he gave no sign. All his focus was on Zeke who knocked his chair over as he jumped up.

Zeke roared back, "What the fuck is that supposed to mean?"

"Exactly what it sounds like. If you can't handle this, you need to go home."

"I can handle it fine. What I can't handle is all of you acting like I can't handle it!"

"Sit down, both of you!" Frankie shouted. She pounded the table. "I'm still running this investigation, and I'm *asking* Agent Darling for his advice. *That's* why he's here."

Still blazingly angry Rob threw Adam a quick look, and Adam couldn't help offering a quick, uncertain smile. He couldn't remember anyone ever leaping to his defense like that.

Not that he'd ever needed anyone leaping to his defense until the Conway case.

Rob abruptly seemed to recall himself. He looked faintly uncomfortable before throwing Zeke one final hostile look.

Zeke glared back at him.

"Will you two idiots sit down?" Frankie requested. Actually it wasn't a request.

Zeke picked up his chair. Rob sat down.

"Look," Adam said to Zeke. He tried to keep his tone neutral. "I'm not part of the Behavioral Analysis Unit, but every FBI special agent is cross-trained to deal with a multitude of situations, including violent crimes. Advise and assist law enforcement is a regular part of what we do." He looked at Frankie. "If you want to kick this up to the Portland Field Office, I understand. In the meantime, you have to proceed with the investigation. You know as well as I do how crucial the first forty-eight hours are."

"Go on then," Zeke said. "Tell us about the victims."

Adam shook his head. "That's not how it works. *You* knew the victims. The three of you knew these women. You need to begin collating that information so that we can analyze what we've got. As you would in any homicide case."

Rob said, "We've never handled a homicide case."

"That we know of," Frankie said darkly.

Rob and Zeke both turned to stare at her.

Adam said, "Since you brought it up, I don't believe you sent for me because you thought this office couldn't handle Cynthia Joseph's murder. You could have turned to Klamath Falls or Medford for any support you require. You wanted me to fly up here because you knew I was working the Ripper case. I think consciously or unconsciously, you *do* suspect you have a serial killer on your hands."

Meeting Rob's disbelieving gaze, Frankie said impatiently, "Am I the only one paying attention around here?"

"To *what*?" Rob demanded.

"The fires, the dead animals." She glared at him. "Pagan symbols scrawled on a church wall. For God's sake, Zeke. You watch all these alphabet soup cop shows. Tell him."

Rob spluttered, apparently unable to believe what he was hearing. "Wait a minute. We've had some vandalism, yes. And, yes, a lot of these kids have guns before they're ready. Hell, everybody around here has a gun."

"You don't see it because you don't want to see it," Frankie said.

"Zeke doesn't see it either!"

Maybe not, but what Frankie was saying made sense to Adam. He'd felt from the first that Frankie knew something was very wrong in her little burg, and one thing he'd learned through the years was to trust cops when it came to what was happening on their own beat.

Zeke said nothing. He was staring at Frankie as intently as if he was lip-reading.

"I've been waiting a long time for the other shoe to drop," Frankie said. "When Dove's body turned up, I thought *this is it.* But I was wrong. Wrong about Dove. Not wrong about the rest of it."

She believed it. Every word. And Adam could see that as much as Rob wanted to argue, dismiss what he was hearing, he had too much respect for Frankie. She knew her job and she knew her town. He looked at Adam.

"She could be wrong," he said.

Adam nodded. She *could* be wrong.

Two murdered women in three days indicated she could also be right.

"Okay," Rob said. "Then let's start pulling everything we've got on every one of these women."

"What about that asshole Gibbs?" Zeke asked. "When do we question him?"

Adam looked at Rob.

Rob said grudgingly. "We didn't find anything at his cabin."

"And the Alaskan police didn't find anything the first time they searched Robert Hansen's house either," Zeke said.

"Who the hell's Robert Hansen?" Frankie demanded.

"The Butcher Baker," Zeke answered.

Frankie shook her head. Rob said, "When did you become such an expert on serial killers?"

"You think you're the only one around here who knows how to do his job?"

"No." Rob held onto his temper with obvious effort. "I'm just saying I don't think we can jump to any conclusions about Gibbs."

"The hell we can't! He's the only freak around here that fits the profile."

"We don't have a profile yet," Adam said.

Zeke looked ready to jump to his feet again and start pounding his chest. Frankie said, "I think a cooling off period might be a good idea for everybody. We'll let Mr. Gibbs chill out in a cell for a bit. We've got plenty to charge him with when the time comes."

That was real life due process. Practicality versus ideals. Adam said, "It's too early to know whether Gibbs is involved or not. What we want to avoid doing is questioning him with an assumption of guilt."

"No? Okay. Thanks for explaining basic interrogation techniques," Zeke said.

Adam sighed inwardly.

"We do have information regarding the museum thefts," Frankie said. "Aggie and I have been going through Cynthia's records. It looks like two items were taken: a large wooden mask in the shape of a raven's head, and a knife. The mask would be very valuable. Worth several thousand dollars."

"There's a healthy market for stolen antiquities," Adam said, "but I don't believe the mask was taken to sell."

"If that was the case, all the masks would have been stolen," Rob agreed. "This nut had time to arrange Cynthia's body in a diorama; he sure as hell had time to cart the rest of the masks out of the museum."

"Then what?" Zeke asked.

Frankie said reluctantly, "The knife wasn't so valuable. However, according to Cynthia's notes, the handle of the stolen knife was also carved in the shape of a raven."

Zeke looked blank. "What are we dealing with?" he said. "Some psycho birdman?"

"I've been reading up on raven legends," Rob said.

"*You've* been reading legends about ravens?" Zeke said. Even Frankie looked surprised.

Rob's expression was sheepish. "I checked a couple of books out of the mobile library last night, that's all. Agent Darling guessed that the missing mask was a raven." He shrugged, not looking at Adam.

"Well, what did you find out?" Frankie asked.

"Nothing. Masks were created to resemble certain animals that were considered sacred or powerful. Sometimes the masks were believed to have magical powers."

"Magical powers!" exclaimed Frankie.

"I'm just telling you what I read. There are a lot of legends and stories about ravens—and crows—but nothing that really fits. In some cultures they're bad luck or harbingers of death. They feed off carrion, so they're sometimes viewed as mediators between the dead and the living. Not according to the stories of the Klamath Tribes. Those are mostly creation stories. In Modoc legends they're tricksters, pranksters. But that doesn't mean they're not the hero of the story."

"You're not looking deep enough," Zeke said.

"They're frightening," Adam said. Zeke gave a harsh laugh. Adam ignored him. "They're a menacing-looking bird. It may be something that simple."

"Go on," Frankie said.

Adam was still formulating his thoughts. "Supposing you're right and Joseph's killer is the same man who attacked, or tried to abduct, the girls in December and January. He was described as wearing war paint, which to me indicates this is someone who identifies with Native American culture and who is developing his persona."

"His *persona*?" Zeke questioned. "Like what? He's becoming a super villain?"

Rob said, "I see what you're saying. He's evolving."

"Yes. He is. He's creating a…self concept."

"He's making it up as he goes along," Zeke said.

"I think that's correct."

"I mean *you*."

"Shut up, Zeke." Frankie seemed to be thinking. She shook her head. "This has to be an outsider. We'd have noticed somebody like that. Some crazy with a raven fetish."

Rob said, "An outsider wouldn't know about the museum."

"You do get a lot of people moving through here during the holidays," Adam said, "All the same, I think this is someone local. The kind of incidents you mentioned the other day: vandalism, animal mutilation, fires…that's classic. It's a serial killer on training wheels. This is someone who has been testing the boundaries for a while."

"Male," Rob said. "Caucasian."

"Probably. In this case, almost certainly."

"Young," Frankie said.

"That's going to be relative."

"Late twenties to early thirties," she qualified with great certainty.

Zeke said, "He's not walking around wearing an *I Love Ravens* T-shirt." He threw Adam a challenging look. "You don't have to be in the FBI to know that much."

No, you just had to watch a few episodes of *Criminal Minds*. If this were a TV show, Zeke would be the unsub. Adam said only, "A lot of those assumptions have been challenged in recent years."

"We do have one piece of good news," Frankie said. "Or maybe good news isn't the word for it. The phone recovered near Echo Falls is definitely Tiffany's. It's pretty smashed up; it looks like she—or someone—dropped it on the rocks near the waterfall. The State Police are doing what they can to retrieve her data. Zeke, I want you to have another talk with the friend Tiffany was supposed to spend the weekend with. Something about that story doesn't sit right with me."

"I'll be happy to." Zeke shoved back his chair and rose.

Frankie glowered at him. "Go easy, Zeke. Azure isn't the only victim. Tiffany is a victim too, until we know otherwise."

After Zeke walked out of Frankie's office, Rob said, "He needs to take some personal time off, Frankie. He's a loose cannon."

Frankie eyed Rob without emotion. "I can't spare anybody, Robbie. Zeke's a good cop. He's just young. It's a temporary situation."

Rob looked unsold. Frankie pushed forward a stack of files. "We've got the personnel files on everyone who ever worked in the museum. Let's see if any names jump out at us." Then she lifted her head and yelled, "Aggie! We need more coffee in here."

It was after seven when they finished reading through the files, and it seemed to Adam that pretty much every kid in Nearby had worked at the museum one time or another. Azure had worked there two years ago, and Tiffany continued to work there, though unofficially. Terry Watterson had worked at the museum the summer he had drowned in Blue Rock Cove.

"What about Bill Constantine?" Adam asked. He kept thinking about that photo on Tiffany's mirror. She was a pretty, popular girl, but there did not seem to be anyone special in her life. Not so much as a Justin Bieber poster decorated the pink walls of her bedroom. The only hint of…well, romance would be too strong a word…was a very old snapshot of two boys: one dead and the other someone everyone insisted Tiffany could never be involved with.

He knew firsthand how wrong everyone could be.

"Billy? No," Frankie said definitely.

"Why? Is he gay?"

"Billy? Not that I know of."

"No," Rob said.

Frankie yawned and stretched. "Boys, I think we need to call it a night. Why don't you two go get some chow and some shut-eye, and meet me back here first thing tomorrow?"

"Why don't *you* go get some rest, Frankie?" Rob retorted. "You never went to bed last night. Aggie said you were still here when she got in this morning."

"I want to know what Zeke found out when he interviewed Tiffany's friend. Anyway, I've got to wait to hear from Doc Cooper. He promised he'd call this evening with the autopsy report on Azure. You two run along."

Adam tried to remember the last time anyone had told him to "run along." The truth was he was starting to feel like someone had thrown him off a mountainside—which wasn't too far from the truth. He wasn't completely sure he hadn't cracked a rib. Even if he hadn't, he was starving, exhausted, and feeling unpleasantly wired from far too many cups of bad coffee. It was going to take him a while to unwind, and a couple of drinks were high on his list of priorities since all the other things he'd have liked—starting with a hot bath and ending with Rob—were not on the agenda.

"Thanks, I think I *will* call it a night," he said.

"Appreciate all your help today, Agent Darling," Frankie said absently, reaching for the files they'd left spread over her desk.

The main floor of the station was unlit and eerily silent after the noise and activity of the day. Aggie still manned the front desk. She didn't answer Adam's "Goodnight," staring gloomily into space as he walked past her and pushed out through the front door.

Hazy lamplight diffused the darkness. What was left of the snow had turned to gray slush.

"Hey!" Rob called from behind him.

Adam stopped on the wooden walkway. The night was clear and cold, and his breath rose in front of him, mingling with Rob's.

Rob asked, "Where's your partner?"

Adam felt a flash of disappointment. What had he expected? He said, "At a guess? Filing an official complaint." He was too tired to care how that sounded.

Rob's grin was lopsided. "He strikes me as a guy with a lot of complaints. That could take a while. Why don't you come over to my place for dinner?"

Exhausted as he was, Adam's heart jumped at the prospect of dinner with Rob. He hesitated, and seeing his hesitation, Rob said, "Look, don't take this the wrong way. I respect that you don't want to get involved with a coworker, but we can still have dinner together, can't we? Coworkers eat dinner together."

"Of course." Hell yes, they did, and Adam's instinctive caution was easily dismissed when he thought of countless meals spent with Jonnie—and Russell—though he'd actually enjoyed the meals with Jonnie.

Seeing that he was wavering, Rob coaxed, "A hot bath. A hot meal. A comfortable bed—in the guest room. You wouldn't object to that, right?"

Adam did his best to remain stoic, but after the day he'd had? Tears of gratitude would not be amiss in the face of such generosity. He admitted, "No, of course not."

"And we can always talk over the case, if it'll make you feel better."

Rob was teasing him. Flirting with him? Adam smiled uncertainly. "True."

"And then we can be back at work bright and early tomorrow morning."

"Yes. That would be…"

Heaven? Sort of.

"See how easy that was?" Rob said. "Easiest decision you'll make tonight."

It was hard to tell in the grainy light, but Adam thought Rob winked.

CHAPTER NINE

They'd been running on caffeine and adrenaline all day, so it wasn't any wonder Adam was quiet on the drive from Nearby. Hopefully that's all it was. Hopefully he wasn't regretting his decision to spend the night?

Rob had mostly been on the level. He wasn't going to try to seduce Adam—although he did make a mean chicken parmesan, and if things moved in that direction, he sure as hell wasn't going to object.

He had been attracted to Adam from the first. That was sexual chemistry. Now he was starting to like Adam, wanting to know more—everything—about Adam. That was something different, something dangerous. Rob wasn't backing away.

When they rounded the bend and the house came into view, Adam drew in a long breath. "You're on the take," he said, and Rob laughed.

It was an amazing house. Maybe not *that* amazing, but on a sheriff's deputy salary, yeah. Pretty fantastic. A 2900 square foot mountain resort of a home surrounded by tall mountains and deep forest. Giant picture windows and long rustic decks looked over the panoramic view. And it had come completely furnished. The previous owners had used it primarily as a vacation rental.

"When the real estate market crashed, a lot of people were selling their second homes and vacation properties for whatever they could get," Rob said. "I lucked out."

"I would say so."

The garage had been built into the hillside beneath the house. Rob hit the remote, the interior light flared on, and the door swung slowly open. They zipped inside the cavernous space.

They exited the SUV and went up the stairs, and Rob unlocked the door to the mudroom. They took off their boots and coats, Adam wincing as he shrugged off his blue FBI jacket.

"You okay?" Rob asked.

"I should have picked up a change of clothes at the campground," Adam admitted. "I think I may have fallen into a pile of bear shit."

Rob smiled. "Then that bear was wearing some nice cologne. Anyway, you can borrow a pair of jeans, and I'll throw your stuff in the laundry."

"Okay. Thanks."

"The kitchen is through here." Rob led the way.

"Nice," Adam murmured. And it was. The kitchen featured white granite counter tops, recessed lighting, dark hardwood floors, and an open view onto the other rooms.

"This is… I think my apartment would fit inside your kitchen," Adam said. "You live here on your own?"

"Just me and seven dwarfs."

Adam laughed.

"You must make a pretty good salary though," Rob said.

"I do," Adam admitted. "I'm never home. That's the real problem. Not that it's a problem." He walked down the long open floor plan of kitchen and dining area to the living room with its towering ceilings, open beams, and gleaming floors.

"Now that is a fire place."

"Quartz and field stone."

Adam nodded at the empty gun case. "Not a hunter I take it?"

"Just with a camera." Rob nodded to the row of framed photographs along the paneled wall.

Adam wandered over to examine the photo gallery, and Rob felt an unfamiliar stab of insecurity. Even in his socks and torn jeans, Adam had a certain air. Austerity? Authority?

Adam said thoughtfully, "I was about to say this is more like a luxury resort than a home. You don't feel cut off here?"

"I don't miss Portland. Even if I did, it's only a few hours away. I've got friends in Klamath Falls, so sometimes I spend the weekend there. Then there's the airport in Medford." Rob shrugged. "I like the peace and quiet. I don't mind my own company."

Adam peered more closely at a study of Blue Rock Cove. "These are all yours?"

"Yep."

Adam threw him a quick, surprised look. "They're really good. I mean, I'm not an expert, but I think anyone would say these were professional quality."

"Thanks. It's not easy making a living as a photographer though. Unless you want to spend your weekends taking wedding pictures."

"And you like spending your weekends hiking in the mountains."

"Oh, I like doing other things too," Rob said with a deliberately wicked grin.

Adam smiled too. Rob thought he looked maybe just a bit unsure. Uneasy? He looked back at the nickel-framed portraits and said, "Black and white."

"It's my Ansel Adams phase."

Adam made a sound of acknowledgement.

Rob suspected things were about to get awkward and he said, "Let me show you the bathroom."

He led the way upstairs and through his bedroom. The master bedroom was another oversized room, painted in neutral earth tones. There was crown molding around the large picture windows, and drapes in a shade of red Rob would never have chosen, but didn't want to spend money to replace. Happily, he'd made the bed that morning and had not left underwear lying on the floor.

Adam was silent, and Rob guessed what he was probably thinking. "There's a shower in the guest bathroom, but the only tub is up here, and I'm guessing after that tumble you'd like to soak in hot water for a while."

He pushed open the door and enjoyed Adam's expression. The bathroom was ridiculously spa-like, with oversized heated tiles, wood accents, a giant glass shower big enough for the entire Nearby sheriff's office, a deep sunken soaker tub next to huge picture windows, and Jack and Jill sinks. The whole shebang.

"That's..." Adam shook his head.

"I know. Crazy. I'll leave you to it. You can drop your clothes by the door. I'll be back with a drink. Gin and tonic okay?"

He didn't think Adam heard him. Rob backed, closed the door, and went downstairs to make a very strong gin and tonic. When he returned, he tapped politely on the door and opened it.

"You want company in there?"

Adam was just stepping into the tub. He glanced over his shoulder, blushed. "Er..."

He was very nicely hung. No question. A clean-cut straight arrow of a cock jutting from a soft, golden bush. Perfect plum-

sized balls nestled beneath. Gorgeous. Rob stopped smiling, stopped admiring, unable to look beyond the ugly black and blue bruises splotching Adam's torso and ass. "What the—why the hell didn't you say something?"

"About—?" Adam glanced down at himself. "Oh." He grimaced. "It's just bruising. Nothing life threatening."

"Bruises? You've got contusions."

"I guess. I didn't even feel them until now. I could do with that drink though." He sat cautiously down in the hot water and leaned back, wincing. "God. That is…" He smiled up at Rob.

Rob's heart did an unexpected flip. In fact, it was probably closer to a cartwheel. Something about that unguarded, pointy smile and the way Adam's green eyes crinkled at the corners. Or maybe it had to do with the width of his shoulders and the length of his neck. Then again, perhaps it was something about Adam sitting uncomplaining for how many hours of briefing and debate after falling off a fucking mountain?

Whatever the hell it was, Rob was sold.

"Here." He thrust the drink at Adam, and Adam took the glass and drained half of it in a gulp.

"Uh…"

Adam blinked. "You make them strong."

"I was going to say. But I figure if you're drinking, have a real drink." The words were spilling from his mouth. Rob had no idea what he was saying. He was still dealing with this unexpected development in his feelings for Special Agent Darling. *Adam*.

No. Not a good development.

"I'm not objecting." Adam tipped the glass in Rob's direction in a salute and took another long swallow. He closed his eyes and tilted his head back. He had a good profile. Probably too sharp, too sculptured to fit most people's ideas of masculine good looks, but Rob thought he was, well, beautiful.

Adam's eyes opened. His mouth curved. "Don't worry. I'm not going to slip under and drown."

Rob chuckled, though that casually flung image felt like a punch in the chest. "You'll miss a nice meal if you do. You have your soak and I'll start dinner."

"You don't have to go to a lot of trouble." Adam closed his eyes again.

"No trouble." Rob picked up Adam's clothes and backed out of the steamy room.

What kind of fool spent his entire life playing the field, and then fell for a guy passing through town? The one guy he couldn't have, *that* was the guy he wanted?

That wasn't only foolish. It was crazy.

Rob tossed Adam's clothes in the washer. He pulled out chicken breasts and shoved them in the microwave to defrost. Peeled the veggies, dumped them in a pan with olive oil and sea salt.

He poured himself a second drink.

A complete emotional dead end. That's what he was headed for. Oh, he could probably get Adam into bed again. He would sure try. He could tell Adam was still attracted, still interested. He didn't want to be. But you always knew. Now sex wasn't going to be enough. For Rob.

His mouth went dry at the idea of taking Adam. Pushing his cock in Adam's trim, tight ass and hearing Adam moan with pleasure. Moan and groan and beg him for more.

Maybe tonight.

Or having Adam inside him again. His legs felt weak at the memory.

Yes. Either. Both. Yes. Sex would be…fantastic. And frequent.

But it was only the starting point. Now, for the first time in his life, he was thinking of, longing for all that might—should—come after. Companionship. Caring.

He set his drink down and dug the first aid kit from under the sink in the mudroom. All those cuts and bruises. Brief as his glimpse of Adam's injuries had been, he'd experienced them viscerally, as though Adam's pain was his own.

How could that be? He barely knew Adam. Somehow it felt like he had known him all his life.

And speaking of Adam, he'd been soaking for about twenty minutes now. Rob jogged upstairs, listened briefly at the bathroom door. Water was running, so Adam was still conscious and alive.

He went back to his dresser and pulled out a clean pair of shorts, jeans, T-shirt, flannel shirt. Green plaid flannel because Adam would look good in that. He liked the idea of seeing Adam wearing his clothes.

Jesus. Christ. *Pull yourself together. You do not want to do this.*

As he passed his dresser, he caught a glimpse in the mirror, and he looked wild-eyed and alarmed. And speaking of needing a shower…

He tapped on the bathroom door and Adam called immediately, "Yes?"

Rob couldn't help it. He opened the door, set the bundle of clothes on the long granite counter. "You want another drink?"

Adam's face was flushed from the steam and his hair was wet and curling in spikes. "Er…sure," he said. And then, "Yes, why not?"

He held his glass toward Rob, but Rob knew if he walked over there he was going to kneel down and kiss Adam, and even if Adam let him, it was liable to guarantee Adam sleeping in the guest room. So he said, "Leave it. I'll bring a clean glass. Nothing's too good for you."

He said it in a joking tone and Adam laughed. The fact was, Rob meant it.

He went downstairs, got Adam another drink, delivered it with only a minimum of scoping Adam out. Adam's nipples were rose-brown, all his body hair pale gold, and he had a surprisingly heavy five o'clock shadow. Well, eight thirty o'clock shadow.

He closed the door firmly, stripped off his own filthy clothes, dropped them in the closet hamper, dug out clean jeans and a shirt he knew he looked hot in.

At least according to his pal in Klamath Falls. Shane. Shane was a nice guy and the sex was great, but Rob had never felt a fraction of what he felt for Adam. He had known from the first that he never would, and maybe in a way that had been part of the attraction.

Which made his reaction to Adam all the more disturbing.

He showered downstairs in the guest bath, and then got back to fixing dinner.

He was just putting the chicken in the oven when he heard Adam coming downstairs, and his heart sped up.

"That was great," Adam said. "Thank you. I feel one hundred percent better."

Rob glanced around, gulped at the vision of Adam in his green plaid shirt—Adam's eyes were gorgeous—and said, "Have a seat. Dinner will be ready in about forty-five minutes."

"Anything I can do to help?"

"Nope. Under control," said Rob.

Adam walked over to the counter, studying the array of bowls and dishes. "Are you sure this isn't too much trouble?"

"Nah. We have to eat, right? Did you want another drink?"

Adam laughed self-consciously. "Better not. You definitely make 'em strong. I'm actually feeling buzzed."

"That's from not eating all day."

"Probably."

Well, hell, they could probably keep up the polite conversation for the rest of the evening.

Please pass the salt.

With pleasure.

Thank you.

You're very welcome.

Given how little time they had—Rob had—he decided to drive right over the No Trespassing sign.

"What was Zeke talking about earlier? That kidnapping case where the victim died."

Adam was still smiling—wryly—but the easy relaxation was gone from his face. "The one I fucked up royally?"

"Don't take anything Zeke says to heart. No one else does."

"Zeke isn't alone in his assessment."

He could tell when Adam was on guard or wary because he started to slip into FBI-speak. Like he was narrating a documentary.

"What happened?"

Adam looked down at the granite counter, then flicked Rob a funny, almost uncertain look. "Bridget Conway was the seventeen-year-old daughter of a wealthy Bakersfield rancher. She was taken on her way to school one morning, and the Bureau was brought in. I was the Special Agent in Charge. The kidnappers demanded one million dollars for her release. That was a figure easily accessible to Tom Conway, so he was able to put the ransom delivery together very quickly."

"But the kidnappers didn't release Bridget?"

Adam sighed. "It's a bit more complicated than that. What we didn't understand was Bridget was complicit in her own abduction. In fact, there's a strong possibility the original idea was hers. She was seeing a young man her family didn't approve of—partly because he was too old for her, and partly because Paul Douglas had a juvenile criminal record."

"Girls go for that bad boy shit," Rob said.

"Do they? Well, I guess some girls do. I guess Bridget did. Anyway, Bridget and Douglas cooked up this scheme to get money from her father so they could run away together. But they needed help to pull it off, and so Douglas brought in a friend by the name of Gary Black. Black was a moronic thug. That's really beside the point. All of this is beside the point. I'm just giving you the background."

"Go on," Rob said.

"The kidnappers gave orders that the police were not to be brought in."

"Of course."

"But Conway phoned the Bureau first thing and we—I—" Adam stopped. "I'll give you the abridged version. When the time came to make the ransom drop, I insisted that we use tracking devices on Conway's car."

"That would be the smart thing to do."

Adam's smile was distracted. "Thanks, Rob. Unfortunately the tracking equipment shorted the electrical system on Conway's car. The alternator failed, the car died, and Conway was stuck on the highway in the middle of the night with no way to contact the kidnappers. He missed the drop completely."

"Hell."

"Finally the kidnappers called Conway on his cell. Conway explained the situation. He said he had the money, he still wanted to make the exchange, and they should come and pick up the ransom. And so they did."

Rob was watching Adam's face. "Conway was on his own?"

"No. He was supposed to be, but no. I insisted on hiding in the backseat."

"So far I don't see you making choices anyone else wouldn't have made."

"The kidnapper arrived on a motorcycle to pick up the money. Things weren't going according to plan, so he was already rattled. And then Tom recognized him as Paul Douglas—"

Rob knew what was coming. Which was probably pretty much how Adam had felt in those final seconds as it all played out on that lonely stretch of highway.

"Douglas panicked and tried to shoot Tom. I shot Douglas. When Douglas didn't return with the money, Black also panicked, executed Bridget, and tried to flee the state."

"Jesus."

"He's about the only person who wasn't on the road that night." Adam sighed. "Maybe I *will* have another drink."

"That is one horrible story," Rob said. "But I don't see how you're to blame for anything that happened."

"Yes, well, what it boils down to is Conway, like a lot of parents, would rather have died than lose his daughter. He argued against the tracking system, and he argued against my being in the backseat of the car. We-I-overruled him. And I ended up being wrong."

"Not from most people's standpoint."

"From the Conway family's standpoint. And probably from Bridget's standpoint. I promised them that I would get Bridget safely back. I promised them that if they did it my way, she'd be home safe and sound."

"You don't think maybe Bridget and her boyfriend were a little bit to blame for what happened?"

"Bridget was a kid, and regardless of her role in the kidnapping, it was my responsibility to get her home safely. I failed to do that. And part of why I failed was it wasn't enough for me that we get Bridget back. I wanted to catch her kidnappers. I wanted the credit. I wanted another gold star. That's the truth."

"Gold star?"

Adam made a face. "Another letter of commendation."

The timer went off. It was a relief to get away from the pain on Adam's face. Rob turned to the stove, poured marinara sauce over the chicken, sprinkled with cheese, and shoved it back in the oven.

He said, "I think I understand now why you believe Tiffany could be involved in her mother's murder."

"I did think there was a strong possibility at first. Despite the fact that Joseph was stripped, there didn't seem to be a sexual element to her murder. Azure's death doesn't fit."

"Unless Tiffany's a serial killer."

"That's really hard to believe," Adam said. "There are teenage serial killers. Not many, and they're mostly male."

"But you do believe Frankie's right? We've got a serial killer on our hands? Just not Tiffany."

"It's too soon to say. We don't know that Azure was killed by the same offender. It doesn't seem like the same weapon was used."

"Now there you're thinking like a city boy," Rob said. "I think it's likely Cynthia's killer took that knife home, cleaned, polished, and sharpened it. He didn't take it for a souvenir, that much I'll guarantee."

Adam looked startled. "That's a good point. I was thinking he'd regard the knife as a relic, a sacred object, but it could be both a weapon and a sacred object."

"Nobody around here would leave a perfectly good knife rusted and useless."

"You're probably right about that."

"It's still hard to believe we've got a serial killer running around Nearby." Or maybe he just didn't want to believe it. Rob wasn't sure.

Adam said, "Serial killers are not the exclusive property of big cities."

"If Tiffany is not involved, where is she? Do you think she's dead?" He hated to think so. She was a good little citizen. Kind of a smartass, but kind-hearted and helpful. If she'd been killed, he hoped it had been quick, that—like her mother—she'd never known what hit her.

Adam said wearily, "If she's dead, I don't know why we don't have a body. There was no attempt to hide Joseph or Azure. Why conceal Tiffany?"

"I don't know either," Rob said. "I think we should forget about it for now. Let's just have a quiet evening. A nice meal, a couple of drinks, a good sleep."

Adam smiled with what looked like genuine relief. "That sounds like a great idea to me."

For the next half hour they chatted about basically nothing. Rob asked Adam if he liked to ski. Adam did not. He asked Rob if he liked to sail. Rob did not. "But we get a lot of people here with sailboats during the summer," he suggested.

"I used to have a boat," Adam said. "I wouldn't have time to go sailing now days anyway."

"Everybody needs time off," Rob said.

Adam frowned like this was an alien concept.

They moved on to movies and books. It turned out that neither of them watched much TV or had a lot of time to read fiction. "I think the last film I saw was a James Bond movie," Adam admitted.

"I like Disney musicals," Rob said. "Especially the ones with princesses. *Little Mermaid? Pocahontas*? That one's *great*."

Adam gave him a funny look and he grinned. "Just kidding."

"You *are* quite the kidder."

"I can be serious too," Rob said.

Adam met his eyes and then looked away.

So it was that kind of conversation. The kind of conversation you made on a first date, except this was not a date.

Rob served the chicken over pasta. They ate in front of the fireplace, sitting at opposite ends of the long leather sofa. Rob talked Adam into having another drink. He thought it was a good sign that he didn't have to try too hard. Adam was fairly relaxed by then, or as relaxed as he probably ever got.

"That was great." Adam set his plate aside and gave a deep, appreciative sigh. "Thank you very much."

Rob shook his head. "I'm a passable cook. You just don't get many home-cooked meals."

"True." Adam's gaze turned speculative. "Is it difficult being a gay man in a small town?"

"In some ways, sure. I don't bring a lot of guys home to dinner. Let me put it that way."

"With a hundred thousand visitors a year, you must not lack for company."

Rob said, "That doesn't mean I'm not choosey about who I spend time with."

"No. I'm not implying anything."

"Imply away." Rob gave him a hard, bright smile. "I never felt any need or desire to settle down."

"Sure. Settling down is not for everyone."

"Not because I wouldn't like to. I just never met the right guy."

"Sometimes that's true too."

"What about you? You said you got involved with a coworker and it ended badly?"

"I feel like I've been doing all the talking." Adam smiled. It was a you're-in-my-space smile. "I'm interested in you. What made you join the sheriff's office?"

Rob pushed his plate away and moved closer to Adam, closing some of that leather-cushioned distance. Adam tilted his head, acknowledging Rob's approach. His mouth quirked.

Rob said, "I don't know. I needed a job. Do you think people get asked why they wanted to become an accountant or a pilot?"

"Nobody wants to kill you for being an accountant. Except maybe at tax time. If you go into law enforcement there are people who want you dead just because you're LE. So it's natural to wonder why someone might choose that path."

"Why did you join the FBI?"

"My father was in the FBI." Adam hesitated. "I admired my dad a lot when I was growing up. I guess I wanted to be just like him."

Rob said cautiously, "Is your dad still around?" He liked the way Adam's face looked in the firelight. His hair seemed gilded, his eyes shone, the silver bracelet glinted. Rob found that bracelet encouraging. It was simple and discreet, but it seemed to hint at a whole other Adam. An Adam who might not object if Rob leaned forward and kissed him.

"He is. I see even less of him now than when he was with the Bureau." Adam's mouth quirked derisively. "I like my job and I'm good at it. I don't have any regrets. I can't think of anything I'd rather do."

Rob stretched his arm along the back of the leather couch and Adam smiled at him. "Would you like another drink?" Rob asked.

Adam moved his head in negation. "If I have another drink, you'll have to carry me to bed."

"I'll carry you to bed."

Adam laughed.

Rob's hand closed on Adam's shoulder, and he drew him closer. "Come here," Rob whispered.

He saw something flash through Adam's eyes. Doubt? Hesitation. Adam tilted his face and their lips brushed. Tentative. Sweet. A much more cautious kiss than Rob was used to. Shy? Something melted in his chest and he kissed Adam again, very gently, as though Adam were a nervous young girl he needed to woo and win.

Adam tasted like alcohol, and he smelled like Rob's shampoo and Rob's soap, which should not have been erotic, but somehow was. His mouth curved beneath Rob's, his lips unexpectedly soft. He liked this approach, he liked being kissed. Rob kissed him again, still gentle, still courting. They breathed together in easy harmony. Rob could feel Adam's heart pounding against his own and Adam's eyelashes flickering against his eyes.

Rob liked kissing—he had wanted to kiss Adam the first night, and had not missed the fact that Adam did not want to be kissed—this was even better than he had imagined. He used every bit of skill and delicacy he had, and he felt the moment Adam stopped thinking and simply surrendered.

Adam's hand landed lightly on the base of Rob's skull, and he applied a little pressure of his own. *More...*

Rob gave him more kisses, hotter, harder, wet kisses. Adam kissed him back openly hungry and feverish. He slid down onto his back, pulling Rob with him. And there they were, having a good old-fashioned necking session right there on Rob's over-sized couch in his under-furnished living room.

All Rob's good intentions flew out the window.

"Jesus, I want you so much."

Adam tore his mouth away and gasped, "What about the guest room?"

"We can do it in the guest room if you want."

Adam's laugh was breathless, his free hand fumbled with Rob's zipper. "No, if we're going to do it, let's do it."

That sounded like there was a chance he was going to change his mind, and Rob wasted no time tearing his clothes off—just about literally—and then remembered protection. Was startled that he'd nearly forgotten. When was the last time *that* had happened?

"Time out."

Adam raised his head. "What the—?"

Rob pounded out of the room, up the stairs, down the hall, and into his bedroom. He rifled through the bedroom drawer and raced back downstairs. As he sprinted through the open floor plan he saw Adam sitting up on the sofa looking beautifully naked, with the expression of someone who has missed his bus.

Rob pounded his chest and gave a Tarzan yell as he sprang for the sofa.

Adam's jaw dropped. He raised an instinctive, defensive leg, and that was almost the end of the evening's proceedings.

"AAAHHHH AH AH AH aa *owww!*" Rob landed half on top of Adam who had watched his advance with astonished disbelief.

Adam offered a strangled, "Uhhhh…"

"OW," Rob repeated. He lifted off, studying the footprint in his chest. "That hurt."

"You're *crazy*." Adam still looked amazed, but he was starting to laugh. "You're the craziest guy I ever met. That I didn't have to arrest."

"Your feet are deadly weapons."

"You're just lucky that kick didn't land where it nearly did." Adam was still amused. He sat up, swinging his legs off the sofa.

Rob watched him with dismay. "Where are you going?"

Adam's smile twisted. He said apologetically, "I think maybe the guest room might be a good idea."

Rob caught his hand and kissed it. "Hey. Don't do that." He kissed the back of Adam's hand again, and felt the tiniest tremor of Adam's fingers. "You don't want to do that." He nuzzled Adam's wrist, feeling the hammering pulse point.

Adam swallowed. His eyelashes flickered. Fluttered? Whatever, it was disarming as hell. "It's not a matter of want to, but I do think—"

"Stop thinking," Rob told him. He kissed the sensitive skin of Adam's inner elbow, gave him a tug, and Adam sat down beside him on the cushions as though his legs had given out.

"We've got an early day tomorrow," Adam said faintly.

Rob kissed his shoulder. Adam's breathing sounded funny. Rob kissed the curve of his neck, nuzzled him beneath his ear. Adam made a soft sound, very close to the moan of Rob's imagination.

Rob said, "Adam, listen, you can still spend the night in the guest room. But that's not what I want, and it's not what you want, and why shouldn't we have what we want?"

Adam was watching him sideways, still breathing those light, shallow inhales and exhales.

Rob kissed him moistly under his jaw, kissed him at the corner of his very firm mouth, which quivered.

"Up to you," Rob said. "You decide."

Adam turned and his mouth covered Rob's.

CHAPTER TEN

He woke several hours later to bright moonlight and a headache.

Rob was still deeply asleep, snoring softly, peacefully, on the other side of the king-size bed.

Adam rose, trying not to jostle the mattress, and found his way to the spa-like bathroom in search of aspirin. He flicked the wall switch, wincing at the flood of bright light, found a bottle in the cupboard and swallowed three tablets—hopefully aspirin—washing them down with water scooped from the sink. He splashed water on his face and stared blearily at his red-eyed reflection. *Ugh*. He was sore and aching. Some of the aches were more pleasant than others, but all guaranteed he would be doing little sleeping for the rest of the night.

He wasn't much for sleep these days anyway. In fact, he'd always had trouble turning off his brain. Alcohol didn't really help because halfway through the night he'd wake up wide-eyed and brain buzzing like now.

He turned off the lights and stepped back into the bedroom where Rob continued his untroubled slumbers.

Adam felt a swell of affectionate amusement. Good for Rob. He'd earned a good night's sleep. Adam's memory of the evening was foggy. He did remember being pleasurably surprised at just how attentive and inventive Rob had been. In fact, he hadn't been with anybody that tuned in to what he wanted since—well, a very long time.

In fact, if Rob didn't live in the back of the Great Beyond, Adam would be tempted to start thinking maybe there was a possibility of…what?

By his own admission Rob was not the From This Day Forward type.

Whereas Adam. Well, he was an FBI agent. The first word of the Bureau's motto was fidelity. *Fidelity, Bravery, and Integrity.* There wasn't any future in it, but it was tough not to give in to the desire to crawl back into bed and let himself be calmed and comforted by Rob's presence. He continued to study the sleeping mound next to the empty stretch of sheet where he'd lain.

Yes, it would be all too easy to care for Rob.

Adam crossed to the picture windows and gazed out.

From this vantage point, Nearby looked like an Alpine village in one of Rob's Disney films. Was there a Disney film set in an Alpine village?

Frankie must have finally gone home because there didn't seem to be a lamp shining in the entire town. In fact, there didn't seem to be a light on in the entire world. Not that it was dark. The reflection of moon and starlight on snow illuminated the mountains and forest in an unearthly silver light.

He shivered. There was a stark, almost aching beauty to it.

A couple of other vacation homes dotted the pristine hillside. There was plenty of room between them so nobody was breathing down anyone else's neck.

As he stood watching he noticed a pale glimmer moving through the house on the ridge across from Rob's.

The next instant it was gone. Maybe it had been a reflection?

Adam waited, watching.

He was growing bored and cold when he saw the single bright dot moving on the top level.

Ghost light? He smiled grimly. No, sure as hell that was a flashlight beam.

He tried to think of a good and lawful reason someone might be tiptoeing around their own house using a flashlight.

Maybe the power was off?

He glanced over at the clock beside the bed. The illuminated numbers read four thirty.

The power wasn't off all across the valley. It didn't mean it wasn't off in that rental. Even so, what was someone doing up and creeping around at four thirty in the morning?

Granted, *he* was up and creeping around.

He watched the light die again.

What are you up to?

Maybe nothing at all. Given the rapidly rising murder rate in the town of Nearby, it seemed worth checking out.

He went back to the bed and sat down on the mattress.

"Rob?" he said quietly.

Rob cut off mid-snore, jerking awake. "Hm? I'm listening!"

"The house across from this one. Does someone live there?"

Rob was silent for a few seconds, processing. "Live there?" he repeated. "It's a rental property."

"Someone's moving around inside with a flashlight."

After a moment, Rob threw back the covers, rolled out of bed, and went to the windows. He said finally, "You could be seeing a reflection from headlights."

"There aren't any cars on the road."

Rob was silent, staring through the window. "I don't see anything."

"It went dark before I woke you up. I watched it move from room to room downstairs and then again upstairs."

Rob turned back to the window. Adam joined him. The windows in the vacation property remained solidly blank.

Rob said, "You want to go check it out?"

The relief was substantial. Adam had been prepared for amusement or exasperation. "I would like to. Yes."

"Okay. Let's go see what's going on over there." Rob turned from the window. "I think we should walk. It'll take us a little longer to get over there, but whoever is in that house won't see or hear us coming."

They dressed quickly, Rob loaning Adam a black sweater, a dark parka, and a pair of wool gloves. Then they armed and headed into the cold night.

The crust of snow crunched softly beneath their boots as they jogged down the road. Ahead, the vacation rental continued to sleep beneath the rafters of clouds.

Adam knew he hadn't imagined that furtive light. He was afraid that whoever was behind it would be long gone by the time they made it down the long, slippery road.

Five minutes into their run, Rob, slightly ahead, stopped so suddenly, that Adam slammed into him. Rob grabbed his arm, steadying him. "What...the...fuck...is...that?" he whispered. He was staring at the ridge above them.

Adam gazed up and his heart seemed to stop for a few crucial seconds.

Gazing down at them, so still he could have been carved from midnight, was a tall, black, winged figure.

Winged.

As in...wings.

Adam tried to wrap his mind around this development, assuring himself they were not real wings, even as his disbelieving eyes took in the details of every glossy black feather. They sure as hell *looked* like real wings.

Rob seemed to recover from his initial shock. He said in a clear, loud voice, "What are you supposed to be?" and pulled his weapon.

The figure drew back, disappearing from view.

Adam saw it all, just as he'd seen it unfold from the backseat of Tom Conway's Porsche on that deserted road in Bakersfield. Intuition? Instinct? He didn't know *how* he knew. He just knew.

He said urgently, "Rob, we've got to get to that house. He didn't come from there. He's after whoever is *in* there."

Rob was already halfway up the slope, pistol in one hand, scrambling for a foothold. He threw over his shoulder, "Then find her. Or whoever it is in there. This guy is mine."

They shouldn't split up. But there wasn't time to argue, and if by some chance Tiffany *was* hiding in that vacation rental, he had to get to her first. Why the hell hadn't they brought a radio? These thoughts flooded Adam's brain as he sprinted down the road, twice nearly losing his balance on patches of ice, racing for the dark and silent house.

God, be careful, he thought. There was light; icy, silvery light, more romantic than useful. That's all he needed. A sprained or broken ankle. But the words were really meant for Rob. Did Rob realize what he was dealing with? Did he understand the danger?

He hit another frozen puddle, his foot slipped and he went with it, skating a couple of inches before regaining solid ground. He ran on. He reached the house at last and went quietly up the snow-piled steps to the front deck. He crossed the deck and tried the front door.

It was locked. It would have been surprising if it hadn't been. He moved on to the sliders a few feet down. Also locked. With a wooden broom handle wedged in the tracks for good measure. He tried to peer through the glass. The drapes had been drawn across.

He didn't want to panic her, if it was Tiffany inside. And he didn't want to get shot by some freaked-out homeowner. He went back down the stairs and went around the side, nearly falling over a metal fire pit concealed beneath the snow. The collision of his shins with the metal lid and the subsequent crash made a fair bit of racket. No lights came on, no draperies twitched open. The house stayed stubbornly still.

Maybe she'd already fled.

That was a disheartening thought.

He tried the two big windows on the first floor. Both were locked. He went to the back door and began searching amongst the weathered and peeling lawn ornament animals populating the built-in flower planters. He struck out a couple of times before he noticed a small, painted stone.

Score.

Why homeowners imagined these decorative hiding places were anything but an invitation to burglary, he would never understand. Tonight he was only grateful to hear the reassuring jingle of metal on resin. He opened the key box, rose, and went to unlock the back door.

The door swung silently open onto a long empty sun porch.

Adam softly closed the door, locked it, and drew his weapon. Carrying at low ready, he moved quietly across the outdoor carpeting and went up the narrow wooden staircase.

The house was cold and smelled of paint and new carpet. It smelled uninhabited, and he began to wonder if he *had* made a mistake.

He reached the next level and found himself in a kitchen. There were half shutters across the windows. Moonlight spilled over the tops, highlighting a can opener and an empty Campbell's soup tin on the island in the center of the kitchen.

"Tiffany?" Adam called. "This is Special Agent Darling. I'm with the FBI and I'm armed. Please show yourself."

Nothing.

He kept his voice calm, tried to sound reassuring. "We don't want anyone getting hurt tonight."

A floorboard squeaked. He brought up his weapon. The doorway was empty. Even so, he could sense her presence, feel a pulsing, live element in the darkness. Close by.

"There's nothing to be afraid of," Adam said. "No one wants to hurt you."

Granted, the fact that he was pointing a Glock in what he surmised was her general direction was probably not reassuring. But he had no way of knowing whether she was also armed or not, whether she was another innocent victim or an accomplice, whether it was even Tiffany he was talking to.

"We can end this right now," Adam said. "Put your hands up and step out slowly. I'm going to count to three. One. Two."

Shrieking, she flew from the darkness like an apparition in a horror movie. Knife upraised, eyes wild in her white face, hair a matted mess.

"Jesus." It happened so fast and the sound she made was so bloodcurdling, he wasn't sure why he didn't shoot her. Somehow he saw her terror for what it was and managed to shoulder his weapon and grab her wrist before she could slash him.

She was strong and wild. Not a match for him, though, and the butcher's knife clattered to the tile floor. Unnervingly she continued to scream, over and over. If there were words, they were unintelligible.

"I'm not going to hurt you," Adam kept saying. He doubted she could hear him over her shrieks. "You're all right now."

She wasn't all right though. She was crazed with whatever she had been through. She writhed in his grip and screamed at the top of her lungs, eyes staring at him but clearly seeing something else. Finally, in a mix of desperation and pity, he wrapped both arms around her and held her tight. Her screams choked off and she went limp.

For a moment he was afraid she'd literally died of fright, but no. When he lowered her to the floor, she was in a dead faint. Beneath the torn and bedraggled flannel sleep shirt her heart was still pounding.

"Adam?" Rob yelled from downstairs.

"Up here!" Relief washed through him. Until that instant, he hadn't realized how worried he was about Rob, how much of his mind had been occupied with what might be happening to Rob.

Rob's boots thudded up the stairs. "What the hell? I could hear screams clear across the ridge."

"It's Tiffany," Adam said. "She's in shock."

Rob reached them. "It *is* Tiffany." He sounded startled, though he too had guessed at the truth earlier. "I'll phone for an ambulance." He reached for his cell phone.

"I don't know how she managed to get over here, but she's been hiding in this house."

"I guess it makes more sense that she'd run toward houses and people rather than the forest."

Adam nodded absently. Given the opportunity, why hadn't she run toward town? What was it in the village of Nearby that frightened her?

"I lost that birdman bastard in the woods. He had too much of a head start. Do you think she saw who killed Cynthia?"

"She sure as hell saw something," Adam said.

Rob said grimly, "One thing we know for sure. Sandy Gibbs isn't our guy." He turned away to speak into his cell phone.

* * * * *

"Well, you boys had a busy night," Frankie said when Adam arrived at the sheriff's office much later Monday morning. He had waited with Rob until Tiffany had been transported to the hospital, then Rob had driven him back to the campground where he'd showered, shaved, checked his email, and returned phone calls before heading over to the sheriff's office.

As he'd seen Rob only a couple of hours earlier, Adam was disconcerted at the way his pulse jumped when he spotted him over by the coffee machine. Rob held the pot up in inquiry. Adam nodded.

Watching him, Frankie said, "I guess I shouldn't ask how you two managed to be working together at five o'clock in the morning."

"Early to bed, early to rise," Rob said. "And no, you shouldn't ask."

Frankie put her hands up. "It's not like I want to know."

"How's Tiffany doing?" Adam asked. "Any change?"

"The doctors are saying she's in deep emotional shock. She's under heavy sedation," Frankie replied. "And nobody is willing to commit as to when we're going to be able to question her."

That did not sound promising.

"And in other news," Frankie continued, "Sandy Gibbs tells me he's planning to sue you."

"Me?"

"The Federal Government in general, and you and my deputy in particular."

"Let him sue." Rob's expression was flinty. He carried over two mugs, handing one to Adam, and leaned against the door frame of Frankie's office.

"I have to agree," Adam said. "The minute he opened up on our searchers with an assault rifle, any legal standing he might have had became shaky." All the same, it was not good news. And it would not be greeted as good news by his SAC. This would be the second citizen in less than a year who was threatening Adam with legal action.

"I think there's room for negotiation," Frankie said.

Mid-sip, Rob paused. "What exactly does that mean?"

"It means I think there's room for negotiation."

Rob opened his mouth and Frankie said, "He says he's got information for us on our killer."

There was a short, sharp silence. "Let me get this straight," Rob said. "You're suggesting we make *a deal* with him?"

Frankie rolled her eyes. "Now don't go getting all bent out of shape until you hear what I have to say."

"I'm listening."

Frankie looked at Adam. "This concerns you too."

Adam hadn't planned on going anywhere. He said mildly, "All right. Go on."

"He says he didn't shoot first."

"Bullshit," said Rob.

Frankie looked at Adam. "I think it's bullshit too. But...we weren't there," Adam admitted.

Rob looked outraged. But it was the truth. Adam and Rob had not been with Zeke's party. They could not say for certain who had fired first.

"He says someone tried to kill him. And he says it's not the first time."

"Horseshit," Rob said. Evidently bullshit couldn't cover this degree of lying. "What does Zeke say?"

"Zeke went down to Portland to break the news about Azure to her family. I'll talk to him about it when he gets back. Here's the thing of it. I don't think Gibbs is lying."

"What?" Rob quit leaning on the door frame and drew himself straight.

"I don't mean about yesterday. I don't know about yesterday," Frankie said. "I do know genuine fear when I see it in a man's eyes, and I believe that someone has tried to kill Gibbs in the past. Maybe not yesterday, but I think part of why he reacted the way he did was because of these past attempts."

Adam said, "Sheriff, Gibbs has an arsenal of illegal weapons in that cabin of his. He opened fire on law enforcement, federal agents, and innocent civilians. He threatened to shoot Rob, and I have no doubt he'd have done his damnedest to shoot me or anyone else in his way as well."

"But he *didn't* shoot anyone. For all that gunfire, nobody got shot. The only injury was a sprained ankle, and Bobby Kane knocking herself cold when she ran into a tree trunk."

"He's a lousy shot," Rob protested. "How is that a legal defense?"

"Haskell, will you sit down and open your ears? The fact of the matter is that Zeke's search team *was* trespassing on Gibbs's property. Nobody talked to Gibbs, nobody warned him of what was going on. It's not like he's keeping up with current events." Frankie headed off Rob's objection before he could voice it. "I *know*. He doesn't have a phone. That doesn't negate his property rights. Gibbs's story is he saw an armed man climbing up the hillside, and that the man fired on him. Now whether anyone fired on him, I don't know. His story is he was just trying to scare off his would-be attacker."

"That's the dumbest story I've ever heard!"

Frankie eyed him with grim sympathy. "I'm not denying I think Gibbs is a few saltines short of a cracker box. But I think he's telling the truth as he knows it. He believes someone is out to get him. Has been trying to get him for years. And he mistook yesterday's search efforts for a full frontal assault."

"Years!"

Adam said, "Why would someone be out to get Gibbs?"

There was a funny gleam in Frankie's eyes. "He says he saw our murderer. And that the murderer knows he saw him."

"I'm confused," Adam said, and that was an understatement. "How could this murderer have been after Gibbs for years when Cynthia Joseph was only killed four nights ago?"

"That's just it," Frankie said. "Gibbs isn't talking about whoever killed Cynthia. He's talking about our other murder."

Rob raised his head. "What other murder? Is he talking about the dead hiker? Or Dove Koletar?"

"No. Well, maybe. I've wondered about that one from the first. But no, Gibbs is talking about Jordan Gaura."

Chapter Eleven

"**H**m." That was all Adam said. Which was sort of annoying—as was his thoughtful tone of voice. As though none of this was coming as any great surprise.

Rob said, "Just how the hell many murderers are supposed to be living locally?"

Adam said, "The Pacific Northwest does produce more than its share of serial killers. I guess it's too soon to have the ME's report on Gaura?"

"You guess right. They haven't even finished excavating him," Frankie said. "I figure it wouldn't hurt to speak to him though. Right? Gibbs, that is."

"What's the deal?" Rob asked.

Frankie looked blank.

"The deal you want to strike with Gibbs? We drop all charges in exchange for the name of Gaura's murderer?"

"I haven't promised anyone any deal," Frankie said. "But you should consider the fact that it's a way to get your—Agent Darling and yourself off the hook. And maybe we'll get some information we need."

Adam met Rob's eyes. "I wouldn't mind hearing what he has to say."

"I don't mind hearing what he has to say," Rob said. "But I'm not in favor of cutting any deals. In my opinion Gibbs is crazy and he needs to be locked up. He's a danger to society and to himself."

"I'm not so sure a good defense attorney couldn't knock that argument on its ass," Frankie said. "But it's your head on the chopping block. Why don't you talk to Gibbs and then see how you feel?"

* * * * *

A skimpy breakfast and a night on the lumpy mattress in their holding cell had put Gibbs in a talkative frame of mind. Cooperative or not, he was not an attractive specimen, but then Rob was predisposed not to like anyone who had pointed a rifle in his face.

Gibbs was a wiry five eleven with balding, sandy hair, and eyes of a reddish-brown color that reminded Rob of a white rat. The rat resemblance was bolstered by Gibbs's nervous habit of twitching his nose.

"I didn't actually see his face," Gibbs hedged. "But it was Bert Berkle. I'm sure of it."

"Bert Berkle?" Rob repeated in disbelief.

Gibbs raised his chin defiantly. "That's right. His southwest property line runs along mine. He used to hunt over that way."

"Yeah, I know," Rob said. "And I also know you two have been feuding over that property line for the last twenty years."

Adam asked, "If you didn't see Berkle's face, how are you so sure it was him?"

"He was a big man, Berkle's size. He was a hunter. And when he spotted me, he took off back across Berkle's property."

"How the hell does that prove anything?" Rob asked. "Berkle is not the only big man in this county, or the only hunter, or the only hunter wandering around in those woods."

"Tell us what you remember about Jordan Gaura's murder, Mr. Gibbs," Adam said.

"Oh, now it's *Mister* Gibbs," Gibbs retorted nastily. "Don't think I'm not going to remember *you, Mister* G-man."

"We're wasting our time," Rob said to Adam. "He's full of shit."

"I'm not!" Gibbs said. "I'm telling you what I saw. You just don't want to believe it, that's all."

Ever patient and persistent, Adam said, "What exactly did you see?"

"Well, I didn't see everything," admitted Gibbs.

"You're kidding," Rob said sarcastically. Adam shot him an impatient look.

"Go on," Adam said. "Start at the beginning. Do you remember the date? What time of day was it?"

"It was night. I remember that. I don't remember the day. It was before the kid disappeared obviously."

Rob sighed.

Gibbs said, "How the hell should I remember what day it was? It was twenty years ago."

"It wasn't twenty years ago. It was seventeen years ago," Rob said. "And if you don't come up with some compelling information pretty fast, I'm walking out that door."

Adam gave him a long, level look.

And Rob gave him a long, level look right back because this was a complete waste of their time whether Adam realized it or not.

"I heard them before I saw anything," Gibbs said. "I didn't *want* to see because from the sounds, I was afraid it was a pair of faggots doing their thing. But then the big man got up. His back was to me and it was dark in the trees, but there was moonlight shining through and I could see that he was holding a big knife."

Gibbs held his hands apart.

"Can you describe the knife?" Adam asked.

"Bloody. I could see the blade was black with blood. The blood dripped right off it. I won't forget that."

"What *type* of knife?" Rob asked with what he felt was great restraint.

"One of those KA-BAR knives, I think. He was breathing real heavy. I was afraid to move. I thought my heart was going to explode. He bent down and wiped the knife in the grass, and then he shoved it in his belt."

"You could see he was wearing a belt, but you never saw his face?"

"I didn't see his belt. I just knew that's what he was doing. What else would he be doing? For a while he was just kneeling there breathing real hard, like I said, and then he got up and pushed and dragged the body until he could throw it into the gully. And then he threw the kid's backpack in too. Maybe there was a sleeping bag or something. I don't remember now."

"Go on," Adam said.

"He was still standing there looking down into the gully, and I thought it would be a good idea to bug out. So I started backing up real quiet and real slow. But he must of heard something because he spun around and he was looking right at me. And I was looking right at him."

"But you couldn't see his face?"

"He was standing in the shadows. But I know he saw me. And he knew I saw him because he turned and ran."

Rob said, "But you didn't see him. Not really."

"I saw enough."

"Why didn't you come forward?" Adam asked. "Why didn't you report what you saw?"

Gibbs laughed unpleasantly. "You think anybody would have believed me? Hell no. They'd have said *I* killed him and that I was trying to cover it up."

"Sounds like a workable theory to me," Rob said.

"See!" Gibbs pointed at Rob. "That's what I mean."

"But if you believed this man recognized you, you must have realized your life was in danger?"

"Not that much danger," Rob said. "Because he's still here seventeen years later."

"He's tried to kill me," Gibbs said. "But he has to make it look like an accident. And I'm smart. And I'm careful."

"Yeah, you're a genius," Rob said.

"Deputy Haskell," Adam said.

"Agent Darling," Rob retorted. "Explain to me why this giant knife-wielding killer didn't slaughter Mr. Gibbs on the spot? He was armed and he sure as hell had motive. But he turns and runs. Why?"

"He didn't know if I was armed or not. I *was* armed and I was fumbling for my rifle."

Rob turned to Adam. Adam said, "Is there anything else you'd like to add, Mr. Gibbs?"

"I want to make a deal. I won't sue you and Deputy Hassle over there if you drop all the charges against me."

Rob laughed. "Fat chance."

"Unfortunately, it's not that simple," Adam said. "Firstly, multiple agencies were involved in yesterday's shooting, and the kind of deal you're asking for would require every single one of them to sign off. That's unlikely to happen. In fact, I can assure you right now, it won't happen. Secondly, regardless of your motives, you opened fire on civilians and law enforcement alike which gave Deputy Haskell and me reasonable grounds for searching your property—whereupon we discovered a number of illegal weapons, including a grenade launcher."

"I made that myself!"

"And thirdly," Rob interrupted, "your story is total bullshit."

"The hell it is! I'm telling you exactly the way it was. Bert Berkle killed that hiker, and he killed the Indian woman, and he killed that green-haired bitch, and he's been *trying* to kill me. And I'll tell you something else. A man has a right to protect his property. And people around here understand that. And they also don't like the federal government butting in where it isn't wanted. So think about *that* before you try taking me to court, Haskell."

* * * * *

"That was a waste of time," Rob said. They had returned Gibbs—loudly protesting the violation to his civil rights—to his cell, and were reporting back to Frankie. Or would have reported, had Frankie not been on the phone to Doc Cooper.

"I'm not so sure," Adam said. "I believed his story. Well, not all of it. The part about where he came across his neighbor throwing Gaura's body in the ravine—that sounded genuine."

"That's because you don't know Berkle. Or the history between those two."

"I understand that there's a dispute over property lines."

"Dispute is not the word. Feud is the word. Blood feud would be more accurate."

"Which doesn't change the fact—"

"No, it doesn't change the fact, because there are *no* facts. There's an accusation from someone in deep legal shit who has a score to settle. I'll tell you another thing. That whole bit about thinking he'd stumbled upon faggots doing their thing in the woods. That was aimed at me. And maybe at you too. It sure as hell wouldn't be aimed at Berkle."

Adam frowned. "Gibbs's hostility is irrelevant."

"I don't see how you can say it's irrelevant. It's the driving force in his life. But okay. I know we've got to talk to Berkle. So let's go get his side of the story."

"Don't go anywhere just yet," Frankie called.

Rob stepped into her office. "News?"

"We've got the autopsy report on Azure."

Rob was glad Zeke was not in the office for this. "And?"

"She wasn't sexually assaulted. Doc believes it's the same assailant. Left-handed, using a—"

"Left-handed?" Rob interrupted. "Cynthia's killer was left-handed? You didn't mention that before."

"Didn't I?" Frankie asked innocently. "Well, maybe I thought it might be a good idea to keep certain facts quiet."

"From your own investigators?" Frankie had her own way of doing things, but this seemed eccentric.

"One of my investigators is left-handed," Frankie observed.

It took Rob a disbelieving moment to find his tongue. "*Zeke*? You think Zeke—" He looked at Adam, and was shocked to see an expression of something like approval on his face.

"Shhh!" Frankie said sharply. "No need to blast it into the atmosphere. The thing is, Doc says Azure put up a real fight. He retrieved what he called a 'significant amount' of DNA evidence from beneath her fingernails."

Adam said, "It's going to take time to get the lab results."

"We may not need lab results," Frankie said. "Doc is pretty sure that whoever killed Azure is going to be wearing an ugly set of scratches for a few days. So I think maybe we're going to hold a local beauty contest and invite the gentlemen of Nearby to take part."

"And what if a gentleman doesn't want to take part?" Rob asked.

Frankie's smile was cold. "I would find that very suspicious, wouldn't you?"

"Have you seen my partner?" Adam asked as they were leaving the office to drive to Berkle's place.

"Don't tell me you lost this one too," Rob said.

"Agent Russell drove down to Medford," Aggie volunteered.

Adam checked his cell. "He didn't leave me a message. Did he say why?"

"Nope." The phone rang Aggie bitterly cursed all reporters everywhere, and reached for it.

"Maybe he flew back to L.A.," Rob said as they walked outside into the bright sunlight. Most of the remaining snow had melted. There were deep puddles everywhere, reflecting startlingly blue sky and fleecy clouds. The morning felt clean and freshly washed. Which was kind of surprising given the grim start to the day.

The night had been nice though. He couldn't help glancing at Adam and smiling.

Adam said, "As much as Russell doesn't like this assignment, he wouldn't leave without informing me. And if he'd been recalled, I'd have been recalled too."

"Did you check your phone messages?" Rob hated the idea that Adam might get recalled. But whether he was recalled or not, sooner or later Adam would be leaving Nearby.

Suddenly the sun didn't seem half as bright as it had a few seconds before.

"Yes. I just checked my messages, and I checked my email this morning. There's nothing from anyone, including Russell."

"Then don't worry. He'll be back."

Adam nodded, though clearly unsatisfied.

They climbed into Rob's SUV, and Rob started the engine. "The Constantine place is on the way to Berkle's. We can stop there on the way back, if you'd like to talk to Bill."

"Doesn't he have a job?"

"Part time. It's more of a hobby, I'd say. Even if Buck hadn't made a fortune in real estate, he married money."

"It usually seems to work that way. I've been thinking about the Watterson boy. Is there any possibility his death wasn't an accident?"

He really had a way of dropping those nasty little bombshells. Adam had one dark imagination, that was for sure. Rob said, "I don't think so. There was never any suggestion that it wasn't an accident."

"How did it happen?"

"There's a giant boulder at Blue Rock Cove. Kids dive off it into the lake. It doesn't matter how many times you post warnings, kids always believe they're invincible. Anyway, Terry jumped off the blue rock, hit his head, and drowned."

"Was he alone when the accident happened?"

"No. There were witnesses. A bunch of kids saw it happen. Well, I shouldn't say 'kids,' because these idiots were all college age, and they were all drinking. And before you ask, both

Billy Constantine and Zeke were among them. Zeke grew up in Nearby. He and Terry were best friends."

He waited for Adam to ask the next question—there was always going to be a next question with Adam—all Adam said was, "It should be a lot quieter around here now that Tiffany's been found and the search and rescue teams have gone home."

"Yep," Rob said. "Now we just have to get rid of these pesky serial killers, and life can get back to normal."

To his surprise, Adam threw him that rare, pointed grin and said, "But it seems to me that maybe serial killers *are* normal for Nearby."

"Oh, *sa-nap*," Rob said, and Adam chuckled.

* * * * *

Bert Berkle bred and trained the best tracking dogs in the county. In fact, some people said he raised the best dogs in the state. Rob liked dogs—they'd always had beagles at home when he was growing up—but he wouldn't have paid twenty-four grand for any dog. Berkle seemed to make a decent living though, so apparently there were enough people willing to dish out big bucks for a pooch.

"You're not afraid of dogs by any chance?" Rob asked as they parked in front of the large single-story cedar cabin. The cabin was nice enough. The real property value lay in that breath-taking lakefront view and the private dock. "Allergic to them?"

Adam raised his brows. "Me? No, I like dogs."

"Good."

A crisp breeze blew across the lake and turned the blue water choppy with white caps as they left the SUV. They started up the wooden walk and the dogs in the kennels behind the house began barking. It sounded like a hunting pack in full cry.

"Imagine listening to that at night," Adam observed.

"Yeah. Luckily the closest neighbor is over there." Rob pointed toward the mountain where they had been searching only the day before. A helicopter was slowly circling the approximate area of Sandy Gibbs's "compound," as the press was dubbing it.

"They're not exactly tripping over each other."

"No, but you know the old this-town-isn't-big-enough-for-both-of-us routine? Well, the county isn't big enough for those two."

They stepped onto the porch, and Rob knocked on the rough hewn cedar door.

There was no answer.

"His truck is parked under the carport. He's probably in the back," Rob said. "Unless he's on the lake." He led the way back down the steps and around the side of the cabin to the kennels in the rear.

He'd been here a couple of times—usually to ask for Berkle's help when some camper or hiker got himself good and lost. Everything looked the same. Rows of tall immaculate dog pens, several long enclosed runs, a big metal barn, a dog trailer, and black semi truck cab adorned with a naked lady on the door.

"Those aren't German Shepherds," Adam observed as they neared the pen with the short-haired fawn-colored dogs.

"Belgian Malinois," Rob said. "They look a lot like Shepherds."

"They're more alert and smarter than GSDs," Berkle said, exiting one of the pens. He locked the gate behind him. "Better looking dog too."

He was a mountain of a man. Big shoulders, big arms, big black beard, big blue eyes. He looked intimidating, though Rob couldn't think of an instance where Berkle had ever tried to bully or use force. He kept to himself mostly, though he was a regular at the Lakehouse Restaurant bar during the summer months. But then pretty much everyone was a regular, given that it was the only real restaurant in almost forty miles.

"Bert, this is Agent Darling of the FBI. He's helping us investigate Cynthia Joseph's murder."

Berkle nodded curtly to Adam. To Rob he said, "I heard you found the Joseph girl. Is she going to be okay?"

"We hope so," Rob said, and Berkle's stern expression seemed to lighten.

"And you finally got Sandy Gibbs in custody?"

"Well, that's what we wanted to talk to you about," Rob said. "We've been questioning Gibbs, and he's come up with a story that we feel we've got to investigate."

"Okay," Berkle said warily. He looked from Rob to Adam.

Adam said, "Can you clarify the situation between yourself and Mr. Gibbs, sir?"

Berkle's black brows drew together. "The *situation*?" he repeated to Rob.

"Gibbs has made some pretty serious allegations," Rob said.

"About what?"

"About an incident several years back," Adam said.

Berkle ignored him, waiting for Rob to speak. Rob said, "Gibbs is claiming that you killed that hiker who disappeared back in '98."

Berkle's jaw dropped. "He said *what*? And I would do that why?"

"Why do you suppose he'd make such an allegation, sir?" Adam inquired.

Probably a liability in social situations, Adam. Then again, he was a guy who used the word "firstly" with a straight face, so Rob was going to cut him all the slack he needed. He was looking severe and serious as he waited for Berkle to respond.

"I'll tell you why he'd make up such an allegation," Berkle told Rob. "He wants my land. He's been after my land for the last twenty years. So he made up this cock-and-bull story about something he probably did himself."

Adam said, "He claims you tried to kill him yesterday."

Berkle looked at Rob and gestured toward Adam in a kind of futile *are you kidding me?* gesture.

"If you could just answer the question, Mr. Berkle," Rob said.

"What question? He's not asking me any questions. He's *accusing* me of murder."

"I'm not accusing you of anything, sir," Adam said. "It's our job to follow up on these allegations."

Rob made a mental note to check for the battery compartment when he got Adam home that night, because if ever a guy sounded like a robot…

"I didn't kill that hiker," Berkle said. "I haven't killed anyone."

Adam looked unimpressed. "What do you do for a living, sir?"

"As you can see, I raise dogs."

Adam indicated the black semi truck cab parked beside the barn. "Do you also drive a big rig?"

"No." Berkle reluctantly qualified, "I used to."

"What route did you use to drive?"

"I drove all over the country."

Adam nodded noncommittally. "And you've lived in the area…how long?"

"My entire life. Sure as hell longer than Sandy Gibbs. I bought this property in '95." Berkle said to Rob, "You know where I was yesterday. I was with the search team to the south, looking for the Joseph girl. My dogs found her cell phone. *My dogs.*"

"I know," Rob said, and despite his best effort, he knew he sounded apologetic.

Knew because Adam gave him a cool, critical look before saying, "Do you mind if we have a look around the premises, sir?"

"Yes, I mind! What the fuck do you think you're looking for?"

Good question. Tiffany had been found. Did Adam think they were going to discover a bloody knife beneath one of the doggie beds? Anyway, Rob was all but positive that the figure he'd seen the night before was not Berkle. Even though the man with wings had been standing on a ridge looking down at them, he had not appeared as big and burly as Berkle did right now.

Despite the fact that he believed Adam was way off track—and that he, Rob, was going to have to live with these people long after Adam returned to the big city—he felt compelled to ask, "Would you mind telling us where you were Saturday morning about three o'clock?"

"Here. In bed!"

"And Thursday night?"

"In bed. At home."

"Can anyone verify that?"

Berkle's glare faded. He suddenly laughed. "Yeah. Sure. Ask the dogs. They'll vouch for me. No, better yet, talk to my lawyer, asshole!"

He shoved through them, striding toward the house.

Rob looked at Adam, who was absently massaging his shoulder and staring after Berkle.

"That sure could have gone better," Rob couldn't help saying.

"It went all right."

"All *right*?"

Adam threw him a quick, surprised look. "Yes."

"Come on, Adam. You know as well as I do Berkle was not who we saw on that hillside last night. Can you imagine him dressing up like a giant bird?"

"No."

"No. We just pissed off the best tracker in the county. And for what? That was a complete waste of time."

"No, it wasn't."

Rob stared at him. "How did you figure that?"

Adam met his gaze, green eyes shining with conviction. "He's our guy, Rob."

CHAPTER TWELVE

Rob preserved a formidable silence all the way back to the SUV.

But once they were inside the vehicle and out of listening range, he said—clearly exercising self-control, "You want to explain to me why you think Berkle, who has been nothing but helpful to the investigation, is *our guy*, but Gibbs, who tried to kill us and everyone else on that mountain yesterday, is somehow a credible witness against him?"

"He's lying. Everything out of his mouth was a lie."

"Even if that were true, and I'm not sure how you think you could know that based on all of five minutes conversation, you already agreed it wasn't Berkle last night. And if there's some nut running around dressed like a raven who *isn't* involved in these murders—"

"I'm not talking about Cynthia Joseph's or Azure's slayings. I'm talking about the Gaura killing."

"The Gaura killing is a cold case."

"Yes. Two—three—different killings. Two different cases," Adam said. "In fact, I think the Koletar killing may be linked to Gaura's murder."

Rob stared at him. "You think we're dealing with *two* serial killers."

"Yes."

"Adam, you're probably my favorite person in the world, so don't take this the wrong way. You're *crazy*."

What was crazy was that he even registered the *favorite person in the world* comment. Adam said patiently, "You suggested the same thing yourself not that long ago."

"I was kidding!"

"No, you weren't."

Rob scowled at him. "Okay, according to Gibbs, who you seem to think is such a reliable witness, Berkle is responsible for all the killings."

"Gibbs is an idiot," Adam said succinctly. "I don't think he's a reliable witness. I do believe he gave us a reasonably accurate accounting of his own personal experience in the woods that night."

"Seventeen years ago!"

"Nobody would forget an experience like that."

Rob shook his head. "*Two* serial killers?"

"Technically there have to be more than two murders to qualify for serial killing," Adam said. "But I think the Raven is just getting started. Berkle…he's been out there for a while, and your woods—or the lake—may hide more bodies than you think."

Rob grimaced. "Don't call him 'the Raven,'" he said. "Don't give him a goddamned name. Imagine if some reporter got hold of that!"

"Sorry."

They were silent, listening to the dogs still barking in the kennels behind the house.

"This isn't just a hunch," Adam said. "It's a matter of logistics. Look at this place. There's no one for miles around. He could do anything to anyone, and no one would see or hear.

Plus, Berkle has a job that allows him to prowl remote areas of the countryside, unquestioned. And if they do question? He's training tracking dogs." He tried to suppress the small shudder the next thought gave him. "*Hunting* dogs."

"You can't think—"

"I don't know, Rob. I know that he's got a large enclosed trailer to haul those dogs around. He can drive country roads pulling that thing behind him, and again, no one would ask questions. And before that, he was a trucker. The entire nation could have been his hunting ground. Why not say what his route was?"

"He did!"

"*All over the country* is not a real answer. He didn't want to say. Why?"

Rob frowned, staring out the window, fingers drumming restlessly on the steering wheel. "Berkle doesn't like you. That could be a lot of what you picked up."

"I know he doesn't like me," Adam replied. He remembered Berkle from the first night he'd arrived in Nearby, back in October. He'd walked into the Lakehouse Restaurant, looked straight at Berkle, and Berkle had looked right back at him and turned his back. As though he knew exactly who and what Adam was. "Nobody likes the FBI. There's more to it than that."

"He's the right age for the Koletar killing, I guess. But then so is half the population of Nearby. What the hell would his motive be?"

"Psychological gratification of some kind. Whatever it is, it's not going to make sense to us. Maybe he robs his victims. Maybe he's a lust killer—"

"Gaura and Koletar were male."

"And men never feel lust for other men?"

Rob's look of outrage would have been amusing in other circumstances. "Bert Berkle is not gay!"

"Is there a Mrs. Berkle?"

"No. There isn't anyone, male or female, in Berkle's life. I told you, he's a loner."

"That inability to form attachments is a classic indicator. Rob, I can't tell you why someone like Berkle turns to murder. Childhood abuse? Maybe he's got an extra chromosome. Maybe he's got a screw loose. Who knows? We're probably never going to find what triggered him either, although there had to be a trigger of some kind."

Rob gave another of those exasperated exhales.

"We caught him off guard," Adam said. "He never expected to fall under suspicion, let alone to be questioned. That won't happen again. And, by the way, that's another indicator—how fast he threatened to lawyer up."

"He wasn't afraid. He was angry."

"He was offended." Adam's smile was caustic. "We pricked his ego. All this time he's been thinking he was so clever, so smart, fooling everyone. And then we came along, and he realizes he's not as smart as he thought."

Rob muttered, "I'll tell you one thing. We've been sitting here talking in his front yard long enough." He started the SUV's engine, and they pulled around and headed slowly back down the road.

"We need to learn everything we can about Berkle," Adam said. "Including his old truck-driving route."

Rob shook his head, but he didn't argue.

* * * * *

Constantine House looked as though someone had picked up an antebellum mansion and plopped it down in the middle of the forest. A large, stately white structure with tall columns, sweeping verandas, and enormous windows, the house nonetheless looked odd, almost grotesque in its setting of pine trees and snowy mountains.

But then what could you expect from a guy who wore fringed buckskin in public?

"That's a lot of house," Adam commented, zipping up his jacket against the cold wind blowing down from the mountains.

"Yeah, it is," Rob said. "Buck built it for Mary. She only got to live there for a couple of years." He grimaced. "Cancer. It was pretty hard on the boys."

"Buck too, I imagine?"

"Sure. Of course." Rob eyed Adam consideringly. "Do me a favor and try to be more tactful with the Constantines than you were with Berkle, okay? I like my job. I want to keep it."

Adam said evenly, "It's a murder investigation, Rob. Getting at the truth isn't always tactful."

Maybe it was the chilly breeze that brought pink to Rob's cheeks. Maybe it was something else. He said, "That's true. However, this is still my—our—investigation. You're here in a support capacity, remember? So I'll decide when and if we're untactful."

That was pointed enough. Adam nodded. Rob nodded back. They went up the wide white steps in silence. Rob rang the doorbell.

After a moment or two, the double doors swung soundlessly open. Adam was expecting a liveried butler, or at the least, a housekeeper. But Buck Constantine stood before them, clad in a blue smoking jacket and leather slippers. He was not smoking. He did carry what looked like a martini glass. And that seemed incongruous with both the mountainous and antebellum backdrops.

"Rob." Buck's surprise was evident. He glanced at Adam. "And…sorry, I forget your name."

"This is Agent Darling," Rob said. "May we come in, Buck?"

"Of course." Buck stepped aside, gesturing for them to enter. "We heard the Joseph girl was found. How's she doing? Has she been questioned?"

"She's undergoing medical treatment right now," Rob said. "We hope to question her shortly."

"I can only imagine what that poor kid has been through. We can talk in the library." Buck led the way through a ridiculously grand hall—marble floors, a high ceiling with decorative panels and cove molding, and three life-sized family portraits—to a formal study. Or, according to Buck, his *library*, although there weren't any books as far as Adam could tell.

The study was furnished in dark wood and green velvet. Somber paintings of Native Americans adorned the walls, though Adam thought most of the paintings featured Plains Indians and Eastern Woodland tribes, and not the indigenous peoples of Southern Oregon.

"Can I get you two something to drink? Coffee? Tea? Something stronger?" He held up his martini glass. "I don't usually start drinking this early, but it's been a stressful week for all of us."

"No thanks," Rob said. "Is Bill home?"

Buck raised his silver brows. "Billy? No. Why?"

"We have a couple of routine questions to ask, that's all."

Adam said, "Mr. Constantine, were you aware of the relationship between your son and Tiffany Joseph?"

Though he felt the irritation in Rob's gaze, Adam's focus was on Buck as he tried to interpret those myriad, fleeting micro expressions. Not surprise. Not fear. Not anger... Something. Disgust? Contempt? A strong and definite emotion, which was instantly suppressed.

"No. I didn't. Because there isn't one."

Rob removed his glare from Adam's profile and turned his attention to Buck. "Are you sure about that? We have reason to believe—"

"Absolutely not," Buck said. "There was no relationship there. She's a kid. Billy is a-a man."

"A young man. And she's a pretty girl. He used to tutor her in biology," Rob pointed out.

"He's tutored half the teenagers in Nearby. That doesn't mean there was ever anything inappropriate going on."

Buck's tone was casual, even humorous, as though the idea were totally ridiculous. Surely the first and most likely problem Cynthia Joseph would have with any romantic connection between her daughter and Bill would be that he was too old.

Would a seventeen-year-old girl agree? Adam thought of Bridget. Not all victims were unwilling.

"No, of course not," Rob was saying.

"Billy is a genius when it comes to science. I don't know where he gets it from. Not from me, not from his mother. Dan never showed any interest in science."

"I know," Rob said. "I remember when he won that scholarship to Oregon Health and Science."

"Exactly. He enjoys that kind of thing. Tutoring. He would have made a good teacher."

"Does Bill have a girlfriend?" Adam asked.

At the same time Rob suggested, "But maybe Tiffany had a crush on Bill?"

"No," Buck said, and Adam wasn't sure if he was answering Rob or himself.

Back off was the message in Rob's hard brown gaze. Was he overstepping? Yes, probably. This was the difficult mix of personal and professional. As easy-going and laid-back as Rob was off the clock, he was still a cop, and a good one, and he didn't need or want Adam trying to do his job for him.

Adam offered an apologetic look and swallowed his next question. Rob said, "When are you expecting Bill home?"

"He doesn't work regular hours. He goes in when they need him."

"Right. Will you let him know we'd like to speak to him when he's got a moment?"

Buck nodded. He looked unhappy and wary.

"We'll see ourselves out," Rob said.

Rob slammed the SUV door hard and said, "What part of *this is my investigation* do you not get, Darling?"

"I agree. I was overzealous," Adam said.

"That's big of you." Rob jammed the key in the ignition. The engine roared into irritable life.

Rob did seem uncharacteristically pissed off. Even so, Adam couldn't help asking, "What's the big secret regarding Bill Constantine?"

Rob's frowned deepened. "What are you talking about?"

"It's obvious there's something going on, some piece of information that you're all aware of but no one discusses openly.

A scholarship he apparently didn't utilize, an expected career path he didn't follow, a part-time job nobody wants to talk about."

Rob stared. "*Jesus*. I'm starting to think you're a fucking *robot*."

The depth of his anger bewildered Adam, flustered him a little. He couldn't see the reason for it.

Rob said, "This is the difference between the way government polices, and the way real people police each other. I *live* here. I care about these people. They're my neighbors and my friends. Unlike you, I don't get to pack up and leave when it's all over. I have to stay here. Live with their pain and their loss and their grief. And I don't want to add to that, if I don't have to. Can you understand that?"

"Of course I understand that."

"We don't have to trample everyone under our hobnail boots."

"Hobnail…"

"We don't have to march in like it's martial law and treat everyone like a suspect."

Adam opened his mouth and Rob cut in, "And even if everyone *is* a suspect, one thing I do know, even if I'm not in the FBI, is that you catch more flies with honey than vinegar."

Stung, Adam said, "That's great if you're trying to catch flies. We're trying to catch a killer."

"Funny." Rob's eyes were cold. "I'll tell you what the big secret is about Bill Constantine. After his mom died, he had a breakdown. Or whatever the proper medical term is for it. He dropped out of college, lost his scholarship, and was hospitalized for a while. And now he's working a shit menial job because the alternative is sitting home all day watching his old man get potted. Okay? I know you were hoping for something a lot deeper and darker. The kid has problems, and most people are sorry for him. Most people get the fact that we all have our weaknesses, our vulnerabilities." Rob was glaring as he finished, "We can't all be high powered hot shot special agents for the government!"

Adam didn't have an answer. Not true. He did have an answer. He was the last person to judge someone like Bill. He hadn't had a breakdown after the Conway case, but it had been close, and for a time he'd been popping Xanax like breath mints, and seeing the departmental counselor on a regular basis. So yes, he understood all about weakness and vulnerability.

But he couldn't explain that to Rob, not when Rob was looking at him with that mix of dislike and disgust. Besides, this was clearly not just about Bill Constantine, and since he couldn't tell Rob what he wanted to hear…maybe it was preferable to be thought a cold-hearted robot than someone terrified to take a chance on being wrong. On getting hurt.

Adam grimaced. "I apologize. I know I overstepped."

"You did. Yeah. And the next interview I conduct will be without you."

That hurt even more than the rest of it, and Adam didn't have a response.

Rob must have felt that he'd won that round because without another word he threw the SUV into gear and they started back to town.

Adam had grown used to Rob's usual chatty friendliness, and the silence made the drive feel twice as long. He almost apologized again. But it wasn't really an apology Rob was looking for. Or maybe it was. Rob had made a point of how he never lacked for company, of how much he enjoyed playing the field. Maybe he was just looking for Adam to grovel. In which case, he could keep looking. Point taken. Move on.

They were still not speaking when they reached the sheriff's office. Adam spotted his rental car parked in front, so Russell had returned from his mysterious trip to Medford. Great.

As they walked through the front doors, Aggie glanced up and said quietly, "Trouble." She seemed to be speaking to Adam.

"It's about time you two wandered home," Frankie called. "Come and say hello. We've got company."

Through the doorway to Frankie's office, Adam could see part of Russell's face. He was smiling at someone on the other side of the room, and Adam's nerves wrenched still tighter.

What the hell was going on?

He mentally squared himself, strolled through the doorway, and found the small room crowded with blue and gold FBI jackets. Russell was seated in Rob's usual chair in front of Frankie's desk. A large, blond man, a stranger to Adam but instantly recognizable as the agent in charge, was taking up a good portion of wall real estate. And a woman—*Jonnie*—sat in the other chair facing Frankie.

Adam's instinctive pleasure at seeing Jonnie was doused by the realization that something was very wrong—confirmed by Jonnie's brief, troubled smile of greeting.

"Looky what I got," Frankie said in that same tone of forced joviality. "I ask the FBI for a little help and before I know it, I've got half the profilers at Quantico taking up all the chairs in my office." She pointed at Rob. "That's my second in command, Robert Haskell. And I guess you already know Special Agent Darling."

"No," the blond man said. "I don't know Agent Darling. I've heard of him though." And clearly it was all bad. His smile was somehow more alarming than other people's scowls.

Jonnie said, "Adam, this is Unit Chief Sam Kennedy." She didn't quite cough when she said *Unit Chief,* but the words did seem to stick in her throat.

And no wonder. Sam Kennedy was a legend. The kind of legend Special Agents in Charge told bad little subordinates who wouldn't eat their vegetables. The Bureau's very own Bogeyman.

He was also BAU, which was confusing. What was Jonnie doing with the BAU? What was Jonnie doing here at all?

Kennedy was dressed casually: a bulky sweater beneath the blue and gold FBI parka. It didn't matter. He was one of the few people in the world you could try and try to picture stark naked and it still wouldn't diffuse the threat.

"Sir," Adam said.

"Agent," Kennedy said. His blue eyes looked like ice chips. "I understand you're attempting to single-handedly run a serial killer investigation."

What the…?

Adam looked at Russell. Russell raised his eyebrows as though in polite inquiry.

"No. That's not the case." He could feel Rob's stare, and his face flamed as he wondered suddenly if it was the case. If it was the general opinion of the Nearby Sheriff's Office that he had overstepped the boundaries. It had certainly been Rob's opinion half an hour ago—and nobody was speaking up on his behalf now.

Kennedy said, "Sheriff McLellan, do you have a spare office where I can speak to Agent Darling in private?"

Frankie's eyes met Adam's. She looked sorry for him. "You can use our interrogation room. Third one off the main room."

Adam turned. He couldn't look at Rob. He left Frankie's office and walked down to the room where he and Rob had interrogated Gibbs that morning—was it only that morning?—listening to the measured tread of Kennedy's feet behind him.

He felt…well, mostly he just felt numb. Hollow. He couldn't believe this was happening. He knew with complete certainty that he was about to be fired, and while he could see that he had made a series of missteps—starting with his failure to realize that Russell was a serious enemy—he still couldn't quite grasp how he'd gotten into this position.

His mouth was dry, there was a block of ice in his belly, and he was desperately afraid that he might look like he was going to cry. He was not going to cry. He was not going to show anything if he could help it.

The door to the interrogation room closed. Kennedy said, "If you've got something to say for yourself, Agent, now would be the time."

Adam turned to face him. He forced himself to sound crisp and unemotional. "Agent Gould and I were here in October on morgue patrol for the Roadside Rip—"

"I already know all this from Gould." Kennedy cut in. "I want to know what the hell you think you're doing usurping the authority of a local sheriff's office and taking over their murder investigation?"

"I've done no such thing. We're here to assist Sheriff McLellan at her request."

"*You're* here," Kennedy said. "Your partner has been trying unsuccessfully to get you to involve the regional office so that the two of you can return to your own jobs and responsibilities. And you have steadily refused. True?"

Adam swallowed. "Not…completely."

Kennedy laughed. It was not a pleasant sound. "Out of curiosity, which part of it's not true?"

"We've only been here ninety-six hours. It's not as though—"

"And an action-packed ninety-six hours they've been. There've been several search and rescue efforts, a second murder, a shootout with a domestic terrorist, and now you've started interrogating suspects in homicide cold cases."

"Sir—"

"Since you enjoy local policing so much, Agent Darling, I suggest you apply for a position with the Nearby Sheriff's Office."

Boom. Done. Quick, clean severing of head from body. He barely even felt it.

He stared at Kennedy. Kennedy stared back, hard-faced and unrelenting. He seemed to be waiting for something.

Oh. Right. Adam's badge and gun. And probably his laptop too, come to think of it. He couldn't seem to make himself reach for his ID. He was afraid his hand might shake. But it wasn't just that. He had worked his entire life—the Bureau *was* his entire life—

Kennedy cocked an eyebrow. An ice cold bastard to the end. He spread his hands. "Nothing?" he asked. "That's it? That's the extent of what you have to say for yourself?"

Adam stared, noncomprehending. Wait. Was it *not* over?

He said, "I didn't volunteer to come up here. Sheriff McLellan asked for our help, and that's what I've been trying to provide. It's a small office, they have limited resources, and yes, I've done everything I've been asked to do. I thought that was why I was here."

"Really? Agent Russell believes you're here because you've formed a particular...friendship with Deputy Haskell. In fact, his words were *gone native*."

Russell had been paying closer attention than Adam realized.

He said, "I don't know what *gone native* means."

"I notice that you're not denying that you and Haskell have a relationship outside of your professional one."

As Adam stared into Kennedy's eyes he realized something totally unexpected. Unexpected, but possibly encouraging. Kennedy was gay. And he suspected that part of Russell's antipathy for Adam was due to Adam's orientation. It was the one sole point on which Adam had Kennedy's sympathy—but it was a big one.

"Haskell and I did not have a relationship before I came up here. And I don't know that our friendship will last beyond this assignment. That's not why I discouraged Russell from dumping this case and returning to L.A. I thought from the first that the case was more complicated than it appeared. I'm now convinced that's true."

Kennedy was back to looking bored and impatient. "Yeah, yeah. You think you've discovered a serial killer. Two murders, an attempted staging of the body, and everybody thinks they've got a serial killer on their hands."

Adam said politely, "Actually, sir, I think we may have two serial killers on our hands."

Kennedy's eyes narrowed. He studied Adam.

"All right," he said finally. "Let's hear it. Start to finish. And make it good."

Chapter Thirteen

"**Y**ou're a shit," Rob told Russell.

Russell turned red and started blustering. Frankie said in warning, "*Robbie.*"

Rob ignored her. "Get out of my chair," he said.

Russell complied, huffily, and Rob took his chair. He stretched his legs, leaned back, and eyed Agent Gould. "Back from your early retirement, I see?"

"Hey," said Gould. "I'm on Adam's side."

"Oh, that's nice!" Russell said.

Gould looked unimpressed. "Nobody likes a backstabber, J.J."

"So we're clear, I'm not taking sides," Frankie said to Russell, "but you haven't been a whole hell of a lotta help. They can send you home with my blessing."

Russell made a disbelieving sound, somewhere between a splutter and a *hmpf.* "Fine. I didn't realize I was sitting with Darling's fan club. I'll wait outside."

"Do," Rob said. "In fact, try the middle of the street."

Gould snorted. Frankie's look was disapproving. Rob didn't care either way. He was worried about Adam—when he had left the office, he'd looked like he'd received a death sentence—and he was sick at the thought that Adam might be on his way home this afternoon. It was too soon. Way too soon. They still needed his help. They needed *him*.

Rob needed him.

He sat there unmoving, angry, stricken, while Frankie and Gould talked. He had no idea about what.

Finally he tuned back in to hear Gould ask, "The girl is still sedated?"

"I spoke to the doctor right before you folks arrived. He said she may not be much help even when she is up and moving again. She might not remember anything."

"Post Traumatic Stress Disorder," Gould said knowledgably. "That's too bad. She's your best witness."

"Yeah. Poor kid."

"Does she have any other family?"

"There's an aunt on her father's side."

The door to the interrogation room was still closed. Rob glanced at his watch. Fifteen minutes and counting.

Frankie and Gould continued to converse. Rob continued to listen to the silence from the room where Adam was. Not completely silent. He could hear the murmur of voices. They weren't raised, so that was something.

"We'll start at nine o'clock tomorrow," Frankie said. "We've just about finished notifying all our residents. So far everyone has been very cooperative. At least on the phone. We'll see who shows up when the exam begins."

"If this was L.A., you'd be slapped with a civil rights suit before the first T-shirt dropped," Gould said.

"But it's not L.A." Frankie's smile was smug. "And anybody who refuses to play ball is going to have some explaining to do."

"You can't force people to take part in this," Rob warned her.

"No, I can't." Her smile faded at the approach of footsteps. "Zeke. How did it go?"

Zeke stopped in the doorway. He looked haggard, his eyes red as though he hadn't slept in days, his normally coiffed hair rumpled. He looked at Gould without interest or curiosity. Rob suspected he didn't really even see her.

"Like you'd think. I couldn't even tell them when we'll be able to release her body so they can bury her."

"I know," Frankie said sympathetically. "It's a terrible thing. Terrible."

Zeke said, "I'm going to take the rest of the day off, if that's okay, Frankie. I'm not going to be any use to anyone today. I'm beat. I haven't slept since..." He stopped.

"Sure, sure," Frankie said. "You go home and get some rest. We'll see you tomorrow morning. Let's say nine o'clock?"

"Yeah. Whatever." Zeke shoved away from the door frame as though he needed that extra momentum to keep him on his feet. He departed without speaking to Aggie, who called a sympathetic goodnight after him—despite the fact that it was only two-thirty in the afternoon.

"Now don't go glaring at me," Frankie told Rob.

"Nine o'clock?" Rob repeated. "So he won't know ahead of time you're planning to strip-search every man in town?"

"What kind of a sheriff would I be if I played favorites with my own department?"

"You want me to take my shirt off?" Rob asked. "I'll be happy to. Hell, no need to wait. I'll strip now."

Frankie was unabashed. "Wouldn't that be a nice treat for Agent Gould and me? But no, I know you haven't killed anybody,

Robbie. So far. Which means I guess I *do* play favorites sometimes." She winked.

Rob shook his head, and rose. He was too restless to sit there any longer waiting to hear what was going to happen to Adam. It wasn't like he wouldn't know soon enough.

He went to his office, sat down at his desk, and began sorting through his mail. Not that he usually got a lot of mail. What he did get had started to stack up over the past few days.

There were a couple of brochures for training courses, a gun catalog, an "anonymous" complaint about a barking dog from someone who'd forgotten he was being anonymous and used his own return address sticker, and a large brown envelope like those used for mailing legal documents. The wobbly address in the upper left-hand corner read M. Koletar.

Rob's spirits jumped, and he tore open the parcel. A couple of photos fell to the desktop. Nothing else. He shook the envelope, checked inside. There was no note.

He picked up the first photo. It was of a boy of about eighteen or nineteen. He was rail thin and wore one of those flat, moppet type haircuts. Sort of cute in a scruffy way. He seemed to be modeling the tattoo on his scrawny chest. To Rob's eye, the tattoo looked amateurish, homemade. It consisted of two figures. The figure on the right looked like a triangle at the end of a stick. Maybe it was supposed to be a flower? The figure on the left looked like a cross with triangles attached to the three upper bars. So maybe a religious symbol? Or a tree?

Or just the effort of someone who couldn't draw very well?

The boy—presumably Dove—smiled with a chipped and cheeky defiance at the camera. It was the face of someone life had kicked in the teeth more than once—but who still hoped this boot would be different.

Studying that boyish and misplaced confidence, Rob felt a pang of sadness. He picked up the second photo. Two boys, arms looped around each other's necks in casual, goofy camaraderie. One boy was Dove. The other…

Was he familiar?

Rob frowned and turned the photo over.

Dove and Buck. August 1983.

Rob whistled silently. *Buck?* Now that was a shocker. He'd never picked up any inkling that Buck Constantine was anything other than a hundred percent obnoxiously heterosexual.

And of course one hug didn't mean these two had been anything besides pals.

Except… Rob turned the photo back over studying Buck's face. There was something in their expressions. A brave and tentative happiness?

Rob frowned, holding the photograph toward the light. Thirty years was a long time and Buck looked nothing like the boy he'd once been. He still wore his hair about the same length. Back then it had been darker and thicker. The face in the photo was rounder, softer. The body was surprisingly stocky. Muscular.

Someone tapped on the door frame. Rob looked up to see Adam standing in his office.

"Hey." He dropped the photo, rose, and then wondered what he planned on doing. What he wanted to do was hug Adam, but Adam was…Adam. And they were not really on a hugging-in-the-workplace basis. Rob was unhappily conscious of that stupid argument on the way back from the Constantine place. What had he been so mad about? He'd even called Adam a robot.

Adam wasn't a robot, and he looked worryingly tired, drained. Flattened. Like someone or something had leeched all the life and energy out of him.

"Are you…?" Rob was afraid to finish the question.

Adam gave a crooked smile. "No. I'm still employed."

"Well, hell. Of course!" Rob said, as though they all hadn't been thinking Adam's head was on the chopping block.

"I think I may even have got a backhanded attaboy from Kennedy for putting the pieces together on Gaura."

"No pun intended?"

Why had he said that? Why did he always have to make a dumbass joke? And it was worse with Adam. He was always playing the fool around Adam.

Adam looked startled, and then gave a weak laugh. "Anyway, Russell and I are flying back to L.A. tomorrow morning. So I wanted to say goodbye."

"Goodbye?" Rob repeated, like he'd never heard the word before. Not like he hadn't known it was coming. But it still felt like a shock, the horrible surprise of reaching into the dark and touching a live wire.

And Adam didn't say anything. As though he didn't know what to make of it either.

"So that's it?" Rob said.

Adam drew a breath. "No. I also wanted to apologize again. I know I probably…did cross a couple of lines. I'm sorry if I seemed insensitive."

"You were fine," Rob said quickly. "I was just…I don't know. Feeling out of sorts."

Adam gave another of those halfhearted laughs. "Yeah, probably not. But BAU has offered their full help and resources to Frankie. Kennedy is a legend at the Bureau, the situation here has his interest, so you're going to get serious support now."

"Great." Happy happy joy joy. More feds. Only this time none of them would be Adam.

"So. Anyway." Adam stuck out his hand as though he'd suddenly remembered that was part of the fare-thee-well ritual.

They shook. Rob was startled to realize Adam's fingers were ice cold.

"Hey, wait a minute," Rob said, still gripping Adam's hand.

Adam waited, his expression almost wary.

"What about dinner?"

"What about it?"

"Are you stuck with them all night, or are you free for dinner?"

Adam freed his hand. "Dinner was not discussed," he said. "I think it's safe to assume we're not all squeezing into the Marina Grill."

"Good. Then have dinner with me. It's your last night here, let's spend it together."

Adam's expression lightened. Then his pleasure faded. "I'd have liked that, but I believe you're working tonight," he told Rob. "That's the way it sounded to me."

"I've got some things to finish up, yes," Rob said, "but Frankie is betting the house on tomorrow's show-and-tell session. If Kennedy thinks she's paying us overtime to sit around and brainstorm cold cases, he's in for a shock. Anyway, I'm whipped. My shift started at four thirty-five this morning. I'm having an early night." He added boldly, "With you."

Adam did that fluttery, disconcerting thing with his eyelashes before meeting Rob's gaze directly. His smile was rueful. "If you think you can swing it, then yes. I'd like to have dinner."

Rob smiled. "I can swing it. I'll pick you up at the campground and we can spend the night at my place. What time's your flight?"

Adam looked apologetic. "Eight."

Rob wouldn't have cared if it had been six. Or four. He felt cheerful again and full of optimism. "Don't worry, I'll have you back at the campground in plenty of time." He was tempted to lean forward and kiss Adam. That was probably pushing things. He could tell Adam was still partially attuned to the sound of Kennedy and Gould speaking down the hall in Frankie's office.

"I'll see you at five," Rob promised. "Don't be late."

"Er, you're picking *me* up. Remember?"

"True." Rob grinned. "It's a date, Darling."

At ten after four, Rob realized Bill Constantine had never shown up at the station or phoned. Knowing what he did now about Buck—or at least what he suspected he knew—he felt it all the more urgent that he talk to Bill.

For the last couple of hours he'd been reading over his notes on the case. Mostly he'd focused on Zeke's possible role, because he found Frankie's suspicions disturbing. But the more he looked over the homicide reports on Cynthia and Azure, the more positive he was that Frankie was off base.

Zeke was a jerk and probably what they used to call a chauvinistic pig, but Rob had never seen any indication that he was violent toward women. In fact, it was irritating the way his numerous ex-girlfriends continued to hang around in hopes of winning him back. The only girl who'd ever had the upper hand with him was Azure, and they'd been off and on for years. It was hard to believe that after all this time Zeke would suddenly go off the deep end and kill her.

There was certainly no motive for him to kill Cynthia Joseph, let alone in such a gruesome way. And the notion of a museum robbery gone wrong didn't fit because Zeke wasn't particularly hard up for money, and even if he had been, he'd have more likely sold one of his motorcycles, which was something he was always talking about doing.

Initially, Rob had been suspicious of the fact that Zeke had once worked at the museum. Until he'd realized that back then there would have been more tourists visiting Nearby, and Zeke would have viewed it as a good way to meet girls. Meeting girls would have always been—and continued to be—a priority for Zeke.

The one thing that niggled at Rob was the idea planted by Adam that maybe there had been more to Terry Watterson's death. But he'd hunted up the old accident report on Terry Watterson, and there was no mystery about it. Watterson had jumped off the rock, hit his head, and unfortunately no one had realized he was in trouble until it was too late.

It might even be the reason Zeke didn't drink. And considering how obnoxious he was cold sober, that was probably a good thing.

As for the idea of Zeke dressing up like a giant raven—or whatever the hell that costume was supposed to have been—no. *Hell no.* Zeke would consider that totally embarrassing. Never in a million years would Zeke dress up like Big Bird's evil twin— and as creepy as that moment had been when Rob had looked up and seen that…thing looking down at him—that's how Zeke would view it. *Big Bird's evil twin.* He could practically hear him now. Zeke would think that was ludicrous.

So no. Frankie could host her naked chest soirée tomorrow. Zeke would not be falling into her net.

Whoever had done this possessed a completely different kind of brain.

And not just from Zeke. From pretty much everyone. This was a seriously disturbed individual, and there would have to be other signs. There would be a history. A pattern.

Which is why he had problems with Adam's theory on Bert Berkle.

Berkle was another one he couldn't picture dressing up in a feathered costume and skipping around the woods.

As far as he could see, the only real grounds for suspecting Berkle were that he had opportunity and he didn't like the FBI.

Okay, and eyewitness testimony.

But eyewitness testimony from a *highly* unreliable source.

Adam had been so sure though.

That certainty was convincing. But that was probably due more to the force of Adam's personality than solid evidence against Berkle.

Berkle had never shown enough interest in his fellow humans for it to seem likely he'd bother killing them.

Rob picked up the photo of Dove Koletar and Buck Constantine, studying it idly. People changed a lot in thirty years…

This was another piece of the puzzle that didn't make sense. Not that he couldn't use it to put together a workable scenario for murder.

The only gay kid in town turned out to not be the only gay kid. Buck had killed him to keep his double life secret.

Except why kill Dove once he'd decided to leave Nearby? Wouldn't his leaving mean the problem was solved?

Ah. But what if Dove *wasn't* leaving? What if Buck had murdered him and written the note to make it *look* like… No. That was getting way too complicated. That was the territory of those TV shows about murder in cute little cottages where the flower boxes were watered with the blood of the local inhabitants.

No. Dove had been leaving. So why kill him? Why kill him *then*?

Because the killer *didn't* want him to go?

Rob considered Dove's murder from this new angle.

Okay. Maybe. Except it was difficult to imagine Buck Constantine so passionate, so desperate he'd commit murder. He'd never struck Rob as particularly emotional.

He'd also never struck him as particularly gay.

Not that Rob was a big believer in gaydar. Yes, sometimes sexuality was obvious, and sometimes not so obvious, but you still knew. And sometimes you had no clue. But Buck… Rob would have been willing to bet money that there was not a gay bone—or boner—in Buck's body.

And yet here was written proof.

Frankie rapped on his half-open door. "Get your coat. We're taking the FBI to dinner. They think we've got *two* serial killers on our hands, and they want to talk over the cases."

"Not me," Rob said. "I've got plans."

"Robbie, you're my second-in-command. I want you there tonight. These feebs already think we're a bunch of dumb hicks. We need to impress—"

Rob looked past her shoulder and called, "Night, Agent Kennedy!"

Frankie jumped, whirled to see the empty hallway, and turned back to Rob. Her expression was sour. "Damn it, Haskell."

Rob grinned. He wasn't kidding though when he said, "I've been up since four thirty-five on sheriff's business. I'm going to talk to Bill Constantine, and then I'm taking the rest of the night off. So put that in your pipe and smoke it, Frankie."

She glowered at him. He met her look calmly.

"I suppose you think I won't know what you're going to get up to this evening?"

"Now you're making me blush," Rob said. "My mother used to knock first."

As Frankie began to splutter, he offered her the photo of Dove and Buck. "Does this look like Buck Constantine to you?"

Frankie took the photo. Frowning, she examined it. Her eyes widened. "Where did you get this?"

"Dove Koletar's mother sent it to me."

"Where would *she* get it?"

Rob shrugged. "No idea. Is it Constantine?"

"Hell no." Frankie met his eyes. She looked flabbergasted. "This is Buck Berkle."

"Buck *Berkle*? You mean Bert Berkle?"

Frankie nodded. She was staring at the photo again. "My God," she murmured. "So I guess it was true."

"Bert Berkle who tracks missing hikers for us? *That* Bert Berkle?"

Another absent nod from Frankie.

"Then why the hell does it say *Buck* on the back of that photo?" Rob demanded.

"That's what we called him. That was his nickname in school. Buck Berkle. He was captain of the football team."

"*Berkle* was? Well, why doesn't anybody call him Buck now?" Rob questioned. He felt aggrieved that this vital piece of information had been withheld.

"Why doesn't anybody call me Peaches?" Frankie retorted. "Nobody keeps their high school nickname."

"Uh…true. Still. I can't believe this is Berkle." Although, as Rob took the photo back from Frankie, he had to admit the boy with Dove looked more like Berkle than Constantine. He'd never seen Berkle without a beard before. That was what had initially thrown him. "You're saying he was captain of the football team? That doesn't sound like Berkle."

"He was different back then. Well, sort of. He was always kind of a loner, but not like he is now. *There* was a kid whose parents did beat the hell out of him at every opportunity. That mother of his was a fishwife."

Whatever that meant. "So Berkle was—is—gay?" That was a shocker. Although, come to think of it, he could more easily believe it of Berkle than Constantine.

"I—there were rumors about him," Frankie said. "Nobody believed them. But I can't believe—why, he used to bully Dove. He used to push him around. I saw him shove him once."

When she looked up, her eyes were frightened. "All this time," she whispered.

CHAPTER FOURTEEN

Adam was shaving when he heard the knock on his cabin door.

He put his razor away—he was nearly packed for the flight home, so he wouldn't have to waste a minute of tomorrow morning's time with Rob—and opened the door.

Jonnie stood on the front stoop. Her smile was tentative. It faded at Adam's expression.

He turned away and she followed him inside.

"Adam…"

"When were you going to tell me?" he asked over his shoulder. He shrugged into a clean shirt.

"Wait a minute," Jonnie said. "If you think this was something I've been keeping from you, you're wrong. Kennedy talked to me about joining BAU4 not long after we were partnered. I turned him down. I liked working with you and I was leaving after the wedding anyway."

"Why didn't you tell me Kennedy approached you?"

"What would have been the point?"

He frowned. "I think that's obvious."

"I was turning down a job we both know you'd have given your eyeteeth for. And it would have bothered you a lot to know I'd been invited to join Kennedy's team and you weren't."

Adam flushed. "I'd have been glad for you. You don't believe that?"

"Yes, you would have. And you'd have insisted on me taking the position too. And I didn't want it. I was happy where I was."

"Morgue patrol?"

"Oh come on, Adam." Jonnie sounded irritated. "I liked working with you. And I like living in Southern California and so does Chris. None of those things would influence your decision, but they did influence mine. And I planned on resigning anyway."

He finished doing up his shirt buttons. "But here you are."

"Yes." She drew a deep breath. "True. Because when it came down to it, I wasn't ready to stay home all day, and I couldn't think of anything I'd find as satisfying or challenging as working for the Bureau. And it happened that Kennedy still had a position on his squad. But the decider was that Chris is getting transferred to Quantico. So it made sense for a lot of reasons." She said more quietly, but still earnestly, "I was going to tell you when you got back. I had no idea we were going to end up working the same case."

"We're not. Russell and I are being sent home tomorrow."

Jonnie bit her lip. "I know. It's all Russell's fault. If Sam kept you on, he'd have to keep Russell, and he hates snitches." She added with a touch of maliciousness, "That's the one bright side. Russell was so sure he would be invited to stay. You should have seen his face when Sam said he wasn't needed."

Adam pictured that and smiled reluctantly.

Watching him, Jonnie said, "Sam's hard to read, but I think he's impressed by how far you brought this case on your own."

"He must be good at hiding his feelings then. And it wasn't on my own. I wouldn't have gotten anywhere without Haskell."

"Yes, Deputy Haskell," murmured Jonnie. She smiled at him and Adam gave in and smiled back, though reluctantly. "I had a feeling there was more going on there than wham-bam-thank-you-ma'am."

"Is that what you and Chris call it?"

She laughed. "For the record, I love being married. I think everybody should get married."

"As many times as possible."

She laughed again. "Do you think—?"

"No," Adam said. "Long distance relationships don't work. And neither of us are in a position to move."

"Have you talked about it?"

"Of course not."

She raised her delicately arched brows. "You don't think maybe it's worth discussing?"

"We've only known each other a couple of days."

"Chris knew the day we met. I knew…well, it took me a bit longer." She checked her phone. "I have to go. We're having dinner with McLellan. But…are we good?"

Adam nodded.

She walked over to him and kissed his cheek. "We'll talk later, okay?"

"Of course."

She hesitated on the threshold. "Night, Adam."

"Goodnight."

As the door closed behind her, he had an unpleasant thought. He went to the window and stood watching her tall, pale figure walking back through the trees. He waited until he saw her go into her cabin and close the door.

He relaxed and returned to the bathroom where he splashed on the aftershave that Rob seemed to like so much.

It was nice of Jonnie to try and soften the disappointment of being sent home in the middle of a case he had worked from scratch.

He was quite sure she was wrong about Kennedy being impressed though. At least in any favorable way.

"Let me see if I understand the situation correctly," Kennedy had said once Adam had finished explaining his reasons for believing not just one but two possible serial killers were at work in a small, remote resort community. "You were originally brought in to investigate the possibility that a John Doe belonged to the Roadside Ripper. You were attempting to verify or rule out the inclusion of this victim in the case the Ripper Taskforce is trying to build?"

"Correct."

"And you ruled John Doe out?"

Adam had hesitated. Kennedy did not like hesitation.

"Yes or no?"

"We ruled him out," Adam said.

Kennedy eyed him for a long moment. Unexpectedly, he smiled. Well, no. That grim twitch of his mouth could not actually be called a smile. He continued to watch Adam as though he were a specimen on a microscope slide. "But?"

"I thought it was highly unlikely," Adam said. "The physical evidence did not support any other conclusion. And a thirty-year gap between killings…" He shook his head.

"You thought there was a slim possibility that this was an origin kill," Kennedy spoke with a weird and unsettling satisfaction.

"I…" Adam really had no idea how to answer that. It had certainly crossed his mind, but he had believed—and continued to believe—that the theory was too far-fetched.

That said, every serial killer had to start somewhere. And the first victim was special for a number of reasons. Either because the predator knew him personally, or because the predator had watched and stalked him for a period of time. The first victim was very often the most meaningful and important to the killer. Subsequent killings were frequently an attempt to reenact the first.

You never forgot your first.

"There's not enough evidence to support that theory," Adam said.

"But that's what you privately believe."

"Suspect," Adam said. "There's not enough evidence to support belief."

Kennedy nodded thoughtfully. He'd said at last, as though delivering some final, grudging judgment. "You're cautious, but you do have excellent instincts."

Maybe it *was* a compliment of sorts, and Adam appreciated Jonnie saying that he probably would have been kept on if not for Russell. It didn't change the fact that he *wasn't* being kept on.

One thing Jonnie was wrong about: he'd never wanted to investigate serial killers. He'd have taken the BAU job if it had been offered to him, but he'd have taken any job to get off morgue patrol and back to real investigation. It was ironic that he'd landed in the middle of two serial killing inquiries, and he'd have liked to see these twin cases through to the end. But he'd also be happy never to hear the words "serial killer" again.

He put his razor and the bottle of aftershave in his kitbag, tucked the kitbag in his carryall. Rob ought to be showing up any minute.

Just as the thought formed, there was a brisk, friendly knock on the cabin door. He went to answer it.

His cell phone rang. Loud. Imperative. *Duty calls.*

He opened the door, and the sky fell in.

* * * * *

Pain jerked him back to consciousness.

Not the pounding of a head that felt ready to split in two, though there was that too, making it harder to think, to understand.

This was much worse. A bright and shining slice across his shoulders and up the length of his arms. So much pain it confused him, panicked him. Fighting made it much, much worse, and he had to stop, calm himself, try and sort out what had happened, what was still happening.

He was naked. *Humiliating.* Enclosed in darkness. *Terrifying.*

He was cold. Freezing. Not a close and stifling absence of light. A frigid, airy blankness that smelled of… Sawdust. Chemicals. Animals. Animals old and new. Dogs.

Yes, he could hear dogs barking nearby.

Kennels. Berkle.

He was in the barn at Berkle's place. Panic flooded him. Adam began to struggle again, and the pain burning through his arms and shoulders expanded horrifically. He cried out.

No. Stop. Think. *Breathe.*

As long as you're breathing, you're still okay.

Or maybe not. But he was still alive. Adam stopped struggling, forced himself to take deep breaths, to take stock. His wrists were tightly bound, arms hauled high above his head. His hands felt numb. That was lack of circulation, and it was bad news. His arms felt heavy. His shoulders ached. The pain eased when he stood on the balls of his feet—and grew agonizing when he lowered his heels. Which he had to do, because no one could stand poised on tiptoe forever.

Tears stung his eyes, and he blinked ferociously. He would drown himself if he wasn't careful. *Just keep breathing. Thinking.*

Berkle had to know he couldn't get away with this. He did know that, right? He couldn't be arrogant enough to think he could snatch an FBI agent, with impunity.

The darkness was not absolute. It grayed at the edges, and there were faint lines of yellow as though lights shone outside the barn. That would be the main entrance.

He made a careful, pivoting turn. There was another faint outline of light on the other side of the barn. Another possible point of egress, if he got the chance.

He had to lower his heels again, drawing in a sobbing breath as the muscles in his shoulders and arms were yanked tight.

Where was Berkle? How much time did he have before Berkle came back? That was as far as he let his thoughts run. If he could get his hands free...

His fingers felt like sausages. He tried to wiggle them, to feel along the...nylon?...plastic?...ties cutting into his wrists. Slick. Slippery. Hard edges. Cable ties? Zip ties? He couldn't picture them, let alone work out how to undo them.

There had to be some way though...

Breathe.

Think.

The dogs barked louder. A deep voice spoke to them. Footsteps ground on gravel or grit. He heard the metallic slide of a bolt, the rattle of metal frame, and the boom-clang of the barn door being shoved open.

He rose up on the balls of his feet again, giving his arms that tiny bit of relief. Through the blur of tears he could see part of the moon, the gleaming corners and fences of the dog cages, and a black silhouette that seemed to fill the square of doorway.

The barn door slid shut again with a clap that sounded like the thunder that followed a bolt of lightning.

Adam kept his gaze pinned on the darkness, waiting for it to separate. Slow, deliberate footsteps approached, and he recognized that Berkle knew exactly what effect this had on his victim, that he had refined his technique over time.

"I guess I hit a nerve," Adam said.

No answer. The hair rose on the back of his neck. The silence added to the uncertainty, and the uncertainty added to the victim's fear. Not that Adam was uncertain. He knew what was going to happen to him. Barring a miracle, he was going to be killed. Horrifically.

Because he was under no illusions—was not sidetracked by the false hope that if he cooperated, didn't fight, he might be spared—he was left free to think of how to make sure Berkle didn't get away with it. If he died tonight, he wanted to make damn sure he was Berkle's final victim.

It would be up to Rob, and Adam had faith in Rob. Had faith in what Rob felt for him. He could acknowledge that now. It was a comfort. Maybe it was crazy, but knowing how much Rob would care if he didn't make it, made it easier to face the fact that he probably wasn't going to make it.

He regretted that he hadn't let Rob know, had resisted admitting even to himself, that he felt the same.

He had to make sure that he gave Rob what he would need to make the case stick. If he could mark Berkle somehow, injure him…because if Berkle didn't show up tomorrow for Frankie's "beauty contest," that was going to turn some unwelcome attention his way. It had been stupid of Berkle to leave Adam's legs free. He was going to make the most of that.

And Rob would have all the help he needed because Sam Kennedy had believed Adam, had even acknowledged that he might be on the right track.

He was mentally prepared, but the attack that came out of the darkness still slipped through his guard. He had to keep turning, dancing on the balls of his feet, and with his arms tethered, his mobility was limited. Berkle lunged forward, and there was a hot blaze across Adam's ribs. He cried out and kicked up—and he kicked hard. His foot connected, but it was with the lower half of Berkle's anatomy. Personally satisfying, but not what Adam was going for.

He heard Berkle's intake of breath. "You *fuck*," Berkle said. He came at Adam again, slashing indiscriminately, giving into temper and outrage that Adam dared to fight back. Adam lashed out again, and the blade cut across his ankle and shin.

He yelped. But he landed that kick too, though without the force he wanted. He thought—hoped—he hit Berkle's chest, but maybe not hard enough to leave a bruise. "Bad fucking idea," he gasped.

Really, it was. Berkle wasn't used to anyone fighting back. That was his mistake.

The problem was, even this much effort had worn Adam out. He was dizzy and tired—losing blood probably, or maybe concussed. Or both. The cut on his ribs stung like a sonofabitch. His arms felt like they were ripping out of their sockets. His hands were throbbing pieces of meat. His feet were raw and aching as he stumbled in the miniature circumference of his prison.

He had to have time to catch his breath. He gasped, "Tell me about it. You must want to talk."

Nothing.

"All these years and no one to know how smart you are? Not the cops. Not the feds. Of course you want to talk."

He could hear Berkle breathing. Closer than he'd thought. It sent a chill down his spine.

"Tell me about the first one. Tell me about Dove."

That got a response.

Berkle growled, "You piece of shit. You think you can talk to me about Dove? *You?*"

This time Adam caught the glint of the blade arcing down toward him. Instinctively, he lifted up and swung back—and made the discovery that his hands were looped over some kind of hook. A meat hook? The ties binding his wrists slid and stretched against the metal. Not enough to snap, unfortunately.

He kept kicking, fiercely, indiscriminately, and thought he grazed Berkle's face, thought he felt the bristling softness of his beard. He felt Berkle back off again, give him space.

Why didn't he turn on a light? Why were they doing this in the dark? What was it that Berkle didn't want to see? Did he enjoy it this way? Or was the fact that Adam was fighting back throwing him off his stride?

"If you feel that way, why'd you kill him?" Adam stretched his fingertips, trying to feel the outline of the hook. Curved steel. Yes, it *was* a hook, and that meant that in theory at least, he could lift his hands over the end of it. He needed to get some lift, some elevation. "Dove was just a kid. You stabbed him right through the heart."

"Don't say his name!"

"Dove," Adam yelled. "*Dove Koletar.*"

"God damn you. I had to. I *had* to," Berkle groaned. "He knew how it was. He knows that."

He came in like a combine harvester, arm scything the darkness, slashing this way and that.

This time Adam was ready. This time instead of kicking Berkle back, he used him as a springboard. His right foot landed on Berkle's thigh, and he jumped as high as he could, thrusting his arms out in front.

To his astonished and ecstatic relief, he cleared the end of the hook and crashed down on the dusty barn floor. The next instant he was up and scrambling for the door. His arms felt like dead logs and his balance was off, but desperate hope gave him jets.

He fell against the door, leaden fingers scrabbling for the bolt.

Berkle, after an incredulous instant, was right behind him as Adam's slippery fingers slid the bolt. He ducked down and Berkle struck the metal door so hard, the blade of his knife pierced it. Adam threw the door open, for a split second taking Berkle's knife with it.

Adam ran from the barn, sprinted down the row of tall cages—the dogs were going crazy—as Berkle snatched his knife free and came after him.

Run.

But as his bare feet pounded the frozen ground, he was working out the logistics and realizing he was never going to make it. Battered, bruised, his arms bound in front of him and throwing him off stride, he was just too slow.

Too slow…

What if Berkle turned the dogs loose? What if Berkle got a rifle?

No. Don't think about that.

He kept running, kept stumbling drunkenly on, barely feeling the rocks and frost cutting into his feet. When he spotted the red and blue lights swirling through the darkness, cresting the hill and speeding toward them down the empty road, he thought he was hallucinating.

He ran toward them, toward the highway. "Hey!" he yelled without the breath for the words to carry.

So far away. They were so far away…

Berkle, on the other hand, was close behind. He was not fast, but he was fast enough given Adam's numerous handicaps.

Adam staggered on.

The lights sped toward them, now close enough for Adam to make out two or more vehicles, an SUV out in front, racing their way. He put on a final burst of speed, stumbling up the short embankment and reaching the wide, country road. He put his hands up in supplication. He didn't have the breath left to yell.

A hard hand dug into his shoulder, spinning him around, hurling him to the ground. Adam hit the pavement. It knocked the wind out of him. Stunned him. He could taste the salt of his own blood and dirty snow. The night was alive with sound. His own strained breathing—and Berkle's too—brakes screeching to a halt, voices… He could smell burning rubber and the hint of pipe smoke on Berkle's clothes. Until that moment, he'd always liked the scent of pipe tobacco. About an inch from his nose there was a crack in the pavement of the road. Through that tiny fissure—bleached of color in the moonlight—grew a wildflower.

"Drop your weapon." The voice was deep, fierce. Familiar. Not familiar. *Rob?*

A hand locked in Adam's hair, dragging him upright. He winced against the pain, half-blinded by the glare of headlights, the flashing halogenic red and blue bars. Yes, Rob, positioned behind the open door of his SUV, weapon trained on Adam. On Berkle, who was using Adam as a shield.

Not that Berkle planned to walk away. His exit strategy would be to inflict as much pain and damage as possible by whatever means available.

"Berkle," Rob said, "Last. Warning."

"Say goodbye," Berkle told Adam. He sounded easy, relaxed.

Adam closed his eyes. The winter night erupted in gunfire.

CHAPTER FIFTEEN

"I hope you're kidding," Adam said.

He was propped against a mound of pillows in Rob's bed. Battered, bruised, bandaged—and still the most beautiful thing Rob had ever seen.

Not a good patient though. That was for sure.

"I don't see how you think you're going to use a fork." Rob indicated Adam's still red and swollen hands.

"You're sure as hell not feeding me."

It was Tuesday afternoon. Adam had been released from Klamath Falls Medical Center only a couple of hours earlier. He'd started the day being interviewed by local law enforcement and the FBI about the events of the previous evening. He'd given a quiet, precise accounting, and maybe he really was as calm as he seemed.

That made one of them.

Rob had not slept in forty-eight hours. He was not sure if he would ever relax enough to sleep again. The night before, he'd spent sitting beside Adam's hospital bed watching every slow, peaceful, sedated rise and fall of Adam's chest. Even if he hadn't been afraid to leave Adam's side…he couldn't close his eyes without seeing himself emptying his pistol into Bert Berkle.

Berkle had not given him a choice. There was no question he would have killed Adam, and when he failed, no question that he hoped Rob and the Nearby Sheriff's Office would kill Adam for him. Rob did not regret his choice. He was never going to forget the horror of seeing Adam come stumbling out of the night, drenched in gore—or the sight of Berkle stalking him, unhurried and purposeful, knife in hand and infrared goggles in place. Every cop in Southern Oregon could have surrounded him, and Berkle wouldn't have cared. He was like a wild animal scenting blood. His only aim was to kill Adam—or die trying.

So, no. Rob had no regrets. He was deeply thankful that he had a good eye, a steady hand, and had faithfully logged all those hours on the gun range though he had never imagined he would have to put his training to use. He would have slaughtered a hundred Bert Berkles to save Adam. But when he'd opened fire last night…something had changed inside him. Life would never go back to the way it was. He couldn't have explained how or why. But it was kind of like the first time you saw butterflies covering carrion. Or noticed soft, white snow angels in a graveyard.

That sounded stupid and maudlin, and it wasn't what he meant anyway. He didn't know what he felt. Except that anything was worth it to have Adam sitting there, whole and in one piece. Mostly whole. He could barely flex his fingers, and he couldn't lift his arms without the muscles shaking badly, but he had been lucky. No nerve damage according to the doctors. He just needed rest and a little time to recover.

Neither of which were in his nature. He planned on flying back to L.A. the following day.

"Well, if you're not hungry," Rob said.

Adam looked indignant. He gazed helplessly at the tray Rob had prepared. The delicious aroma of garlic and oregano wafted from the lasagna. Grocery store lasagna, but still.

"You could always try licking the plate," Rob suggested helpfully.

"You're a crack up, Haskell."

"No one says 'crack up' anymore," Rob told him. He sat down on the edge of the bed, companionably close to Adam, and picked up the fork. "Aw, come on. Let someone take care of you, for a change. It's not going to cost you anything."

Adam flicked him an uncertain look. "It's not that."

"Really? What is it?" Rob used the fork to break off a piece of lasagna. He lifted the fork to Adam's lips, and Adam wrinkled his nose and took a bite. He chewed, swallowed.

"See, not so bad," Rob said.

"No, it's good." Adam licked his bottom lip self-consciously.

Rob smiled faintly. Not an easy guy to know, Adam. But Rob would have been willing to try. Was still willing. It wasn't going to happen.

When Adam had asked Rob how he'd guessed that Berkle had snatched him, Rob had shown him the photos of Dove Koletar. Adam had studied the photos for a long time, and then he'd asked Rob to get Sam Kennedy back to the hospital. When Kennedy had arrived—wearing the expression of one who knows it's his job to humor the injured-in-the-line-of-duty—Adam had asked Rob to show him the photos of Dove Koletar.

Like Adam, Kennedy had pored over the photographs for a long time.

"What?" Rob had asked, finally, irritated with all the mystery. "What are you two looking at?"

"Koletar's tattoos," Adam said. "It's cuneiform for bird."

"Oh. That's interesting." Rob knew he shouldn't be surprised that Adam's mind was already back on work, back on chasing the next mankiller.

"These are also the symbols the Roadside Ripper carves into the chests of his victims."

"*Maybe*," Kennedy cautioned. "We can't be positive yet. But…" He eyed Adam thoughtfully. "I think you're correct."

Some of the color had come back into Adam's face. He smiled at Rob, though Rob had no part in any of this. Not his world. They were welcome to it.

After that, Kennedy and Adam had a pleasant little chat about serial killers, and finally Kennedy had offered Adam a place on the BAU4 squad. Or rather, he had said a position would be coming up and he wanted Adam to consider it. And Adam said he would. He'd still been a bit groggy with pain meds, but Rob had no doubt Adam would take the job, and if L.A. had seemed a long way away, Quantico felt like the ends of the earth.

Hello goodbye. When Adam had opened his eyes that morning and seen Rob sitting beside his bed, he'd smiled a tired smile and twitched his fingers in Rob's direction. It had felt like the start of something. But he had been smiling at Rob after Kennedy offered him a job, and that was definitely the end of Rob's tentative hopes.

In the meantime… "Open," Rob said.

Adam gave him a much put-upon look, and opened.

Rob's cell phone rang. He put the fork down, rose, and answered Frankie's call.

The news was not good.

His face must have shown it because when he returned to Adam's bedside, Adam said, "What's wrong?"

"Bill Constantine killed himself last night."

"*What?*" Adam sat up, nearly knocking over the tray. He tried to save it, but his hands still weren't cooperating, and he knocked over the water glass. "Hell. How? What happened?"

Rob lifted the tray with the now soggy lasagna off the bed and set it on the floor. He needed a couple of seconds to get his face under control. "Eden found him this morning."

"Eden…" Adam repeated doubtfully, watching him.

"Ed Eden. He's the director of Mountain Mortuary where Bill worked the last couple of years. He came in this morning and found him in the Preparation Room. Bill was lying on the metal autopsy table." Rob stood up. "He was wearing the raven mask stolen from the museum and a…a garment made of raven feathers. Like giant wings." He gestured vaguely to his own shoulders.

He could see Adam thinking it over, putting two and two together. "How did he do it?"

Rob said flatly, "He stabbed himself through the heart with the raven knife he stole."

Adam released a long, slow breath. "I didn't realize he worked at the mortuary."

Rob said, "There's a reason some of the kids around here called him Creepy Billy."

"I never heard anyone call him that."

"Azure called him that." Here was a weird thing. Rob felt zero pity for Bert Berkle, yet Bill Constantine had been just as fucked up in his own way. He had killed people, ruined lives. So why did Rob feel…the way he felt? Like he could have—should have—done something, done more.

Adam said thoughtfully, "Frankie and her mandatory strip search."

"He must have panicked," Rob agreed.

"I imagine so. It would be his DNA under Azure's fingernails."

"Frankie says Buck is swearing he's going to sue. He claims that even if Bill stole the artifacts, he would never have killed anyone."

"That's to be expected."

Was it? Probably. Recognizing that someone you loved was insane would be hard enough. Believing them capable of murder?

"He was there for Dove's autopsy. You may not have noticed him. He was assisting Doc Cooper."

Adam's eyes narrowed, but there was no recognition. He nodded.

"I planned to stop by and talk to him last night," Rob said. "If I had—

"I'd be dead," Adam said.

Rob's eyes flashed to his.

"Listen, Rob. You can't save everybody," Adam said quietly. "I know what you're feeling right now, but it's the truth. And if I didn't say it before, thank you for saving my life."

"He was sick," Rob said. "I know that. He left a nine-page letter to Tiffany explaining everything, but it sounds like it's just a bunch of rambling nonsense. It seems like maybe he thought her mother was preventing them from being together. But that's a guess. It's *all* guesswork because Frankie says Tiffany regained consciousness last night, but she still doesn't remember anything. Or says she doesn't."

"That's probably the best thing that could happen to her." Adam's tone was noncommittal. But then he'd suspected Tiffany of having a crush on Bill at one time. That was another thing they would probably never know the truth about.

"Bill wrote in that letter that when he saw Koletar's skeleton, he knew he'd been murdered, and he couldn't get it out of his head. He became obsessed with death and dying."

Adam said almost gently, "You're not going to understand this, you know. You're not going to find logic in madness."

"Yeah, I know." It was hard to say it aloud, but Adam was probably the only person he could admit this to. "I feel like I should have done something more."

"You did what you could with the facts available to you at the time." Adam held out a shaky arm. "Come here," he said.

All this sympathy from Adam made Rob feel foolish, but he joined him on the bed, and was reassured and comforted by the strength of the arm that wrapped around his shoulders.

They sat there for some time. So long and so quietly, he thought maybe Adam had fallen asleep, but when he glanced over, Adam was frowning into space.

He heard himself say, "What if you didn't go?"

Adam's brows drew together. He opened his mouth. He said, "What if you came to L.A.?"

"The thing is, I've tried living in a city. It's not for me." Rob smiled. "Anyway, it's not going to be L.A. for long, is it? It'll be Virginia. Quantico."

"I don't know. I hope so." Adam said hesitantly, "Even if I didn't take the BAU job... What would I do here? Let's say I tried to get a transfer to Portland. Even if they had an opening, even if I could get in there—and I don't know that I can. I probably *can't*. It would still be a lot of commuting back and forth."

"Not as far a commute as Quantico. Or even L.A."

"No."

Rob stared out the window. "No. I know this isn't fair. It would be crazy not to take the job. You've been working for this, waiting for this. And now it's here." He tried to joke, "Anyway, I guess I can't in good conscience ask you to live in the serial killer capital of Oregon."

"It is a lot to ask of a G-man." Adam's effort at humor was equally weak. He said, "I don't believe in long distance relationships. But…maybe we could try."

"Long distance relationship. Isn't that a contradiction in terms?"

"Yes," Adam said a little bitterly. "But we could try."

Rob pulled away from him, carefully. He didn't want to hurt Adam. Not in any way. Not ever. "Is this because of the colleague you got involved with? The relationship that ended badly?"

"Yes." Adam's mouth twisted. "I have to take my share of the responsibility though. We were having problems. We were both ambitious, both preoccupied with our careers. Me in particular. He was transferred to Washington. State, that is. And we agreed that it might be good for us to have a little time apart, a little space. But…I never had any doubt that we were going to work it out. I thought… But he phoned the first week and said he'd met someone else. That he knew this was the guy."

"How could he know that?" What Rob was thinking was, *the first time I met you, I knew you were the guy.* A one-way street, it seemed. "Did the other guy feel the same?"

"I guess he did. They're still together." Adam said, "So I don't have a lot of faith in long distance. But we could try. It's not ideal, but I…care for you. I don't know how it happened so fast. We don't really know each other. And that's what I mean. We should take it slow, get to know each other a lot better before we…" His voice trailed.

Take it, Rob told himself. *It's the best offer you'll get. It's the only offer you'll get.*

He was dismayed to hear himself saying, "Okay. But best case scenario is that eventually we're going to have this conversation again, right? Sooner or later aren't we going to be back at this point?"

Adam rubbed his forehead. "I don't know. We've known each other all of five days. We're discussing...well, what *are* we discussing?"

"Retiring together in about twenty years?" It wasn't really funny though.

Adam looked pained. "I can't turn this job down, Rob. I've got to take it. This kind of opportunity only comes once. If it comes at all."

"I know."

"But it doesn't mean that I can't have a personal life. Planes fly both ways across the country."

"Yep. They do."

"We could figure out some kind of schedule. It won't be easy, but if it's important to both of us, we can make it work."

"Yes. We should be able to do that."

"We don't have to decide this now," Adam said. "Right?"

"Right," Rob reassured.

But he knew—they both knew—the decision had already been made.

EPILOGUE

A man travels the world over in search of what he needs, and returns home to find it.

That had been the message on Cynthia Joseph's wall, and maybe there was some truth to it, but when Adam's front door closed behind him and he dropped his carryall, he wasn't searching for much beyond a shower and a good sleep.

He still felt frustratingly weak, and the effort of carrying his own luggage had left him shaking and drenched in sweat. That was probably the reason for his inexplicable depression.

Not totally inexplicable. He already missed Rob. Badly.

He was glad to be home, of course. Grateful for sunshine and the absence of snow, glad for peace and privacy. But surely home was more than a supply of hot water, clean towels, and a safe place to sleep.

Of course it was. And one day he would recapture that... feeling he'd had with Rob.

One thing he did not believe—had never believed—was that there was only one right person for anyone. Soulmates? He didn't buy into that concept. But there was no denying he had felt something for Rob he'd never experienced with anyone else. Not even with Tucker, whom he'd always thought of as the one who got away.

What he did believe—had learned the hard way—was that timing was everything. Life did not guarantee second chances. Sometimes you only got one shot.

Which was why he was so happy—yes, *happy*—about this job with the BAU. Why he *had* to take it. Why he could not, *must not*, turn down this opportunity. Kennedy was offering him his life back. He would be on track once more. Reputation restored, future reinstated. The work would be challenging and absorbing—and he'd be doing it with Jonnie instead of Russell.

Except.

Except he'd be chasing serial killers. Something he'd never wanted to do. Fascinating, maybe, but he wasn't sure he'd ever get another good night's sleep.

And he'd be living in Virginia, over two thousand miles away from Rob.

Which didn't change the fact that almost anyone he knew would jump at this chance. Russell would jump at it. Russell would probably be willing to kill him for it. Actually Russell was probably ready to kill him on general principles.

Well, he wouldn't have to put up with Russell for much longer.

If he took the job.

And of course he was going to take the job. It would be irresponsible not to. Even Rob had said he'd be crazy not to take it.

Sam Kennedy wouldn't ask twice. This was a one-time offer. Take it or leave it.

The problem was, he couldn't shake the feeling that by taking the position on Kennedy's team he was passing up another and more important opportunity. A chance at something that was even more rare than the chance to become one of Kennedy's elite man hunters.

Adam got out a bottle of gin, carefully poured a drink, and wandered to the window, gazing down at the glitter of lights. The frenetic winking and blinking of a city that never slept.

He sipped his drink and thought of Rob's snowy retreat where the lights came from the stars.

It was after ten. What was Rob doing right now? Filling out a mountain of paperwork probably. Maybe having a drink at the Marina Grill? Or maybe he'd decided to visit his friend in Klamath Falls.

Agent Darling, I think I may be in love.

Adam smiled. His smile faded. Okay, but you couldn't just…follow your heart.

Could you?

That was not the way he'd been raised.

He knew what his father would say if he told him he was throwing away everything he'd worked for, everything he'd achieved. Being accepted into the FBI was about the only thing he'd ever done that made his father proud.

His father was a lonely old man with a wall full of commendations, a wife who cared more about breeding poodles, and two kids who were too busy trying to emulate his successes to find time to phone home between official, major holidays.

Was it "throwing it away" if you realized your priorities had changed?

He put his drink down and fished out his cell phone. It didn't hurt to call. To say hello? *Thanks again for saving my life.*

The phone rang and rang. And rang.

It was too late.

Sweat broke out on Adam's forehead. His palms were wet. Been here and done that. He pressed Redial and the phone began to ring all over again.

I know you meant it. You can't have changed your mind already.

The phone picked up and Rob—sounding no farther away than the next room—said, "'Lo?"

It took Adam a moment to find his voice. He really had been rattled for a moment. "Did I wake you?"

There was a pause before Rob said in a very different tone of voice, "I didn't think I'd be hearing from you again."

That delivered another jolt to Adam's nervous system. Had their goodbye been that final? He thought back to the airport. It had been a little awkward with the distractions of other people and luggage and timetables. "Not at all?"

"Well, I was expecting a Christmas card." Rob's tone was rueful. "So this is definitely a bonus."

Adam said, "But when we spoke this morning, I said I would…let you know how things were going."

"Yes, you did," Rob said. He sounded kind, like he was humoring Adam.

Adam thought back to the rushed coffee and toast they'd shared that morning. It felt like five minutes. And it felt like forever.

Rob was right. This wasn't going to work.

Adam said, "I got back about twenty minutes ago."

"Yeah? Did you have a nice flight?"

"It was okay. I thought I was coming home. Before I walked through this door I thought I had everything I wanted. I *did* have everything I wanted."

"And then you realized you'd been robbed?" Rob was joking, but his heart didn't seem to be in it.

Adam drew a deep breath—it felt like he was going for the high dive. "When I walked through this door I realized the one thing I really want—need—isn't here. Because you're not here."

Silence.

Adam swallowed noisily. "I want—"

At the same time Rob said, "I can't—"

They both stopped. The silence was excruciating.

Adam said, "You go ahead."

"I interrupted you. Go on."

"Right. Well. What if I made a mistake?"

"Did you?"

Rob was not making this easy, but why should he? He had put it all out there, laid it on the line, and Adam had basically said his career needed to come first. So no more hedging, no more equivocating, no more safety net.

"Yes," Adam said. "I think I made one hell of a mistake."

The silence on the other end felt alive, electric. "So what are you saying, Adam?"

"I'm saying that if you meant the things you said yesterday—"

"I meant every word."

"Then I want to give this a try. I want to make this work."

Rob said slowly, "Okay. Well, I don't think I'm going to be happy living in L.A. or Virginia or wherever we end up, but I don't think I'm going to be happy without you either. So—"

"So I feel the same." Adam rushed in because Rob shouldn't always be the one making concessions, giving ground. "And like you said, you've tried city living. It wasn't a good fit. I guess I can give the wide open spaces a shot."

There was another of those disconcerting pauses before Rob said with almost touching uncertainty, "Are you sure, Adam?"

"The only thing I'm sure of is wherever you are is where I belong." Adam glanced at his watch. "It's after ten. I don't know if I can get a flight out tonight, but—"

"Try."

"I'm going to try."

Rob said, "It's about an hour from here to the airport. I'm looking for my keys now."

"Maybe you should wait to hear if I catch the red-eye."

"It doesn't matter," Rob replied. "Whenever you get here, I'll be waiting."

About the Author

Author of over sixty titles of classic Male/Male fiction featuring twisty mystery, kickass adventure, and unapologetic man-on-man romance, JOSH LANYON'S work has been translated into twelve languages. Her FBI thriller *Fair Game* was the first Male/Male title to be published by Harlequin Mondadori, then the largest romance publisher in Italy. *Stranger on the Shore* (Harper Collins Italia) was the first M/M title to be published in print. In 2016 *Fatal Shadows* placed #5 in Japan's annual Boy Love novel list (the first and only title by a foreign author to place on the list). The Adrien English series was awarded the All Time Favorite Couple by the Goodreads M/M Romance Group. In 2019, *Fatal Shadows* became the first LGBTQ mobile game created by Moments: Choose Your Story.

She is an Eppie Award winner, a four-time Lambda Literary Award finalist (twice for Gay Mystery), An Edgar nominee, and the first ever recipient of the Goodreads All Time Favorite M/M Author award.

Josh is married and lives in Southern California.

Find other Josh Lanyon titles at www.joshlanyon.com, and follow Josh on Twitter, Facebook, Goodreads, Instagram and Tumblr.

For extras and exclusives, join Josh on Patreon.

ALSO BY JOSH LANYON

NOVELS

The ADRIEN ENGLISH Mysteries

Fatal Shadows • A Dangerous Thing • The Hell You Say
Death of a Pirate King • The Dark Tide
So This is Christmas • Stranger Things Have Happened

The HOLMES & MORIARITY Mysteries

Somebody Killed His Editor • All She Wrote
The Boy with the Painful Tattoo • In Other Words...Murder

The ALL'S FAIR Series

Fair Game • Fair Play • Fair Chance

The ART OF MURDER Series

The Mermaid Murders •The Monet Murders
The Magician Murders • The Monuments Men Murders

OTHER NOVELS

The Ghost Wore Yellow Socks
Mexican Heat (with Laura Baumbach)
Strange Fortune • Come Unto These Yellow Sands
This Rough Magic • Stranger on the Shore • Winter Kill
Murder in Pastel • Jefferson Blythe, Esquire
The Curse of the Blue Scarab • Murder Takes the High Road
Séance on a Summer's Night
The Ghost Had an Early Check-Out

NOVELLAS

The DANGEROUS GROUND Series

Dangerous Ground • Old Poison • Blood Heat
Dead Run • Kick Start

The I SPY Series

I Spy Something Bloody • I Spy Something Wicked
I Spy Something Christmas

The IN A DARK WOOD Series

In a Dark Wood • The Parting Glass

The DARK HORSE Series

The Dark Horse • The White Knight

The DOYLE & SPAIN Series

Snowball in Hell

The HAUNTED HEART Series

Haunted Heart Winter

The XOXO FILES Series

Mummie Dearest

OTHER NOVELLAS

Cards on the Table • The Dark Farewell •The Darkling Thrush
The Dickens with Love • Don't Look Back • A Ghost of a Chance
Lovers and Other Strangers • Out of the Blue
A Vintage Affair • Lone Star (in Men Under the Mistletoe)
Green Glass Beads (in Irregulars) • Blood Red Butterfly
Everything I Know • Baby, It's Cold • A Case of Christmas
Murder Between the Pages • Slay Ride

SHORT STORIES

A Limited Engagement • The French Have a Word for It
In Sunshine or In Shadow • Until We Meet Once More
Icecapade (in His for the Holidays) • Perfect Day
Heart Trouble • In Plain Sight • Wedding Favors
Wizard's Moon • Fade to Black • Night Watch
Plenty of Fish • The Boy Next Door
Halloween is Murder

COLLECTIONS

Stories (Vol. 1) • Sweet Spot (the Petit Morts)
Merry Christmas, Darling (Holiday Codas)
Christmas Waltz (Holiday Codas 2)
I Spy...Three Novellas
Point Blank (Five Dangerous Ground Novellas)
Dark Horse, White Knight (Two Novellas)
The Adrien English Mysteries
The Adrien English Mysteries 2